REBELS,
TURN OUT
YOUR DEAD

REBELS,
TURN OUT
YOUR DEAD

Michael Drinkard

HARCOURT, INC.

Orlando   Austin   New York   San Diego   Toronto   London

MAR — 2006

www.HarcourtBooks.com

Library of Congress Cataloging-in-Publication Data
Drinkard, Michael.
Rebels, turn out your dead/Michael Drinkard.—1st ed.
p. cm.
1. New York (State)—History—Revolution, 1775–1783—Fiction.
2. Prisoners of war—Fiction. 3. Farmers—Fiction. 4. United States—
History—Revolution, 1775–1783—Fiction. 5. Domestic fiction. I. Title.
PS3554.R495R43 2006
813'.54—dc22 2005027539
ISBN-13: 978-0151-01119-3 ISBN-10: 0-15-101119-2

Text set in Adobe Caslon
Designed by Cathy Riggs

Printed in the United States of America

First edition
A C E G I K J H F D B

For Jill

REBELS,
TURN OUT
YOUR DEAD

I

1

JAMES HATED moccasins. He wore big boots that cracked twigs. Seventeen and newly conscious, he was given to symbol and metaphor. When there was nothing to be excited about James was especially. Day or night, indoors or out, coarse woolen trousers or no trousers at all, girl or no, he was often hard. He wondered if this happened to all seventeen-year-olds, but his curiosity was never satisfied because he never whispered his question aloud.

"Mend the fence," demanded Salt, the father, the moccasin-wearer. Tall and ruddy, today he turned forty. With three ax blows he felled a balsam fir a half-foot in diameter and dragged it to his son's pile. Work well done was backmaking, not backbreaking, a message he was determined his son learn. Thick red hair grew on Salt's head and down his cheeks, stubble battling to overtake his face. He wore buckskin leggings and a hemp shirt that his wife, Molly, had sewn.

"Who broke it should fix it," James said.

"Boots don't make a man." Salt timbered another tree. The zinging woodchips incensed a half dozen sap-drunk yellowjackets, which in turn spurred the blue jays to jerk their crests and squawk.

Drinky Crow, Salt's farmhand, winked at James. At least somebody was listening. Where moccasins were false on his father, they were true on Drinky Crow. Because he was Indian. Plus Drinky Crow, James had been told, died already seven times. Nobody believed this literally. But anybody that dead everybody liked.

Drinky Crow looked younger than sixty, or older, depending. His black face had soaked up the decades. Jet hair ruffled like the feathers of his namesake. His squint made eyeballs seem unnecessary. The offspring of rape—a runaway negro, a squaw—Drinky Crow had been sold on a platform in Newport to a tobacco farmer. When he turned nineteen his master died, leaving a will that stipulated his slaves be manumitted, and Drinky Crow most significantly, with one-sixty-fourth of the estate. Drinky Crow had been a capitalist ever since. He lived with four or five women on a spit of sand at land's end in Rockaway. Maybe there were six women.

Squatting opposite each other, he and Salt hoisted the naked trunks, lifting in parallel choreography, interlacing the logs six high at a slight angle, like fingers at the top knuckle, while James bound the projecting butts to a post with rope. The next section would zag, followed by one that zigged, and so on.

"Why go to pains when they're going to tear it down again?" James fumed.

"I won't do something but the right way." Salt knew they could save time and trees by setting the fence in a straight line, without the slight angles, the way they did in Virginia. Some people said the South was about fast money, others that there weren't trees enough. Everyone admitted that straight Southern fences toppled after a season or three.

"What good is a fence, for that matter?"

"What kind of a question is that?"

"There's no purpose for it."

Salt scratched his sideburns. "To keep the cows from the corn, for one."

"What cows? Thieves got every last one."

"Careful who you call thieves."

It made Salt happy, physical labor. And the blue sky made him happy, too, and the small ears of corn each stalk yielded, and the fresh scent of hewn wood, and the dangling legs of flying yellowjackets, and the companionship of son and farmhand, and his moccasins and hemp shirt.

James spat. "It's not even *your* fence."

Until just this moment, Salt had been able to forget that he was not in fact working for himself. "What's good for your granddad is good for us all."

James was quick, the rope a blur, hands a flash. In a snap the joint was lashed.

"Now can we eat?" Unlike his father, James did not like toil. Nor did he share his father's illusions about the task at hand. This work was not backmaking; it was the opposite. *Some people*—and everyone knew who those *some people* were—had broken the fence and taken the logs for their own purposes. *Some people* had stolen not just the fence but the hours that had gone into its construction. It frustrated James that his father did not share his rage. As for Drinky Crow, James did not hold him to account in the normal constellation of human emotion; Drinky Crow was mad.

On this job, as on all jobs, James got it over with—this required less effort than to make a statement by not doing it, or to prolong agony by doing it negligently—so he could get back to shooting things with guns.

Seventeen was too young to matter, too old not to. James thrust his hand into his pocket to rearrange himself, but first he gave it a yank. Another. And one last. Then he got his pistol out of its holster, which was set on a fallen tree. His father and Drinky Crow both had Pennsylvania rifles. You could bark a squirrel in a tree at three hundred yards with a Pennsylvania rifle. But all James got was a pistol. He was lucky when he hit a turkey ten feet from his face. It wasn't fair. The pistol was just better than nothing. It was made in Britain, a gift from his grandfather. The handle's walnut grain gave him comfort, the bullet inside reason to care.

"Rope?" Salt offered a leather pouch to Drinky Crow.

Drinky Crow took out a pinch of dried hemp, brought it to his nose and sniffed. Eyes lost in wrinkles, he loaded up his pipe. It was made of white clay with a tapered cooling stem. They smoked. Drinky Crow had been the one to show

Salt a type of seed that produced hemp that was fibrous and useful. But Drinky Crow's purple seed had a unique quality.

The sparrows sang in the trees, a treble chitter that was in fact dozens of interwoven, contrapuntal melodies, with no bass notes to anchor. Three chords were all that were required for Salt's moment of perfect happiness, maybe two. Just one, if a minor seventh. Another smoke and he knew he'd hear it.

"Good rope."

Molly had packed Salt and James a lunch of roast turkey, boiled yams, and cinnamon buns. Fine sticky things, sweetened with honey. Molly saw to it that desires Salt didn't even know he had were met. A wave of relaxation passed through him. The yellowjackets, buzzing loudly, held still, and the world around them bobbed.

Drinky Crow offered Salt a slab of dried and salted cod. In his pack there was also a tangle of seaweed, and a boiled phalarope egg. Despite its glistening greenness, or maybe because of it, the seaweed looked appetizing—another effect of the hemp. Salt helped himself, and offered Drinky Crow a sweet potato and a drumstick.

The yellowjackets descended upon the cod, the cinnamon buns, and neither Drinky Crow nor Salt made any attempt to wave them away. The blue jays hopped from branch to branch, eyeing the pickings.

"Father, can I practice with your...Penn...Pennsylvania rifle?" James asked. He was careful about his word choice. *Practice* instead of *shoot. Pennsylvania,* a mere modifier, as if the gun were more important than the colony.

Salt heard the appeal as self-conscious and stammering. He did not encourage his son's interest in guns. James was gawky, pimply, Adam's apple abob in a too-thin neck. Engrossed in firearms and solitude and two-shilling pamphlets. Hands too often moving about in front pockets.

"Eat something. Your mother went to trouble."

"Later."

"Now."

"Why can't I join the Continentals?" James blurted. Next to him was a leather hunting bag, its contents spilled: lead balls, a knife, patching material and powder horn.

"I told you we'll discuss it when you turn eighteen," Salt snapped, worn by the topic.

"Yes sir," James dutifully glowered.

"What's that in your hand?"

James held up a small wasp nest. "Wadding." It looked like a cross between a daisy and a piece of coral, a stem opening to a bloom with a colony of holes, some of them covered with a membrane, pupae inside. Two or three wasps darted here and there in its defense. "For the...rifle."

"Pistol. You may practice with your pistol." Despite himself, Salt was pleased with his son's resourcefulness. The papery nest would indeed make good wadding to cram down the barrel after the powder and the lead ball. "But only if you eat afterward."

"Die!" Drinky Crow slapped the back of his neck. In the palm of his hand was a crushed yellowjacket. He brought it to his mouth and, with his incisors, carefully extracted the stinger. Drinky Crow's teeth looked new, elegant, the tiniest serrations not yet ground away, the canines true as daylight; they took the attention his eyes denied, but his smile did not express joy. Drinky Crow knew that Salt would make slaves of people like himself if given the chance. And he knew too that James was a spoiled thing, born of privilege, incapable of seeing any point of view outside his own, content to grope himself and lick gunpowder from his fingertips.

Just then a team of horsemen rounded the bend, a-trot, not a-gallop. The clamor Salt felt, then, was likely his own. Rope did that. Made you suspicious, then made suspicion itself suspect. Inhaling deeply through his nose and letting the breath out through parted lips, Salt brushed the crumbs off his lap. His rifle was nearby. "Keep that pistol hidden like I showed you, James. And don't say anything."

"But—"

"Sit until I say stand."

"They're the ones wrecked this fence! Stole our cows! Ate our corn!"

"The cows weren't yours. Nor the corn."

"Would have been. Will be yet."

"Sit on that fence. Or...to bed no dinner."

"It's only common sense!" James sulked, and just to make sure, pouted too.

The leader wore scarlet, gold epaulets bouncing to the lope of his bay horse—a British officer. His teeth were clenched, a ball of jaw muscle. Two blue-uniformed mercenaries held slightly behind, the nags underneath them hard rode.

"God save the King!" said the British officer, by way of greeting. He had no fat on his bones yet. For Salt, this boded ill. A newly commissioned officer's world consisted of slights and challenges.

"Aye, sir, and us all." Salt offered the canteen, but the officer waved him off. The Hessian stepped forward to grab it. He was large-headed with a black beard, and when he gulped he was oddly careful not to touch his mouth to the spout, like a dainty ogre.

Lifting the bucket, Drinky Crow watered the horses, first the officer's bay and then the Hessians' mares. Salt saw the foam at their gumflaps, the lather on their bellies, the quivering flanks, and met Drinky Crow's eyes. Drinky Crow stroked their muzzles and bid them easy. The horses accepted his calm, and slurped from the oaken buckets. One of them was gimp and lifted her leg, revealing quittor that attracted green bottle flies.

"Why is your negro so put out?" asked the officer.

"He's not, sir," Salt said. "That's the face he was born with."

The Hessian ogre stopped drinking, rivulets suspended on his beard, and shuddered.

"Any slave joins my army earns freedom." The officer dismounted.

"He's no slave," Salt said.

"I didn't ask your opinion." The officer tugged at the fingers of his glove, removed it, then the other, folded them together and tucked them under his belt, next to his pistol. It was a gesture long imagined, and had about it the stink of pride.

"Aren't those Old Man Jones's mares?" asked James. Ever since the British pounded Washington in Brooklyn a few years ago, the King's army had been entrenched in New York City. It was said there were twenty-thousand troops. To feed and quarter them all, the army was consuming more farm-land, billeting in more houses, appropriating more stock—first Ebenezer's cows, and now, it appeared, Old Man Jones's mares. Salt frowned. Just because it was true didn't make his son's utterance any less foolish.

"Do you think a commissioned officer cares to ride this sorry beast?" growled the Briton. Salt saw the truth for what it was: the young warrior had given up home for glory. Instead what he got was a teenager's sneer. "Ignorant American."

"Ignorant?" If James had been allowed to enlist, he could kill this redcoat now. With bare hands.

The second Hessian spurned water. "Where rum?" The mercenary was ruggedly handsome but for toothlessness. The two Hessians stood side by side in their tattered blue uniforms, tongues lolling. Salt wondered at their situation. What kind of man would war for money? Where was the feeling in that? And these men were not young.

"You heard him," said the British officer. "It would please the King that his soldier's thirst be quenched. Where is rum?"

"I have none, sir."

"What, then, is in your skin?"

"Coffee, sir." Every time Salt said "sir" James felt a stab. Why did his father have to be so truckling? Salt was older, taller, broader in the shoulder, better looking, and most important, in the right. All qualities that merited respect, not insult. These crooks stripped the fence in the first place!

"Coffee?"

"Yes, sir," said Salt. Even though a tiny fib just now might save him, save Drinky Crow and James, Salt was incapable of it. He had many faults, as his son constantly reminded him, but his one good quality, he felt, was telling the truth. *Tea*, he should have lied. Because tea was taxed, most colonists did not drink it. Those who did were on the side of the British.

"Coffee slurpers."

"Sir, I am no slurper, neither rebel nor loyalist," said Salt. "I am not even a landowner." He hated this war. Nothing good had yet come from it. "A family man is what I am. A farmer at work where I live. I treat everyone the same, no matter from which corner he comes."

"Lovely speech," said the officer, applauding. "You should see that your son memorizes it. But first, he must help your negro load those logs."

Drinky Crow had already begun the job. Long used to usufruct, both perfect and imperfect, he carefully fit a log in the litter and rolled it to balance. This, like most human interactions, was just another battle in a larger war. In the end, whoever stuck around longest won, because there is no appetite in any man for frustration.

"Will we be compensated for the wood, for the work?" Salt had to ask.

"You shall receive the Crown's gratitude," said the officer. "In the form of a letter of credit."

Salt knew these l.c.'s were worthless, and would be even if the Brits did end up winning the war.

"Where rum?" asked the mercenary again, a note of iron in his accent.

Salt joined Drinky Crow in loading the wood. The sparrows sang with comic delight.

The officer strolled into a patch of sun, plucked an ear of corn off a young stalk. He had eaten well this morning, eggs and cheese at officers' mess, taken from a Dutch farmer. The Dutch were agreeable and did make tasty cheese. And the Quakers were pliable, good with lathes. One wished they could be made to craft cannonades as well as kitchen tables. As for the rebels, they were easy. Either bayonet them or fire away. Scalp the worst to send a message.

It was civilians that were such trouble.

The officer shucked the corn. It was tender and young, the ear slender, the kernels the palest yellow and sweet, but slightly woody too. A yellowjacket buzzed at the cob, banging off his lip.

"Cow corn," said James. The officer stopped mid-chew, then swallowed. James pointed to stalks in another field. "People corn grows yonder."

"I'll make your eyes roll for the last time." The officer's scarlet coat was a torment of rank and discomfort. It left his underarms raw and blistered. The bloody epaulets weighed a pound each and he could never keep them properly polished. Redcoats scorned them for their tarnish, rebels for their shine. An officer in the British Army, the world's most formidable force, and yet he was accompanied by two drunks riding pinched nags. The Crown's mission had been reduced to stealing logs from a useless fence. The facts made plain by a teenager's insult. I'll show you, he thought. But a voice in his own head answered, Show you what? And so he leveled his bayonet. "Get busy."

James wasn't sure what to do. Years later, when he looked back, this is where a jumble of images tumbled forth in an uncertain timeline. As he would remember it, just now he stayed on the fence, as his father told him to. But in another version he let his hand fall to his side, every finger alive to the pistol tucked into the waistband at the small of his back.

"Now, sir, there's no call to show blade." Any threat to his son raised Salt's hackles. Instinctively, he moved toward his rifle. "We'll load you up with wood promptly, sir, so that you may be on your way."

"Put your son to work," growled the Brit, pumping the ball where jaw and temple met. With the bayonet, he jabbed at a yellowjacket.

"If you want wood, *sir*, get it yourself." James felt calm, assured as the singing sparrows. Here was a chance. If father would shrink, son would not, to do backmaking work. "And give back my grandpa's cows."

"Cows?" The officer cocked his gun. The yellowjacket was

persistent, ricocheting off his nose, darting at his eyes. And then he saw the paper nest at the teenager's feet, torn asunder. The saucy fry should know better than to stir such a thing. If he didn't, well, it was a lesson the officer himself could teach.

Maybe now James grabbed the pistol; maybe he already had.

A shot went off. Then another. The sparrows stopped singing.

———•·•———

ON THE PORCH, Molly looked down the road again for signs of Salt and James.

The house behind her was a white clapboard two-story set in a grass clearing surrounded by planted fields, a barn and stables. There were brick chimneys on either end, shutters painted black. The double-doored entry opened to a foyer, where across the rifle rack lay a broom. Molly grabbed it and instead of sweeping the porch took aim at the horizon.

"Why hasn't that husband of yours fixed these loose boards yet?" grouched her father, Ebenezer. He stomped, making them jump.

She didn't bother to answer, but swept.

"You gave him honey." Ebenezer stomped again; again the board jumped. "Why?"

"It doesn't mean we—he has joined the sugar boycott." Molly sighed. "Some Americans prefer honey."

Ebenezer owned a thousand acres of prime Hempstead Plain land. He called his estate Bury. In addition to his farm, there was a pond, a trout stream, and hayfields he leased out. Chestnut, elm, maple, sycamore, and oak trees grew, along with a few evergreens. Deer, turkeys, pigeons, and hedgehogs once lived here, but in the past couple of years most had been shot for food, and the porcupines, skunks and squirrels for sport. Long Island Road, which ran from Montauk to Jamaica, had to make a long loop around Bury and cross a toll bridge, a costly inconvenience for commercial traffic. Ebenezer let preferred customers shortcut through his land, which lopped an hour off the trip and saved the toll. The British had paid for access; troops knew him as "the rich old troll."

"Where's the boy?" Ebenezer asked. "I've got something for him."

"You spoil him." Molly stopped sweeping and looked Ebenezer in the eye. "I wish you wouldn't."

"I've something for you, too." Ebenezer held out an inlaid box.

"Don't keep giving things!"

"Give me pleasure. Open it!"

Inside was a delicate sapphire ring. She slipped it on her right finger, opposite the one that held her plain gold wedding band. The faceted sapphire was large, its color otherworldly, especially against the dirt under her ragged fingernails. "It was Mother's."

"God rest her hallowed soul. If that husband of yours won't appreciate you, I will."

"Father, don't say such things."

"Give me a hand." Ebenezer squatted before the planters

on the porch. Hair as white as tufts of cotton, blue eyes set in a pink face, her father looked like a pretty old woman. His skin was finely wrinkled, but there were no deep creases, no scars or marks of weather. He didn't stoop or slouch or hunch, rather he bent at his wide hips and kept his spine straight, then squatted with feminine delicacy, and used his hands as if every last thing he touched was fragile and had a tiny beating heart inside. He took charge of the English ivy near the door—it was his house after all, and his land. But it was, Molly felt, a shame, because that's where flowers should be. One should be greeted at the door by fragrant blossoms instead of creeping vines.

"There you go, there, a few more slips, that's all." It was his way of asking her to fetch the ivy shoots, roots clumped with soil, lying in a neat pile a few feet away. Her father simply did not want to have to rise from his squat to get them himself. Though he never complained, she saw that he was going lame from the gout, that wherever inside his body two bones met, they met in pain.

"Father, all the work you do, you should get some help."

"If by help you mean slaves, you can have another think."

"Of course I don't mean—"

"Not you, but your husband. I know his mind. How is it the greatest yelpers for freedom are the drivers of negroes?"

"We have money enough to hire a few hands."

"I won't hire a bloody hand to lift a bloody finger till you bury my bloody body."

Molly, too used to his indirection to be irritated, bathed

in the sparkle of the sapphire. More than she missed her mother, she missed her patient father, Sparrow's adoring husband, the Ebenezer of the past. The farm in full bloom, the cattle fenced, the man of property returning from a day of business to the embrace of his wife in a pretty gown on this very porch, their daughter skipping stones on the pond. Everything in its right order.

She checked the skyline for a sign of her husband and son; none. The sun going down tinged the clouds orange. The winds had shifted and now blew warmly from the south, bringing the tidal—even fishy—scent of the great Atlantic. Not cold, it nonetheless gave her a shiver. Being home alone with her father put her in charge. She worried about thieves, runners, other dangers. Molly handed him the ivy.

"When I look at you I feel her absence." Ebenezer inserted the plant into the manured soil of the limestone planter, and with his fingertips patted it home. English ivy, robust, purple stemmed, three veined leaves combined into one, a verdant trinity that reminded him of home. True, he owned this house, this farm. True, his daughter had been born here, as had Sparrow, God rest her serendipitous soul. And yet what felt foreign the day he first set foot on the continent felt foreign still.

"Why hasn't your husband tended to this decking?"

"He's been busy with hemp."

"The way others are busy with the bottle."

"Aaron Lopez negotiated to buy Salt's hemp for his sailing fleet."

"Oh yes, the merchant prince. With the British navy in New York, the merchant prince's slave brigs won't be sailing anywhere soon."

Molly raised the rifle above her head, then stretched backward, easing the tension in her muscles. "They say the British army took Old Man Jones's horses."

"The Crown will recompense Old Man Jones."

"What could they give him, and when?"

"Why, pounds sterling in good time." Her father accidentally slopped mud on the steps, which Molly felt compelled to sweep. "They're gluebuckets on legs anyhow."

"It seems to me they should buy the horses outright."

"The British will act with honor, you shall see. Better them than these damn rebel runners, robbing people at night, stealing their candlesticks and killing their negroes. And with impunity! Impunity!"

Two horsemen rounded the bend, hoofbeats raising dust puffs, followed by a third horse dragging a litter.

"James!"

Ebenezer struggled to one knee and squinted, opening an eyelid with thumb and forefinger. An ivy tendril tangled in his shoe buckle and on rising he uprooted much of his recent work. "Cursed soil!"

THE BRITISH chose red uniforms so blood wouldn't show, maybe because gore demoralized the unwounded, or because soldiers hoped for immortality. But blood did show, always.

A muddy clot on the crimson breast, darkening even the brass buttons. It smelled like tin. The boy was not much older than James. Indeed, his expression looked familiar to Molly—she had seen it before on her son, his napping face misshapen by the pillow.

"It's my fault," blurted Salt.

"James!" Molly panted. She had sprinted from the house to meet them at the barn. She had wrapped her arms around James and clutched him suffocatingly tight.

"He's still breathing." Salt's voice cracked. "But he needs a surgeon."

"The British have taken possession of the surgeon." Molly ripped herself free of James to kneel and place her cheek near the officer's face. "He's twitching."

"Is he?"

Nobody said a thing. James stood off to the side, gazing away. The horses stomped and riffled, wanting water.

"No," Molly said. "He is not. Twitching."

Salt put a finger to the boy's lips. They were hard and pale.

Just then the dead boy sputtered and hacked up flecks of pink foam.

Salt flinched, but Molly didn't. Instead, she bent to cradle the lad's head. The young man's eyes opened, blue and dry and haunted, and they locked on Molly's. He convulsed once, twice, then fell back, staring into the sky.

Molly hung on to the boy.

No one dared break the silence. Fireflies danced.

When Molly finally let go, she looked at James, who could not return her gaze. "Who shot him?" She hadn't intended it as an accusation.

Salt smelled her hair, sweet with a slight bite of witch hazel. Then he frowned at the sapphire on her finger.

———

EBENEZER SLAMMED open James's door.

"Don't bother knocking."

The lantern took a few seconds to settle. James was sprawled belly down on his horsehair mattress. Ebenezer had insisted on horsehair. It gave, he said. One of James's legs hung off the bed, his foot tapping the air. He had a pillow made of goosefeathers under his chest, another of buckwheat to the side. Several pamphlets lay about, open, shut, rightside up and upside down.

"Your mother wants that you return the pistol."

James did not look up from the page. "Did you know that Tom Paine put the *e* at the end of his name when he got here?"

"Don't read trash."

"His father was Joe Pain. P A I N."

"You should be reading Montesquieu."

"You should be reading *Common Sense*. It has sold five hundred thousand copies." When Thomas Paine was young he had been a stay-maker, turning whalebones into corsets. Imagine where his hands had roamed.

Ebenezer sat at the foot of the bed, the same bed in

which James had been born. He remembered when. Sparrow had been in the early days of her forgetfulness, alternately fretful and giggling. Salt was away on a courier run. There was nobody else to help. The contractions came fast and hard, but Molly was shy in front of her father and would not spread her legs. Thunder cracked and the sky turned green. Hail clattered against the windows. Out in the hall, Sparrow crawled on all fours, meowing like a kitten, and Ebenezer worried she might hurt herself. *"Push!"* Molly would not. Ebenezer had never stared so nakedly even at his own wife. The baby crowned, plum purple with dark fuzz, and disappeared inside again. Hours passed. There were several crownings, but James refused to emerge fully. "Stubborn as sunshine," Ebenezer always said. Sparrow fell asleep, curled on the floor, purring. The skies cleared. Then Molly let out a yelp and the baby shot from her, slick, buttery and blue. Ebenezer had bobbled and clutched, but caught his grandson and held on.

"You were born a conehead," Ebenezer said. "Your mother was horrified!"

James chuckled, as Ebenezer knew he would. He always did at this part of the story.

"And your head's still pointy to this day," Ebenezer said, indicating the pamphlets. "Which your father blames me for. Where was he when the job needed doing?"

James went back to reading. When Paine was James's age he'd defied his father and become a privateer on a ship named *Terrible,* under command of Captain William Death. Oh, for a chance at adventure like that!

Quietly, Ebenezer said, "They're going to come looking for you."

James kept his nose in the pamphlet. "'A thirst for absolute power is the natural disease of monarchy.'"

"Nonsense."

"There it is." James jutted his chin toward the dresser. The pistol and ammo pouch were on top. "Now who's going to protect us from runners?"

"He was a British officer, for heaven's sake! He was fighting for us!"

"Them."

Ebenezer sighed. "I've managed to make it to sixty-seven without killing anybody."

"You don't really want to punish me."

"It's your father should be punished."

———◆———

THEY WALKED arm in arm, Molly letting Salt lead for a change. The barn and carriage house were set a ways down a gentle, sloping road bordered on either side by cornrows, potato patches. Beyond them were more planted fields— corn, hemp, and hay—surrounded by a shadowy deciduous forest that held in its deepest interior a trout stream coursing north that ran cold even during midsummer. It fed a great pond and, here and there, small mossy bogs. The night was warming up, the blowsy easterly getting fishier, bringing with it a haze that blurred the stars, robbing them of twinkle. They both knew the lay of the land so well that they could walk it in the dark with ease. Even so, Molly had brought a rifle. Runners knew the land too, and the Bury shortcut that bisected the property.

Salt turned to Molly. She was not what might commonly be considered beautiful. With her rolls of dark hair bursting loose, her thin hooked nose, pale brow, and exaggerated upper lip, she looked haughty, arrogant even, though she was not. Today, as on most work days, she wore men's clothes. When they went into town on errands, the townsfolk whispered, "Yes sir." And behind Salt's back, "Yes ma'am."

"I'm responsible for the death of the British officer," Salt said. The line sounded rehearsed. Yet Molly knew her husband was incapable of lying.

"What happened exactly?"

Salt wanted a smoke. "The Brit came at us with a bayonet."

"Came at who, you or James?" Molly asked. "Who shot him?"

Salt shook his head as if to clear it. "If James had only obeyed me. Sat on that fence like I told him."

"He never does what you tell him. Why do you expect him to start now?" She hadn't meant this as a criticism, and so to soften the sting she added, "He's just a boy."

"A boy who has no respect. You spoil him. Your father spoils him."

"That doesn't make him a murderer!" Molly said. "The magistrate understands self defense."

"A concept the redcoats reject."

They halted at a rocky outcrop by the hemp field. There were two acres' worth, thousands of plants, each one female. They gave off a citrusy scent that cut through the fishy wafts. Early on, Salt had plucked and burned the males. It was Drinky Crow's trick. Longing, the females became extra attractive. Their allure—meant to entice the bees and pollination—was palpable, and Salt worked hard to ensure that desire went unrequited. Lust not only made hemp flower, but rendered its stem fibers strong and silky. Salt pinched off a flower and admired it.

Molly cleared her throat.

Salt said, "Every last plant contracted for by the merchant prince's fleet of fifty. With the profit we can buy slaves to work ten acres. Ten acres of our own. You'll see."

Molly nodded, knowing most of what he was about to say, hoping for something new.

"From ten acres we'll go to twenty, double that again. Think of all the ships! The rope, the rigging! There can be no such thing as too much hemp." He took hold of her, smiled in the dark. "And you and I will walk through fields of it arm in arm. We'll get a thrasher, a pounder, looms. We'll grow it, harvest it, beat it, thrash it, weave it and braid it. From seed to mainsail. Think!" He shut his eyes and jammed his nose into a hemp flower, sniffing deeply.

Salt thought he had secrets, but Molly knew them all.

She knew about his stash of seed money hidden in the barn, for instance, got from some partnership in Drinky Crow's black market trade. She knew hemp fueled Salt's fantasies, even as it siphoned his energies. And although he never lied, Molly understood he could not fully be trusted. To fix the loose boards, for instance. To discipline his son. To finish a thing.

Perhaps he had been born in the wrong time. What was intransigence in him might have been leadership in another man, or era—what was dreamy now might have been visionary then. His selflessness did not come from lack of ambition. Like all men, he was defined by his failures. But in Salt's case, too often the definition stopped there.

At times she hated the plants—hated looking at them, in their naked feminine yearning. They were a threat. And, yet, she saw in them devotion—Salt's, and theirs. Endlessly delayed gratification turned desire into something transcendent. This was Salt's gift.

Molly was a pragmatist. There was no dream she valued more than the life she had. Still, you thought about commitment: what you gave up, what you got. At least Molly did. Had she made a mistake by marrying Salt? Did she ever wish he was dead? Well, yes.

She pulled Salt's arm against her, closer. She supposed there was some discontent in every marriage. And yet what had thrilled her the day they met thrilled still. Attraction, her mother had told her, was the pulse of marriage. Actually, what Sparrow had said was *blood.*

Molly's thoughts returned to the dead officer laid out in the carriage house. She scratched her leg with the rifle butt. "Maybe there is somebody we can pay."

Salt sighed. "Pay off?"

"Father has money. He cannot say no to me."

Ebenezer was a known loyalist, a royalist even. His British-born pedigree had kept the family whole and the farm intact after the ignominious rout of Washington's Continentals in Brooklyn last summer. Cash from him could, perhaps, soften tragedy.

"Why did you let him give you that ring?"

"I gave you honey." Gone with the boycott, against Ebenezer, when she herself preferred sugar.

At last, Salt could no longer resist. He knelt and took a pinch from his pouch, dried hemp from last year's harvest. He tamped it into his clay pipe, and with a mechanism designed for a musket, ignited it. The smoke was sweet and not harsh and filled his lungs entirely, perfectly. When he exhaled his muscles slackened. He offered the pipe to Molly, not expecting her to take it. She had smoked with him in the past, but the last few times the hemp had turned her mute and furtive. When she came out of it she vowed that it had unlocked something inside her, something that was better left shut tight. Through that opening, she claimed, came spirits. They had not possessed her, but they frightened her and stole her powers of discernment. The world was filled with all kinds of spirits, she thought, good and bad and indifferent, and they were all opportunistic.

"What if we just bury him?" she said. "Nobody has to know."

Salt had already given this thought. Drinky Crow was witness, though he could be counted on to keep quiet. But the Hessians had jumped on Old Farmer Jones's mares and trotted away. They were sure to tell. "James knows."

"It's James we have to protect."

"It's James who needs us to set a good example."

"There's a war going on," Molly said.

"He—"

"He what?"

"He was right. Fixing that fence was useless. I don't know why I insisted. Your father would rather I had fixed the porch. Useless, useless, useless."

Salt bent to kiss Molly's lips. He was scared.

Another man might have delivered her from her father. Another man might have worn the pants. Another man might have brought her the gift of requited desire.

If such a thing existed.

"Tell me what you want me to do," she whispered. "I want you to tell me what to do. For once."

Salt ordered her to take off her breeches, to get down on her hands and knees in the hemp fields, the plants pining, dripping, oozing, wanting, and made what might be called love while the stars whistled and the wind carried the stink of seashells. She was wearing the ring her father had given her mother. He told her to howl and she did that too.

2

TAKE THAT PITCH off the boil," said Jabez Boocock, chicken farmer, pointing a stick. A half dozen of his followers guzzled rum at the dump. It was located on the main road east of Hempstead village, around a large bend in a valley that looked as if it had been scooped gently from a hillside, long ago a graveyard for the Matinecock Indians. There were old shoes, broken bottles, tattered upholstery, moldering bed pelts, wigs, cobs, cores, oxtail bones. Vapors piped from yeasty slag piles. Sunrise was an hour away, but the skyline was pink.

"We don't want to kill him, just make him wish he were dead."

Hands wrapped in water-soaked rags, his men went about their work as if they had done it before. They tilted the barrel with a blacksmith's tongs and rolled it out of the fire. Drops of water hit the resinous swill and sizzled and foamed. Their charcoaled faces made their eyes buggy and wet in the firelight. Some wrapped their heads in kerchiefs, others wore bands with feathers, imitating storybook Indians. Boocock himself had a coonskin cap, the ringed tail hanging in back. He lifted his nose and sniffed, then jammed the stick into the back of his victim, hogtied in the dirt.

"I hate the smell of fish. Don't you?"

The bound man, George Sowell, writhed. A warty gourd had been jammed into his mouth.

"The stink of the South."

George Sowell, town solicitor, was a large man with dainty feet. He wore a suit of blue Dover worsted over a silk shirt. A ruffled cravat was tied at his neck. On his head sat a large wig powdered white, three rows of curls on each side. It framed his jowly face. "Illegal," he tried to say, "against the law," but the words remained lumpy vowels in his gullet.

"T'ain't polite to yammer with a full gob." Jabez Boocock tugged off Sowell's peruke. "I always wanted to be a bigwig." Boocock raised an eyebrow, turned down the corners of his mouth, and replaced his own raccoon cap with the hairpiece. Abruptly, he plunged his stick into the hot pitch, pulled it out, and dabbed the top of Sowell's head. Sowell winced; the bituminous stew raised an instant blister. "I do hereby knight thee Lord Chicken Bawk Bawk!" Boocock sprinkled a handful of feathers over Sowell, and a few stuck to the tar atop his head in a sullen tuft. "Now, now, Lord   Bawk, don't look so...so crestfallen."

His rabble exploded in rum-blown laughter.

George Sowell groaned, his jaws ached from the gourd.

How fitting that these goons gravitated to the village midden. They belonged there, with the trash. In the eerie dawn, rats scuttled about the steaming ash tussocks, heaps of oyster shells, chicken bones, rusted nails, broken pottery, glass. A seagull hunched its neck like a winged gargoyle and cawed at a rival, guarding something black and glistering. In the distance, pigs rooted about, but they weren't pigs, they were a poor family on all fours. George Sowell moaned, the blister on his head stinging. The injustice hurt worse.

"I know what you're thinking," said Jabez Boocock. "'Rule of Law.' Without it men run afoul." Again, the gang danced and crowed, piling more wood on the bonfire. "And I say you very well may be correct, Lord Bawk Bawk! *Vive la Rule of Law!* But by that reasoning Law, not Man, must be the controlling authority. Tell your King George that so says Jabez Boocock, man and chicken farmer."

George Sowell writhed. At his cheek was a broken polychrome creamware cup, a yellow butterfly painted on it. A blue glass shard refused from the apothecary. A bag of feathers.

"It is not your place, Lord Bawk Bawk, to let the Crown occupy our church and use it as headquarters for so-called 'officers.' It is not your place, My Lord, to help the Englishman take our food and steal our homes!" To Boocock, the barrister was worse than the occupiers themselves. Hadn't George Sowell factored food and supplies for the British? At first the invaders were content to take Boocock's eggs, but then they appropriated his chickens, claiming to have given him fair market value in credit. "British credit is less than worthless, Sir Bawk Bawk, because there is nothing to buy with it, except passage to Dover." After they took his chickens, the British had commanded Boocock's slaves to kill and pluck them. "They insubordinated me by ordering my negroes! Then they fucked my wench! Thirteen years old! Three times they did!" Jabez Boocock took a deep breath and calmed himself. With his staff, he stirred the reeking slurry. "No, sir."

George Sowell structured deals to favor his client, no matter which side. He'd established a line of credit for Jabez Boocock, contingent upon Ebenezer granting an easement that would enable Boocock to shortcut his foods to British commercial centers. Boocock had done well in the negotiation. And now he was pretending to be aggrieved! Sowell twisted and gargled in protest.

"Gobble on, Lord Bawk Bawk!" Jabez Boocock knew chickens, and the money they made him. Chickens had bestowed upon him land, a family, health and, up till now, wealth. Born to a London scullery maid and a drunken footman, he could never have risen to this station had he stayed in England. There, it was not what you did, but whom.

It might very well be that a young country trying to establish itself needed incorruptible leaders at the top. Like Washington, and Adams, the ornery one—statesmen who fought without regard to personal gain. But a young country struggling to throw off the yoke of indenture also needed what an ordinary chicken farmer could provide. The audacity, to take his eggs, swipe his pullets, make his negroes kill and pluck them, leaving Boocock with nothing more than this gunnysack of feathers. "Three times they fucked my wench! Thirteen, and black as a moonless night! Worth a pretty ducat on the auction block!"

As the sun rose above the dunghill, the Liberty Boys fell upon George Sowell, tearing away his clothes. His pale skin was spotted with moles. He looked, with his big belly and jiggly buttocks and spindly legs bound at the ankle, like a toddler, which, for Jabez Boocock, took some of the pleasure out of the retribution. Much better to tar and feather an equal. Nevertheless, using huckaback rags, the men smeared Sowell's shoulder and torso with the tar, even ladling some upon his bald head. The stuff had cooled somewhat, and no longer scalded. But it was itchy and sticky and vile as it dripped down his scalp, rankling his spine, seeping into the crack of his buttocks.

Next came the feathers. White ones, orange ones, black and gray, handfuls. Down they floated, singly and in clumps, each with its own flutter, some whirling, some hanging aloft and rising even, feathers stinking of Boocock's chickens. They stuck to Sowell's shoulders, back, chest, head.

"Three times! And cry she did, I'll tell you that. That child wailed!"

"Yonder comes a mount!" Guns were pulled.

A horse and wagon had rounded the bend at a clip, the wheels squealing to protest the curve. The horse reared back and whinnied, the rider simultaneously whipping and shushing. The wagon stopped with a clack, backed up an inch, and held in a skid of dust. The rider, dressed for business in knee breeches and a brown velvet jacket, jumped down and glanced back at the tarped payload.

"Salt! How nice of you to join us." Jabez Boocock knew Salt had patriot leanings, but a Tory father-in-law. And a wife with a rifle.

"Good morning, sir." Salt remained tranquil on behalf of his spooked horse, a tactic that served his interests as well. The odor of tar mingled with the sweet scent of composting dung, slightly turning his stomach and reminding him that he hadn't yet breakfasted. And above it all hung the fishy Bermuda funk. He did not recognize the man in the pompous wig, regally holding aloft a shillelagh, or his crew, empty rum scuttles scattered at their feet. Salt could not tell if, behind their face paint, they were patriots or loyalists.

"It's me, Jabez Boocock, chicken farmer!"

Under Salt's hand, the horse shuddered twice. "Mr. Boocock, my good man! And commercial partner. I hear that you will be shipping yardfowl through my father-in-law's easement."

Jabez Boocock frowned. This was not knowledge that he wanted made common. And just what did Salt mean by *yardfowl*? "Roll up your sleeves, dear countryman, and abet our cause of freedom."

The tarred victim was fat as a plundered turkey, a warty squash sticking from his face like a beak.

"Who is he, what has he done?"

"It's George Sowell, now known as Lord Chicken Bawk Bawk!" Boocock's followers broke into chicken dances, squawking. The horse blinked.

"Why Mr. Sowell, is that really you?" Sowell squirmed. Salt turned to Boocock. "What has he done?"

"He sided wrong. And then there's the matter of legitimizing the swindle of my birds to feed the swarming redcoats. And turning my negroes against me."

"Swear a warrant. Air your grievance before the magistrate."

Boocock spat. "The magistrate has run away to Philadelphia, escaping with his life but nothing more. A British commander has anointed himself King of the Town!"

Salt had heard as much. The occupying force had dismissed the local selectmen—those who hadn't joined Washington—and assumed constabulary duties. It amounted to a change of players, Salt had assumed, but the roles were largely the same. "Sowell must be set loose. I have an appointment with this very barrister."

Boocock thrust his chin in Salt's face. Under the wig he looked mad. A few tiny feathers stuck to his eyelashes. "They fucked my wench."

Salt held firm. "The country I call home does not abide tosspot justice."

"If I didn't see it with my own eyeballs, I'd say you hadn't climbed down from your high horse."

"I've got lawyer business and I need a business lawyer."

Boocock took a step toward the wagon. "What business have you with the Crown?"

"No business of yours."

Boocock's followers armlocked Salt.

"What's under the tarp? Ammo?" Boocock ripped off the cover. Laid out in the wagon was the British officer, crisply uniformed, supine, head resting atop a blanket roll, hands at his sides.

"Wake him up!" slurred one of the men.

Boocock took note of the officer's puffy face, blonde hair carefully combed and parted, the brown crusty stain at his heart, and understood that this boy would not be roused. With the overlarge epaulets at the shoulders, and the sleeves and trouser legs hanging slack, he looked like a marionette cut from its strings. "Whoever plugged this boy is a crack shot." He looked up at Salt. "It's that wife of yours, isn't it?"

"She prefers a butcher knife," Salt said. Molly had dressed and coiffed the boy, which annoyed Salt, even though it was what the dead deserved. She had carefully unbuttoned the jacket and sponged the bloody chest, the skin there pale and hairless. Then she turned him over and washed his back, where gristly strings had fallen out of the exit wound. Afterward, she had washed his shirt and dressed him, then combed his hair and, using her fingertips, even attempted to arrange the expression on the boy's face, to make it what? His? Hers?

"Unbind me, citizens!" bellowed George Sowell. He had

somehow yawned the warty gourd from his mouth. "There's a problem that needs be solved."

———••———

THE BRITISH had installed themselves in Jamaica Church. Made of brick with a wooden clapboard belfry, it was planted in the town square, an important commercial crossroads. To the east lay Montauk and the tip of Long Island, to the west Brooklyn and Manhattan, to the south Jamaica Bay, and to the north Flushing and Long Island Sound. Two-thirds of Jamaica supported King George, or at least had proclaimed so on paper, signing loyalty oaths. The rest had fled west, or to Nova Scotia. Troops billeted in the houses they left behind—the Light Dragoons, the Irish Volunteers, Delancey's Brigade, the 64th Company of Grenadiers. Two Hessian regiments had dug themselves huts in the northern rampart. The streets bustled with carts catering to soldiers' wants: meat, whiskey, gunpowder, knives, muskets, daggers, pistols. No women were visible save for the occasional lady peeking from behind stagecoach drapes, and the whores from the windows above Higbie Tavern.

A British flag hung limply from the steeple, and Salt spied a sniper posted in the belfry. Prodded by infantry bayonets, just-freed slaves, heads wrapped in kerchiefs, and others fresh from the Indies with their jipijapas and bare feet, were busy building fortress walls. Using ropes run through squeaky pulleys and split beams as levers, they hoisted rectangular white stones off flatbed wagons pulled by oxen with wicker muzzles, and fixed them into place. Two black men harnessed to a pine spoke turned a pug mill. Round the rutted circle they trudged, grinding oyster shells into mortar. By aligning themselves with the British, slaves and indentured servants had been granted emancipation by King George, but in reality they had traded one form of servitude for another, and earned the murderous enmity of their former owners in the bargain. Carpenters hewed wood into doorframes, sending pulses of shavings, and a black-smith in a flatcrown hat hammered red-hot iron. A coal-fired forge spit sparks and oily smoke. It was cacophonic work, the heat and humidity stifling, redolent of sweat and sawdust and the omnipresent littoral reek that rode the Bermuda high. The workers seemed zombified, as if walking through roles imagined for them by a derelict, dream-paralyzed host. In the middle of the hubbub a grinning idiot played hoops and sticks with a baton and a petticoat stay.

In the field beside the church, the army drilled to drum-beats. The rank and file were boys, cast-offs, bachelors of suspect habits—the unskilled, the poverty-chased, and the un-loved—except for the officers, whose commissions were ac-quired through the gentry of their fathers. Off to the side was a deadcart filled with a dozen corpses wrapped in cloth, their dozen pairs of boots stacked in a nearby wheelbarrow. Salt saw the two Hessians who had served the dead British officer, the delicate, bearded ogre and the other, handsome but for the toothless hole of a mouth. Chained and cuffed, bruised and bloodied, the Hessians looked as they had been beaten. A guard led them, stumbling and clinking, into an outbuilding.

"Those men are witness to the—the incident," said Salt.

"Good then, we shall call them to the stand," said George Sowell. He had cleaned himself up as best he could, with Salt's help. There was no removing the tar on his back and shoulders, but his silk shirt hid most signs of his recent humiliation, save for a rough black patch that clung to the nape of his neck. Like Salt's, Sowell's tailored overcoat fell to the back of his legs, and he too wore boots that reached his knee, though his had polished silver buckles. In a low voice he asked, "How's Molly?"

Salt frowned.

"Everything will work out."

"You believe that?"

"It's not a matter of faith."

"What Boocock's posse did to you embarrasses me."

"No man is higher than the law."

No man isn't, was Salt's feeling, when it comes to the blood of his son. What a strange creature George Sowell was to think otherwise. Salt had never defined himself by any abstraction. Not country, not religion, not belief. There was no flag, book, or cause to which he swore allegiance. What he was first he was to other people: a father, a husband, a son-in-law. Law was mere words. But mere words were what all this warring was about.

"Remember, tell the truth, but nothing more," said Sowell. "I am confident that justice will be served."

Salt's doubts about Sowell's improbably august ideals did nothing to diminish his confidence in the lawyer's integrity. He was glad that such men existed, and not only for their professional skills. Sowell had negotiated the contract for the sale of Salt's small hemp crop to Aaron Lopez of Philadelphia. Because Sowell was not, like most men, motivated by personal gain, Salt felt him to be incorruptible.

"Stand and present yourself!" cried the bailiff, half as tall as the pike he clenched.

The British commander occupied the pulpit. He wore a fancy scarlet jacket, and at his shoulders were overlarge gold-fringed epaulets. His name was William Cunningham, and he was reputed to be a rising star in the British chain of command. The rest of the reputation: American-born black Irish and therefore much put-upon, self-made, altogether too smart, fond of the vine, personally connected to General Howe, at the molten core of the current conflict, and quite often outspoken on behalf of the victim while not unsympathetic to the victor. A marksman in the apse had a rifle trained.

"What is it you want?" Cunningham asked now, surrounded by chalices, candles, pews, minions armed and not, a life-sized crucifix behind him, the buzz of forced labor and martial discipline just outside the doors. His face was a fireball of competing rashes, crimson eyelids jellied.

"God save the King," said George Sowell, not rhetorically, his voice booming in the cool stone interior. In the first pew sat a half dozen redactor clerks, scribbling every spoken word. "Commander, most humbly I—"

"Call me 'Your Honor,' as I am not yet commissioned Commander-in-Chief or otherwise."

"Yes...Your Honor," said Sowell. "My client—"

"Get to the point. Fresh recruits arrive today. We will crush this rebellion and punish every wayward tendency. Don't let me interrupt you." Cunningham abruptly stood, purple robe swaying behind him, and strode to the corpse, which was laid out on a reliquary. Carefully he peeled back the veil, and the dead officer was bathed in honeyed light. "A fine-looking youngster." Cunningham's voice sounded like rocks rubbed together. "Who killed him?"

"It was self defense." Sowell told what happened.

"This officer has a mother, you know. A father. A wife who is very young. A whelp of his own." Cunningham was making this up. He knew nothing of the sort. What he did know was that this dead officer was about the same age his own son would be. John, to whom he hadn't spoken in fifteen years, who might just as well be this deceased greenhorn laid out before him. The only way to take the dead was personally, or not at all. At both options Cunningham was expert. "What say you, sirrah?"

Salt stood up, approached the pulpit. "Your Honor, I am responsible—"

"Sir," Sowell interrupted. "Your Honor, excuse me, but my client cannot be called upon to testify against himself. Stipulations—"

"Counsel," said Cunningham, and beckoned him forward.

Sowell, without realizing it, tiptoed.

Cunningham slowly reached out a hand, and with a violent flick ripped free a feather stuck under Sowell's ear. "Who tarred you?"

"Sir, if I tell you, I sign my own death sentence."

"So you won't testify on your own behalf, he won't testify on his own behalf, nobody speaks for himself in these miserable colonies except for John Fucking Hancock who purports to speak for you all!"

"Nobody should be forced to incriminate himself—"

"Your objection is surely worthy of debate," said Cunningham. "And we must take it up in the future. But just now we haven't time." Cunningham had been tarred, too. Years ago in New York, on a business trip from Philadelphia. He had brokered a line of credit for a British merchant fleet, which competing Americans called seditious. The Liberty Boys dragged him to the Liberty Pole on Wall Street, forced him to tear up the bond and damn King George. He did. They hoisted him up the pole anyway, along with three dead chickens. A born American, bred in the City of Brotherly Love! Ever since, his skin had developed a scurfy mien. It was as if he was allergic to his own emotions, a condition he was determined to turn to his advantage. To have every feeling given countenance had been a handicap for a man of power like himself. "I am not asking for self-testification. I am asking what he saw. Tell me!"

"But your honor," fumbled Sowell, "precedent shows—"

"Rewrite the bloody precedent," Cunningham spat.

"Everybody else is doing so!" He felt his face burn, and he was glad of it. "Lord Chicken Bawk Bawk."

Sowell shrank. So, Cunningham's intelligence network already had the report.

Salt spoke again. "From my heart I regret that the young officer is dead—"

"The confession booths are over there," Cunningham snapped. "The *bench*, where you stand now, is reserved for the facts. Please adhere to them."

"We cooperated with the officer's orders, giving over the fence logs. I saw the very same logs just moments ago out in your churchyard, logs I myself felled, stripped, and hewed—"

"Passable workmanship, the Crown commends you," Cunningham interrupted.

Salt blurted, "That child wanted to shoot my child!"

"*Wanted?* I *want* a million pounds. I *want* clotted cream and scones and roses in bloom every day of the year."

"Bayonet."

"A French invention."

"He charged."

"You are charged with murder."

"It was self defense."

"Was it?"

"In the sense that—"

"Were there witnesses?"

"Yes, Your Honor. Two of your Hessians, which I saw being led away in chains—"

"Deserters. And to think, the Crown pays the German baron ten pence a day for such—or, I should say, paid. Those expenditures will end, starting yesterday. The Hessians will be hanged for their crime."

"What crime?"

"Desertion."

Salt and Sowell exchanged frowns.

"Answer me! Were there any other witnesses?"

"My hired hand."

"Your boy?"

"He is not my *boy*, he is my hired hand."

"I mean your *son*, fool. I'm a Yankee, goddamn it. Treat me as such."

"Two witnesses, Your Honor. My hired hand *and* my son."

Cunningham ran a tongue over the place his lips would have been had he any to speak of. "Very well. Pillory the prisoner. He is to be hanged on the morrow, along with the Hessian dodgers. And apprehend the, ahem, *hired hand*. And the son."

"But Your Honor!" cried Sowell. "This is to be a fair trial!"

"The first truth you've uttered all day."

"Not an auto-da-fe!"

"Language, please! We are in a house of God!"

———•·•———

SALT COULD STAND the stocks. His wrists and neck were scraped raw by the rough oaken yoke, his rear end was exposed. When he'd given in to the urge to relieve himself, he'd remained uncleaned. Hazy sunshine and a steamy breeze brought up a sweat, salty drips stung his eyes, crept into the corners of his mouth, tantalizing his sticky tongue. He was stiff and sore and every breath hurt like a blade in the ribs. But all this Salt could stand. Forty years had given him plenty of practice in tolerating discomfort.

"American!" shouted one of the Hessians. "Them hang us tomorrow!" They were caged in the old animal pen, not far from Salt. The churchyard walls had been spiked with hundreds of two-inch dowels, each sharpened to a point and angled alternately inward and outward. Both Hessians wore ankle irons, and their hands were manacled behind their backs. A third Hessian who was uncaged, an older man with a more distinguished uniform, addressed them in German, a language of burbles and coughs to Salt's ears, until the prisoners nodded enthusiastically. "Yah! Yah!"

The older Hessian clapped once and the grinning idiot, who had been scooping dirt with a spoon, ran to him like a dog. The Hessian gave him a copper. The idiot bit it, held it aloft, ogled it, and then, after pocketing it, smilingly reached through the cage bars to unbutton the prisoners' uniforms, and remove them. He delivered the uniforms to the older Hessian, who in return handed over a jug and two rolled cigarettes. The idiot stuck the cigarettes into the caged prisoners' mouths, lighting one and then the other. This excited him greatly. Next he offered them a drink from the jug. It was too big to fit between the bars, so the idiot helped each to a long guzzle from the spout, before sniffing it himself. "Rum!" they cried. "More!"

"Sir, please, a smoke." Salt wanted, no, needed hemp. He felt that smoking was the root need from which all others derived. Even tobacco would do. He pantomimed. "Smoke?"

The older Hessian barked something in German, ending with, "Yah?"

"Yah," Salt nodded, setting the Hessians in the cage into an uproar of laughter. They rolled and rattled their chains, guffawing until the dainty ogre exploded into a tussive fit. The idiot jumped up and down, chattering like an ape and rubbing a palm through his lank hair.

"He say, he miss his wife long time," translated the toothless Hessian. "He say, he want loving you. Yah?"

"Smoke."

The older Hessian plucked a cornflower—they grew like weeds—and gently placed it behind Salt's ear. He leaned in close. The Hessian's eyes were deep brown, and he was wheezing. From a pouch he tapped out tobacco stems into a cornhusk, spindled it, ignited it with a flintlock, and puffed rapidly, getting it fired. Extracting the cigarette from his mouth, he placed it, slick with saliva, into Salt's lips. It was repulsive, but Salt bit it and inhaled deeply. The relief was instant and fleeting.

The old Hessian placed his lips next to Salt's ear. Cheek to cheek, Salt felt the old man's scratchy whiskers. *"Liebchen."*

"Smoke."

The old man disappeared behind him. Salt felt a splash

of lukewarm water on his backside, then another. The water pooled at his knees. Several of the workmen stopped to watch. The idiot lost his grin and jammed a hand down the front of his pants, then gaped as if dislocating his jaw. Salt looked from face to face, trying to read there what was happening behind him. A redcoat smirked. A freed slave made the sign of a cross. A bricklayer swallowed. The Hessians in the cage drank rum and cackled, the first one clasping the jug in his chained feet and lifting it to the mouth of the second.

Behind him, Salt heard a belt unbuckle.

———•••———

IN THE CLERGY's quarters, Ebenezer sat in a hand-carved rosewood chair. A hint of frankincense hung in the cavernous room, chilled by the marble floors. Behind the desk Cunningham's fingertips lightly plied the pile of paper money Ebenezer had paid him. Cheeks red-patched, nose threaded with veins, forehead a band of pimples, if Cunningham's skin was any indication of his personality, Ebenezer reflected, he was a generous host to pain and discomfort.

"In addition to currency, I'm able to offer the Crown provisions, billets for officers, and a significant line of credit." Ebenezer cleared his throat, still parched from the breakneck gallop. He'd just as soon see his son-in-law hanged, but Molly had been anguished, and it was her sob that had driven Ebenezer forth like a horseman of twenty. His spurs had streaked blood over the church's threshold. And it wasn't just for Molly; James's fate was at stake. If Ebenezer would die for his daughter, he would kill for his grandson. Unfortunately, this passion robbed him of negotiating skills, a lack he felt keenly as he dipped a quill into an inkwell, spilling a droplet off to the side, and sketched a map to Drinky Crow's beach flat, south of Jamaica through wetlands to a small inlet off a spit in Hempstead Bay, then across the channel to Rockaway. Now everything was on the table.

When Ebenezer looked up, Cunningham was regarding him intently. The man had no lips, which to Ebenezer made him seem alien, inhuman. He said, "General, you look familiar."

"Call me Your Honor. I am not yet made general." Cunningham kept his red eyes on Ebenezer's.

How could the man see past all that bloodshot? Ebenezer regarded Cunningham's elaborate costume, the gold fringed epaulets, the badges and pins festooning his breast, the purple robe. "Your uniform led me to believe—"

"Your travails have rendered you tired and dusty." Now that terms were defined, Cunningham could afford civilities. He turned to his sentry, a crisply uniformed mulatto carrying a rifle. "Refreshments for our guest." The sentry swiftly exited, leaving Cunningham and Ebenezer alone. "Your generosity is well appreciated by his Majesty. I am sure that the gifts you bestow come without contingency. That said, I wish to offer you something in recompense. The safety of your family—your daughter and grandson—is your right as a British subject, and I'll see to it that that right is enforced. Protected. Ensured. What have you."

Ebenezer let out a shudder.

"As you know, I cannot release the prisoner." Cunning-ham extracted a key from his vest pocket, gently stroking it.

Ebenezer thought of Molly. There was no question that his daughter's pain outweighed Ebenezer's pleasure should Salt be gone from their lives, and Ebenezer felt a quiver of guilt even for checking the equation. But wasn't he only doing what any old man would do?

Cunningham studied Ebenezer. This was one of Cun-ningham's purest joys, watching a man struggle with such a dilemma—whether to help a loved one by betraying her. And this joy coupled so well the less pure satisfaction of ex-tracting cash for the Crown, and in the process advancing his own career. People said that a born American could advance so far and no farther in the Royal Army. Well, Cunningham would test that truism. He beckoned Ebenezer close, and placed his lips to the old man's cheeks. "However, we can do a bit of nuncupative business," he whispered, and the moist rasp in Ebenezer's ear was oddly familiar. "On your way out of the compound you will pass the stockade." Cunningham pushed the key across the desk. "The prisoner must flee. At once. To Ohio or some other ghastly locale. No goodbyes. He goes with nothing but his clothes. If he dares show his nose at home, he will be strung from a sycamore."

"Thank you, Ge—Your Honor." Ebenezer stood to bow.

The mulatto sentry returned with a silver platter loaded with quail eggs, cured meats, sliced pineapple. "Kickshaws?" Cunningham entreated. "Wine!" A servant poured goblets of claret and pulled doilies from bread baskets and rounds of cheese.

"To his Majesty's health," said Ebenezer. "And to your mercy."

"Bah!" cried Cunningham. "We have done what we must."

They toasted, Ebenezer noticed, with chalices used for Sunday services.

Cunningham called in the scribe to notarize the transactions. "We'll not be subject to accusations that ours is a rule of bribery and extortion."

Ebenezer knew that his daughter, and most certainly his son-in-law, would see this business as just that, notwithstanding the official registry. Cunningham unrolled a parchment, fought it flat. A monocle magnified one glaucous eye, the other was squeezed shut. "Tell me. 'He has refused his assent to laws the most wholesome and necessary for the public good.' This, about King George! What the bloody hell does that sentence mean?"

Ebenezer's thirst overcame his reluctance to sip from the chalice. "I wouldn't know, sir, though I would guess it's a reference to—"

"Blah. It means blah. Did you know that our Jefferson's first draft consisted of a page and a half in longhand blaming the King of England for the shameful institution of slavery?" Cunningham read aloud. "'He has waged cruel war against human nature itself, violating its most sacred rights of life and liberty in the persons of a distant people'—negroes, he means—'who never offended him, captivating and carrying them into slavery in another hemisphere, or to incur miserable death in their transportation thither.' And here. 'He has prostituted his negative for suppressing every legislative attempt to prohibit or to restrain this execrable commerce determining to keep open a market where MEN should be bought and sold: and that this assemblage of horrors might want no fact of distinguished die, he is now exciting those very people to rise in arms among us, and to purchase that liberty of which he has deprived them, by murdering the people upon whom he also obtruded them: thus paying off former crimes committed against the liberties of one people, with crimes which he urges them to commit against the lives of another.' *'Prostituted his negative?'* That is one piece of horrific writing. Your Southern colonists would not stand for this outburst—coming from one who himself enslaves the mother of his child—and thus had it excised."

"Slavery, an abomination."

"He found her pretty."

"Slavery, I said."

"An institution bigger than you or me."

"Like holding a wolf by the ears."

"The Declaration of *Ineptness*, he should have titled it!" Cunningham bared his teeth. "Of *Indebtedness*. Your rich Virginia slave drivers call themselves statesmen? They are not statesmen—this incoherent document is proof of that. They are not even rich. That Jefferson owes bags of money to his London bankers."

Ebenezer extended his hand. "We have concluded business then. Call on me when need arises. I am Your Majesty's servant."

"Honor, not Majesty. But we have not quite finished." Cunningham did not bother to rise. "The boy. Your grandson. James, is it?"

Ebenezer froze. "Yes."

"He is to be quartered here. We shall give him military training, school him for the dragoons." Cunningham sipped his wine, ran a tongue over his teeth. "You look ill-pleased."

"His mother will be anxious."

"She'll get him back every Sunday. Think of it as boarding school."

Ebenezer did not know what to say. "The boy was not made for war."

"He might say differently." Cunningham jabbed a thumb toward the dead officer.

Ebenezer considered what else he might offer, but there was nothing. He had already given up Drinky Crow, Salt. "My grandson was born in this country. It won't do to turn him against it."

"Ha! I was born in this country, and this country is called Great Britain. We'll make a leader of him." Cunningham summoned an officer. "After all, we've got to replace like with like."

In strode a strong-backed officer with half his face burnt off. An unblinking eye peered out, like a hock in a ham.

"Major General Michael Drayton, awaiting your orders."
The scar did not elicit pity. Its owner smiled, or rather, the
lips on the unburned side of his face rose and a dimple
formed in that cheek, a double dimple, as if an extra one
could make up for its missing counterpart. While one eye
stared openly and drooled, the other scanned the table, taking note of the cash, the map, the wine and cheese, the documents. Ebenezer looked for a reflection of his own shame
in either eye, but could find none. The Major General appeared to be a disciplined soldier with an unimpeachable
sense of duty, his wound likely incurred in battle. In this he
was the antidote to Cunningham, and he made Ebenezer
proud to be British. "Thank you kindly, Major General." He
turned. "Almost forgot." He gave Cunningham a wallet.
"The dead boy's papers. My daughter cleaned and bathed
him, but neglected to return this to his person."

Major General Michael Drayton bowed to Cunningham
and escorted Ebenezer out.

Cunningham waited till they were gone to open the wallet. Out fell a sheaf of notes, paper money, and an officer's
commission. *John Cunningham,* it said, giving him a start.
The name was fairly common, but even so…Cunningham
rifled through the papers, looking for a birthplace, a mother's
name, some clue.

He examined the dead boy. The merely sleeping never
looked so pale, so absolutely alone. Cunningham sniffed,
and through the frankincense and beeswax, in the marble

cool air, smelled death. Water in a drain. Carefully, he rebut-toned one of the brass studs that had come undone on the boy's uniform.

"Sentry!" Cunningham picked up the map that Ebenezer had so reluctantly sketched.

"Sir?" The mulatto sentry's long hair fell in loose curls about his shoulders, and his uniform was immaculately pressed. He tugged on one cuff, then the other, to fit them just right. Each finger was adorned with at least one ring, even the thumbs.

Cunningham let his eye rest a moment on his underling. Who said a man cannot be beautiful? "Assemble a dozen sol-diers. Equip them with muskets, sabers, and torches. Have them dull their bayonets." He handed over the map. "Make it hurt."

"Pleasure." The sentry bowed and left.

———

In the churchyard, sun fell like a clash of tin. Ebenezer squinted into it. Workers sawed, hammered, dug, troweled, and hauled. White men spit, slopped, wrenched, bound, awled, punched, and sank, doing the anonymous rag and bone work of civilization. The black men yoked to the grind-stone still tromped their endless circle. Sparrows bathed themselves in dust, rubbing their wings in it, beaking it, spilling it over themselves as if it were rainwater. The idiot skipped about, flying a butterfly like a kite tethered by a thread. It was a disgrace, Ebenezer felt, this commandeering of hallowed grounds. But the Royal Army needed someplace to call home, and the rebels forced them to it, and so had only themselves to blame.

They passed through a gate into a field where negroes hoisted white blocks to form a wall. A disgrace too, that they had been gammoned into believing forced labor was freedom.

"What bricks are those?" asked Ebenezer.

"Sir, they are headstones."

"Why?"

"Why?" It was not a question Drayton was often asked, and one he rarely asked himself.

"Why headstones? And whose?"

Drayton motioned left, and suddenly there was Salt, on his knees, head thrusting from the stock, hands flapping. His forehead was sunburned, cheeks streaked with mud, and somebody had placed a cornflower sprig behind his ear. On his back was an old Hessian, trousers around his ankles.

"Excuse me." Drayton cracked the Hessian's head with his rifle butt, and the Hessian crumpled to the ground.

On seeing his father-in-law, Salt flushed. Disgrace made him want to turn away even from himself. But he couldn't hide, nor could he stand tall. Perhaps he deserved to be pilloried—a middle-aged man dependent on the father of the girl he loved for everything, even this release.

Ebenezer sneered. "Molly sends her love."

The two Hessian soldiers, hands tied behind their backs, feet chained together, hooted in their cage. One of them grasped the jug with his feet and the other, using his chin and lips, found the spout and guzzled, the spilled liquor glinting in his beard. "Papa come for me?"

Salt glumly held mute. The only thing he possessed of value was a bunghole, which the British officer had arrived just in time to save.

"Whose headstones are those?" Ebenezer asked, as if Salt had personally given the order for the conscripts to take them.

An armed guard jabbed a large key into the enormous clasp locking the stocks.

"Don't release me!" Salt barked.

The guard fumbled with the key.

"Don't be stupid," Ebenezer said, distracted by the headstones. "Do you realize how much you are costing me?"

The guard continued.

"Stop!"

"Go!"

The guard followed Ebenezer's orders, disregarding Salt's. A bawling infant would command more respect.

"Bring key here, Papa!" shouted the bearded Hessian, neck veins abulge, his spiflicated mug slick with tears.

"Papa, please!" echoed the other Hessian, craning his neck sideways, gumming the rum bottle like a teething baby. "Me too!"

"Tombstones! You can't build a fortress with tombstones!" Ebenezer stalked to the wall for a closer look.

"Get up." With his rifle butt, the guard prodded Salt.

Salt stiffly uncoiled. His body hurt, the muscles in his neck and shoulders rigid as jerky. Right and wrong, truth, justice, character, virtue, none of it counted. It all came down to coin changing hands.

The idiot clapped with delight, the only free soul among them, and let go of the butterfly. Up it went, disappearing over the wall, string trailing behind. As the idiot watched, jaw thrust skyward, he wept with happiness or horror, Salt couldn't tell which.

The Hessian buggerer met Salt's eyes and shrugged, and Salt understood that it wasn't anything about his ass in particular, any ass would serve. Salt forgave him. Loneliness wasn't personal.

"Go," said Drayton. He explained to Salt the conditions of his freedom. "You have been granted safe passage to New York City. From there, go west. If you return, you will be shot dead."

"Put me out of my misery."

The guard kissed the rifle butt. "I'd be well pleased to."

Ebenezer cursed. "She gave you honey."

Salt smiled, pleased that at the old man's anger. "And that's why you got me banished? If we abandon the sugar boycott you'll let me stay?"

But Ebenezer wasn't listening. He crouched in the gauzy haze reflected by the white headstones. His fingers caressed a marble block atop a row stacked three deep. Engraved on it were the words *Sparrow Bowers Woodstock, Wife, Mother 1710-1767.*

"Damn!" Ebenezer reached under his jacket and swiftly pulled out his pistol.

The guard raised his rifle uncertainly. All around, work ceased. Cicadas took advantage of the silence to announce themselves, a dozen serried rasps. The idiot trundled forward and put a finger in the barrel of Ebenezer's pistol.

"Papa," cried the toothless Hessian. "Me want free."

Ebenezer whispered, "Who dug that up?"

Drayton understood. He crisply addressed a subordinate. "See to it that the headstone is returned to its proper place." The soldier did not move. "As well as the others. Put them all back where they belong."

"But, sir, you contradict His Honor's direct orders."

"Return the headstones now, or I will cage you with the hacks."

The soldier, sulking, did as commanded. The negroes began to disassemble the wall, putting the headstones back on the wagon. Slowly, the buzz of activity in the churchyard picked up. "You have my promise," said Drayton. The idiot extracted his finger from Ebenezer's pistol and Ebenezer tucked it back into his waistband. He let Drayton lead him down the path out the gate. "They didn't unbury *her*, did they?"

"Papa," cried the drunken Hessian, blinking against the sticky light. "Me?"

———·—·———

By FIRELIGHT, Drinky Crow's skin glowed red. He sat at a table of pine, next to a large stump. A gentle twilight bathed the settlement of four wooden houses, built among a stand of elms a hundred yards from shore. His daughters' husbands had gone down coast to trade cod for guns, leaving Drinky Crow to look after the three of them, their daughters, and Drinky Crow's wife, Roquat. The women wore beaded necklaces, sparkling bracelets. They were pretty and attentive and devoted to him above all men. Above, a single star twinkled green, red, white. It was the same star that Drinky Crow had wished on thousands of times. Only tonight he had nothing to wish for, because there was nothing he lacked. Family, health, his mother's land. Ancestral heritage and ownership mattered, everybody agreed, but not as much as fifty dollars an acre. White man's culture was one of moments seldom revisited, which had its advantages.

And yet, Drinky Crow recognized that this feeling of contentment, while enjoyable, was an illusion. The incident at Salt's had not been resolved. Drinky Crow had fled unobserved. The Hessians would not know his name or whereabouts, and Drinky Crow was certain that Salt would not give him up. But there was the matter of the dead redcoat.

Drinky Crow's daughters and granddaughters laughed while they plaited one another's tresses with jay, cardinal, and kite feathers. The youngest, Erie, was just six. She giggled, trying to hold still, while Roquat squatted before a bowl of luminescent powder, golden and coppery, stripped from the wings of monarch butterflies. She dipped in a fingertip and applied it to her daughter's eyelid. Femininity was a balm, a salve, that like music both soothed and stirred. Roquat was thin and hard, deeply wrinkled. Her dark hair was piled atop her head and her ears hung low, weighted with earrings made of scallop shells. Her eyelids sparkled as well as she turned to her husband. "Get off your ass and poke the fire."

If Drinky Crow had been capable of smiling, he would have just then. He threw a piece of split maple onto the fire, sending yellow sparks into the twilight, and a cloud of sweet smoke mixed with the salt air. The sand beneath his feet was cool and moist, as if it too was breathing peacefully, and the surf yielded no waves, just tiny shelves of crumbling foam. "You are an ill-mannered queen who doesn't know how to ask politely for her pleasure."

Roquat had a large iron kettle aboil. By her side, lobsters clicked lethargically in a net. "I take my pleasure where I can."

"Your pleasure is my pleasure."

"Say what you mean." Roquat dropped lobsters into the pot, one at a time, each emitting a high-pitched whistle of finality as it plunged.

"Mean what you say." Depending on how it was spoken, each word carried, at the very least, a meaning and its opposite. Drinky Crow gently placed a hand on Roquat's buttocks. It had been awhile. "And though I've had a long life and there is much I have mastered—" he squared his hips to hers "—I am still mastered by intent."

Roquat backed her rear into him, wiggling. Drinky Crow was at the age where he observed each feeling as if for the last time, which was remarkably like meeting it for the first time. Just as every word communicated its opposite, every emotion carried its loss. Approached this way, even pain gave pleasure. He held his wife firmly by the hips and gave a little thrust.

"Disgusting," cried their daughters. "Take it indoors."

There was corn on the cob, stewed dandelion greens, and fry bread. Boiled, the lobsters had turned bright red. Roquat placed each on the stump and cracked its shell with a mallet. Their daughters tore out the sweet flesh and piled it on a wooden platter. The creamy tail meat steamed. Drinky Crow ate with his fingers because he liked touching his food. He also liked the admonitions of his daughters: "Use a fork like a gentleman." He dangled threads of leg meat into his raised mouth, purposely slurping.

He knew the white men would come after him. It was their war.

White men were more superstitious than Indians. Their *independence*, for example. No such thing existed. Everything a man could name was interdependent with him, most especially his enemy. It wasn't that Drinky Crow didn't harbor his own superstitions. *Freedom*, for example. Life as a slave, Drinky Crow believed, had turned his father into a rapist. Unable to shape his own destiny, he did what he could to seize that of a creature more powerless than himself, a Rockawakian girl. And Drinky Crow, a free man, the result. This land he had bought back from the same white men who killed his mother's people. He recognized in himself the rage and pain that went into his making.

Above the suss of low surf sounded hoofbeats. The girls brightened, thinking their men were home early from their journey. Drinky Crow knew otherwise.

Two dozen dragoons, riding in formation, stampeded into camp, circling Drinky Crow's clan. Their leader was a mulatto, but blacker than Drinky Crow himself, and so pretty as to be almost angelic, with full lips and jet hair that fell to his shoulders in perfect curls. He ran the backs of his fingers through it, tucking a lock behind one ear, then another. On his fingers were bright and gaudy rings.

Without bothering to dismount, each soldier drew a weapon.

It appeared to Drinky Crow that the troops were intent on making quick work of their task. And in his experience, wishing on a star had answered his prayers once or twice, but never in a practical matter. When the stakes were high and the need immediate, money worked best. "Spare the women and there is gold for you."

"If there's gold here we'll find it without your help." The pretty one, raising a scabbard in his clenched fist, rings reflecting the firelight, was the first to strike.

———•—•———

JAMES HAD TAKEN up Molly's post on the porch. Master of his nerves, he neither paced nor cursed. Nor did he spit or grimace or sigh. But he was unable to stop himself from grabbing a rifle off the rack across from the broom. If they didn't want him taking it then why did they leave it lying around? Grown-ups. His father had been captured, humiliated again. Always the loser. And, as always, his mother had to send his grandfather to the rescue. It wasn't fair they always put her in charge. James would help her. He would be the man to answer to. He looked down the long barrel of the rifle and vowed to shoot the first creature to land in his sights, but when he saw a team of horsemen rounding the bend, he scurried quickly to replace the gun in the rack. He picked up a broom and busied himself sweeping.

Ebenezer was accompanied, or escorted, by a British soldier whose face had melted into a swirl of hard flesh, like the palm of a hand, creased. Out of this shone a blue eye, steady and wet, that seemed to see everything, or nothing at all. James watched for it to blink, but it didn't, or wouldn't.

Ebenezer dismounted, and so did the troops behind him. Unlike the Hessians and the bitter redcoat James had confronted yesterday, these regiments had new English rifles, shiny and well oiled. Their uniforms were pressed, spotless, expensive. The burnt-faced man had two pistols holstered in a green sash that crossed his chest. "Where's your mother?"

"Doing chores," said James, a phrase that he and his grandfather both knew meant butchering a pig. Molly could bring herself to slaughter only when distraught; unpleasant tasks for unpleasant times.

"That's a man's job."

James flushed at the broom in his hands. Why had he picked it up? Too late now to put it back without calling extra attention. "Try telling her that."

The burnt-faced officer removed his hat and strode forward. "Major General Michael Drayton. Your father is unharmed."

James gripped the broom hard, wishing that it was the rifle, then glad that it wasn't. What would Tom Paine do? This soldier Drayton was all spine, crisp of syllable, battle-scarred, lethally armed—the very embodiment of Common Sense. "I didn't ask you," James addressed him.

Ebenezer took note of the fierce grasp with which James held the ridiculous broom, Molly's broom, thanking God it wasn't the rifle. "Your father has made his choice."

To James, his grandfather looked pinched, embattled, with his receding gums and constant grimace. Nothing unusual in that. But there was something amiss, in his sticky blinks, now the thumb wipe to an eye. "What's wrong, Grandpa?"

"The inhuman turds…"

James squinted.

"…disinterred her!" Ebenezer blew his nose into a kerchief. "They dug her up!" When he opened his mouth as if to say more, out came a single sob.

"Your father has gone," said Drayton. "And until the hostilities are resolved, must stay gone."

"I know my father," said James, believing it. "You cannot keep him from Mother and me."

"I'm afraid we can."

"He will come."

"He will not," said Drayton. "He is fully aware that to do so would be to invite violence upon those he loves."

James considered the statement, then considered the speaker. "How did your face get like that?"

"James, hush," Ebenezer said.

Seeing no reaction in Drayton, James continued, "So, me and Mother are hostages?"

Ebenezer sputtered at the accusation. The troops stomped their boots and clattered their weapons. Somebody wearing a wide-brimmed hat was stumbling up the path, pushing a wheelbarrow. From the cross-holsters on his sash, Drayton drew both pistols. The economy of the gesture, born of years of training, impressed James. "Halt!"

The figure wore buckskin pants and a cotton smock sparged in blood. Under the belt was a long knife. Whatever was in the wheelbarrow was hidden by a tarp streaked with red.

"Ma!"

Drayton sleeved sweat from his forehead, and combed his hair with his fingers. His men tore away the tarp, revealing a fresh pig carcass with tongue hanging out, bits of straw sticking to an eyeball, blanketed by flies. When Molly removed the wide-brimmed hat, chestnut hair fell past her shoulders. Drayton was struck by her dark eyes, her white cheeks, the spattered blood. She was not beautiful, but her resolve attracted.

James bounded to her. She hugged the boy hard, and

at her glance, Drayton felt caught between a mother and her cub.

Feelings, Drayton's own and others', had always been a mystery to him, the taxonomy of human emotions more opaque and intimidating than Thucydides. He had to see a thing to believe it, and he knew this for the weakness it was. He reseated his pistols over his heart and studied the woman, waiting for her eyes, which she kept to herself.

"Did you get something to eat?" Molly asked James. She set her bloody smock atop the barrow, and with one arm tightly around her son, grabbed Ebenezer with the other. "What's wrong, Father?" The three of them, arms linked, climbed to the porch. The show of solidarity was not lost on Drayton. Molly released her son and father and picked up the broom, sweeping aside the dust the soldiers had tracked. Her shirt was loose, unbuttoned at the neck, and, as she swept, the muslin there swayed a half-second later than her hips. All that had initially been masculine in her appearance was transformed. It was a performance of sorts, Drayton felt, a stay against him, a rejection of fate.

Molly turned to the man with the burnt face. "Who's in charge here?" she asked, as if she didn't know the answer.

"Major General Michael Drayton, ma'am." Drayton climbed onto the porch. "Your husband takes the blame for killing the young officer." As he explained the terms of Salt's punishment, his gaze strayed to Molly's open collar, but she appeared unshaken by either the terms or the gaze.

"You're telling me I will never see my husband again?"

"You might. At war's end." He noticed that while her voice remained steady, her lips had parted, her breath had quickened, and she looked past him toward the fields.

Molly had wished upon her broomstick and been rewarded. There was Salt, crouching behind a large hemp plant, one hand on a stalk, the other holding back a branch. Not a minute after this self-important Brit said he wouldn't, Molly's man came home for her. For James. What Salt lacked for was not loyalty. And that loyalty she would return in kind. But she would not betray him by showing relief.

Drayton paused in his recitation of James's syllabus— mathematics, combat, Latin—puzzled by Molly's lack of response, made awkward by it. "Rest assured he will be well schooled. I will attend to his training myself." Still she did not reply. He shifted on his feet. "And I will personally deliver him to and fro."

No word of thanks from Molly, and barely a nod before her eyes ranged past him. This time he turned to see what she saw. A cultivated field, some weedy crop. "What plant is that?"

"Hemp," Ebenezer sputtered. "A fool's fortune's worth." Then, to his daughter, "This officer has just made an extraordinary offer. The boy will be tutored and trained in a royal capacity by a decorated soldier of the highest integrity."

Molly cried, "Haven't you caused enough trouble for one day?"

3

EBENEZER SHUFFLED into the room, his bare feet scuffing the lemon-oiled pine boards. He would not walk on the handloomed Persians, unwilling to add wear. To Molly, her father's conservatism seemed a sickness, progressive and deeply annoying. As was the why-me pinch of his eyes.

"I'll be mad if you're sad," he said.

"You expect joy?" Molly pulled aside the Irish lace and gazed out the darkened window. Two posted sentries, muskets slung over their shoulders, peered up at her. She shut the curtains in disgust.

"The gallows awaited him," Ebenezer protested. Candlelight painted his teeth gold and drew shadows in the hollows of his cheeks and eyes, giving him, to Molly, the appearance of a chattering skull. "They had Salt in the stocks. Nude, befouled, on his knees. A mercenary degrading him beastly."

"Hush!" Molly hurriedly escorted him out of the room,

shutting the door behind them. "Are you doing this on purpose?"

"Explaining myself?"

"You know what."

"You sound like your mother."

"Painting such pictures," Molly said. "No son should remember his father so."

Ebenezer exploded. "What's wrong with the truth? I saved his life, by God!"

Molly stomped across the carpets and slammed the door behind her. Ebenezer trailed her downstairs and into the library, where two armed guards were playing cards. The house was patrolled front and back and on the sides, seven soldiers by her count. In the kitchen were three more, including the pretty mulatto, exquisitely coiffed, rings on all of his fingers.

Molly removed Sparrow's sapphire from her finger and fled back upstairs, seeking a place free of occupiers. The candle in her hand guttered, its spawn of phantoms jigged on the oak wainscoting. Ebenezer followed. He insisted that he had invited the troops, and that since it all belonged to him—the lace, the candlestick, the Persian carpets underfoot and the roof overhead—he had the right.

At least there were no soldiers in her bedroom. She led Ebenezer inside and shut and locked the door. Her bed was crisply made, the quilt taut, two pillows aligned on top. She stood the candle on the cherrywood nightstand. Ebenezer owned the pillows, the bed, the lock on the door, and the cherrywood nightstand itself.

"Take it back." Molly threw the ring at him. "Take it!"

"Ingrate!" Ebenezer said. He plucked the ring off the floor and sat himself down in the rocking chair, its wickerwork creaking.

"Finally you get what you want."

"I want my Sparrow back!" Ebenezer bellowed. He stood up fast, upsetting the rocking chair. "I want the you I knew!"

"You got the me you raised—"

"Not this shrew."

"—all to yourself!"

"Go find your husband then." Ebenezer sat down on the bed. "No, you won't go." He wouldn't stand on the rugs he'd bought himself, Molly noted, but felt free to rest his bony buttocks on the duvet she'd sewn with her own hands. "He can't take care of you like I do."

"Get off my bed."

Ebenezer put the ring on his pinky finger and jabbed it at her. "You won't give up your comforts!" His neck was knotty and corded, his face positively apoplectic, and then, abruptly, he silenced himself and seemed to shrink, transfixed by banging on the door. He unlocked it, and two guards stuck their heads inside, features etched with threat.

"You won't give up the past!"

"Dug up…" Ebenezer babbled. "Ripped from eternal peace….I saw her."

The soldiers left, gingerly.

"Who?"

"Your mother, God rest—" Ebenezer collapsed into the rocker.

———

MICHAEL DRAYTON cursed the crickets. The chirruping came in waves from all directions, in varying timbres, rendering other sounds indistinct and hard to identify. Like the crack of a twig, if it was that, just now. He held his bayonet in both hands, loosely, professionally, riding the fulcrum, letting the blade lead him to the man he must kill.

Drayton excelled in the arts of war. From the beginning of his career, he had performed well and pleased his superiors, and they had rewarded him by making him Major General. Drayton was a commander of men, and respected himself as such. He could sharpshoot, grapple hand to hand, drill and stalk better than most. Few had his gift for strategy, wit for tactics. Instructed by Howe, Drayton had seen firsthand the lethal effectiveness of surprise and amassed power. Not far from here, in Brooklyn, they had broken Washington's back. Drayton had shot dead seven rebels, including two officers, by his count. The humiliated Americans with their coonskins and pitchforks had been forced to retreat in dories over the East River under cover of a lucky fog. Drayton himself had broken a wrist, had his thigh rent by a hot blade, his ears concussed by grapeshot. There had been no pain yet visited upon him that he couldn't have taken doubled. And though he had heard bullets whistling his own

name—there were Americans who could shoot a rifle too—
none had found its mark. He brought his fingertips to his
face, the skin there ticklish in the way a sole can be.

Drayton's unblinking eye watered. It was a tear with no
beginning, endlessly rolling down his cheek. That eye saw
things as they are instead of how they might appear, and its
tear had no manners or breeding, dripping on fife and drum,
blade and map, into tea and coffee, onto porcelain and pork
chop. It was a stream of a tear willed by its master to add its
payload of salt to the sea, and upon it float vessels destined
to change the world. But the truth was that most often the
tear got not much farther than Drayton's lip, where it was
quickly surrendered to a tongue that, in its middle-aged life,
had tasted its share of salt and now wanted sweet. The old
man Ebenezer was nothing to him, a bribe-dealing sympa-
thizer. Wronged, it was true, by the unnatural exhuming of
his wife's grave. But what of it? The son, James, promising,
dangerous. And the wife, Molly...

Drayton figured duty could be served if he spared the
family but ended the man. Molly had given him up without
realizing it. Had she thought a professional such as Drayton
would not notice her furtive glances toward the hemp field,
the relief she registered when she spotted who she hoped to
see? But before he dispatched the husband, Drayton wanted
some acknowledgment. To begin with, an admission that life
was unfair. The man—Salt—was loved, anybody could see
that. His wife was a vision of fidelity. Together they had

produced a child, thereby engendering more love. Drayton wanted Salt to recognize the gifts he had been granted, to see that all men were not so endowed. Ultimately, in the course of human events, Salt's gifts must be transferred— no, too strong a word—*entrusted* to Drayton. How Salt responded to this fact would determine how Drayton would kill him, mercifully or not.

Another crunch of stems underfoot startled him. Drayton swiveled, slicing the night air, but the source was lost in the crickets.

Self-pity drove his envy, as always. Drayton knew this. Now, however, there was excitement, too. Salt was a rival, and the prospect gave Drayton a rise. Competition was— like whiskey, like war—an acquired taste, and its own reward.

Suddenly, Drayton was lassoed from behind, the cord binding his arms to his body, his legs kicked out from under him. His rifle cartwheeled away. A knee ground into his spine. Face down, he got dirt in his eye, the one that couldn't blink it away.

"Who are you and what do you want?" Tears ran like salt water wrung from a rag. Drayton cursed the lost lid.

"These parts are crawling with runners. Old Man Jones gave up his mares to them."

Drayton guessed to whom the voice belonged. How had he, a military man, let himself get caught by surprise? It had never happened until now, until this woman, Molly, had got him all tangled up in his thoughts. The enemy above and behind him smelled of rough smoke. Drayton summoned his soldier's voice. "My orders are shoot to kill."

"Hogtied you bluster."

"The house is defended by seven soldiers, all highly disciplined."

"Like yourself."

Drayton couldn't think fast enough to return the insult. "Like myself."

"Unfamiliar with the land. Its people."

"It is my duty to become..." and now his wit returned, "...familiar." Drayton gasped as the knee drove into his kidney.

"You provoke infidelity."

"There is no greater infidelity than betrayal of the Crown."

"You are an authority, then, on fidelity." This was spoken as a statement rather than a question, with a chilling absence of malice.

"I can assure you that the household will be protected." A sigh.

Drayton continued. "Are you a man that lives here?"

"I would be a man who lives here freely."

"One who did has been banished for the murder of a British officer. If he returns, I am duty-bound to kill not only him but his wife, his family."

The knee pressure eased. "I take you at your word."

There was a flash nearby, a cry, the sting of gunpowder in the nose. A lantern blazed, washing the field in scraps of light. Salt leapt and fled, stumbling over a rock. Drayton, freed, shook the coil of rope from his body and gave chase. Three British soldiers followed. More gunfire. "Run!" "Halt!" "There!" "Where?" The lantern went black. A few moments later, the soldiers reappeared, panting. "He escaped."

Drayton absentmindedly fingered the rope.

"Blood," said a soldier, kneeling to touch the black-stained grass. "Shall I prepare the lady for punishment?"

"Fool," Drayton said, meaning himself.

"Lord Cunningham's decree—"

"Cunningham's no Lord." Drayton snapped the rope. "Gather the troops at the house. Am I understood?"

The soldier didn't reply, instead sniffed the blood on his fingers. Then he turned to Drayton and raised his snout, as if catching a whiff of humiliation.

"Am I understood?" Drayton coiled the rope and tucked it into his waistband.

"Yes, sir." The soldier barked at his squad, "Get on back now! Nothing to see here."

Molly and James were pacing the porch when the soldiers returned. Moths fluttered around the lamps they held, creating a dizzying galaxy of shadows on the beadboard. The sentries stood stick-straight, muskets slung over shoulders, awaiting orders. The mulatto with the curly locks and the bejeweled fingers alone held his musket at the ready. He watched Drayton closely.

"We heard shots," Molly said. Her eyes were puffy, her cheeks red-patched.

"It was nobody."

"Then nobody was hurt?" She raised an eyebrow.

Drayton raised one of his in return. "Nobody got hurt, not badly anyhow."

Ebenezer staggered onto the porch, his arms full of bricks, their edges glinting in the lamplight. One of them slipped loose and slammed down with a *thunk*, gouging a pine plank. He thrust the others into the hands of any soldier who would take one. "Ingots! Bullion!"

"Sir, there is no need," Drayton said gently. Still Ebenezer doled. Finally Drayton ordered, "Stop!"

The command paralyzed Ebenezer, and there he stooped, chest heaving, until, unable to contain his hoard any longer, he unclenched and down it tumbled.

"Put away your gold, old man, before you buy your death with it."

Drayton produced the rope from behind his back and uncoiled it. Molly's face betrayed nothing, but the boy's eyes flickered from the rope to his mother, then back to Drayton. "The trespasser was a runner, common enough. These woods are crawling with thieves and smugglers." As Drayton described the ambush, he fashioned the rope into a hangman's noose. "By way of a boast, the runner alluded to the theft of Old Man Jones's mares last month." Drayton sharply tightened the noose. He turned to the soldier whose fists were armored with rings. "Corporal, your orders are to protect the family from such threats."

"Yes, sir."

"We are not the Old Bailey here."

"No, sir."

"We will not waste time entertaining petitions, claims, suasions of love or such."

"No, sir."

"We will swat runners same as mosquitoes."

"Yes, sir."

Drayton turned to go, then said, as if in afterthought, "He left behind his rope." He looked at Molly, then flung the noose to the corporal. "Save it in case he returns."

Molly had recognized the rope as Salt's, handspun from hemp grown in their own field. Had she underestimated Drayton? Unless Salt had gotten the best of Drayton—which Molly thought unlikely—then Drayton had let him go, and he had lied to his own soldiers. Warily, she wondered what he expected in return.

SALT'S MOUTH was cotton as he crashed through the brambles. He had been shot through the side, but the bullet hole had, best he could tell, both an entrance and an exit. It hurt like a side stitch, no worse, and was already starting to clot. He had covered miles since fleeing his attackers, running from Bury toward Hempstead Bay along Indian paths. Dirt underfoot yielded to sand. He knew there was poison ivy about, though he couldn't see it in the dark. In the next week his skin might erupt. Which imparted comfort, the possibility of a next week.

Because he was not dead, Salt could not arrive at Drinky Crow's empty-handed. To come without a gift was tantamount to a challenge, exile and bullet wound notwithstanding. But what could he bring? There was hemp in the drawstring bag in his britches pocket. Drinky Crow had his own crop, but Salt's was stronger and better, because Ebenezer's fields were more fertile than Drinky Crow's sandy spit, and Drinky Crow had taught Salt well how to baby the plant, to bring it to sweetness. It was a case of the pupil surpassing the master.

The sea air grew heavy, and Salt's foot stuck in tidal silt, which released it with a fart of marsh gas. Rather than go the long way, a three-mile half-circle, Salt decided to cross the channel, just a couple of hundred yards. He had done it before, and remembered the ebb tide running about waist deep. But as he began to wade he saw that the sea was rising, and so he hurried, up to his knees, to his hips, and when the saltwater reached his bullet hole it scalded. Was he being tested? If so, what exactly was being tested? Not faith, because Salt didn't believe. There was no God but feeling. Not endurance, because flesh was weak, and death undefeated. Not character, because Salt had none in particular. He was ordinary, except, perhaps, in how terribly he loved his family.

The eastern sky brightened, light like pink brush strokes on the tips of a thousand tiny wavelets. Seabirds flew west, their wings skimming the surface, then spiraled up like a waterspout. One by one, they dove, each hitting the water with a splash. A school of menhaden popped into the air—

inch-long minnows of silvery orange, battering his chest, one slapping his cheek. And then they were gone, the channel placid again, a trace of fishiness. A single gull hovered. There was a red spot on its beak, which scissored open, and its eye was blue. "Law, law, law," it screamed. "Law!"

By the time Salt made it across, the sun had risen, the sea emblazoned white, as if skimcoated with tallow. His britches were tattered and there were scratches all over his legs. His throat ached with thirst. The sand at his feet was streaked with foam. Scallop shells were cast about, aligned toward the surf like penitents toward a holy place.

A plume of smoke rose from Drinky Crow's settlement. At first Salt thought it was from a cooking fire, but as he neared he saw that the smoke was black, and shot up in a column that collapsed upon itself. A wet burn. Hurriedly, he shuffled around the stand of sycamore trees, their bark mottled and flaking, some leaves already shriveled and yellow. Crackled ash was all that remained of Drinky Crow's simple frame house atop its riprap foundation. Salt called out; the only answer the suss of the sea. A loud pop startled the gulls picking through the midden—a steaming pile of chicken and fish bones, shells of all sorts, including clams, scallops, crab and lobsters, a creeping burn in its fissures, every now and then a snap and a hiss. A single gull hopped backward, and Salt saw, among the rubbish where it had been pecking, a human jawbone, the flesh burned off, the teeth intact, molars and all. Nearby was the skull, bashed in as if by a rock, face and hair burnt off, a bit of brain bubbling inside like stew. Competing seagulls eyeballed it, waiting for it to cool. Ribs, a thigh bone.

"Law!" screamed the gull, chancing a peck at a molar. "Law! Law!"

Using a branch, Salt sifted through the sizzling bones. There were no clothes, no clues as to identity. Worriedly, he stumbled from squat to squat, peering into the steam, hunting for bodies. But there were none.

Choking with thirst, Salt staggered to the well. It had always surprised him that Drinky Crow was able to get fresh water on this strand. But if you dug deep enough, past the strata of brack, you got aquifer, the water there glacial. Salt had trouble raising the bucket. The rope yielded, but only just. He looped it around a nearby post to make a pulley, and then around the cross-post above the well. Using all his strength, he was able to get a purchase, and slowly hoist.

When he got the bucket to the top, he saw what had made the task so difficult. Tangled in the line was the body of Drinky Crow's granddaughter, Erie, gut-bayoneted, entrails hanging out through a fine blue dress with yellow daisies beaded into the bodice. Her fingernails were painted red, and plaited into her hair were bits of feather and pink ribbon.

———·—·———

"SANGRE DE CRISTO! Is there nobody left to kill?" The Spaniard, De la Luz, swayed back and forth, still on sea legs. A ponytail escaped from his British officer's hat, stolen and ill-fitting. He panted, and his eyebrows twitched. Unruly black whiskers sprouted from his nostrils above a grin full of black teeth. "Where is the Indio?"

"There is no god but Allah." The Arab, Mohammed, wore a woven skullcap. His clenched prayer beads hung like a pendulum stilled, while his body rolled and pitched.

"*Coño,* for why you pick fights?"

"It is a prayer."

"Praying is asking not telling." One cheek bulging with coca leaves, De la Luz's eyebrows fibrillated, as did his upper lip, as if each feature had a will of its own. He spat a gob of juice onto the sand where Salt lay curled around the dead girl. "*Muerto?*"

Mohammed stuck a boot in his back. "He breathes."

"Half to you, half to me."

The seagulls were busily picking at simmering remains. A few wisps of smoke still rose from the smoldering foundations, a late-afternoon breeze off the surf erasing them before they got head high. The blue sky held puffy white clouds, their peaceful appearance at odds with the scent of burnt flesh.

De la Luz chewed and spit, spit and chewed. He twirled one coarse hair of his moustache, then another. An eyelid fluttered until he ground a thumb into it. "*Malo.*"

"Lamentable." Mohammed sighed. "What monster did this?" He smiled, teeth gleaming.

De la Luz cocked his stolen hat, stuck his nose down the well, and sniffed. Then he cupped his hand over his mouth. "What you think is down there?"

"What?"

"Who?"

"Maybe the Indio."

"Don't smell like Indio."

"Don't worry. Murder is not catching."

De la Luz spoke through his fingers. "I worry."

Mohammed regarded the dead child. "Little girls need proper graves."

"Don't we all?"

"Rape and pillage, pillage and rape," said Mohammed, worrying a single bead between thumb and forefinger.

De la Luz squinted suspiciously, baring his fuzzy teeth. "Don't forget plunder."

Mohammed frowned. If one of them were to find loot first, he would kill the other and escape inland with the booty, deserting the ship. "Nothing of value left here."

"El Indio was dependable."

"No one will believe he's gone."

"If we return empty-handed the Captain will flog us."

"Let's take the guns and the powder in the skiff and sell them ourselves."

"And then what?"

"Land runners become."

"I don't know the job."

The pirates scowled at each other. For years, Drinky Crow had been one of their best fences. Even so, it had been foolish of them not to consider an alternative.

"What I want to know, for why they kill *la niña*? *Animales*."

"Make you want your mama." Mohammed grinned relentlessly. "The acts man commits." Black flies buzzed about the dead girl, an orange crab worked on her insides.

"Who is this one?" De la Luz gave a swift kick with a leather boot made crusty by saltwater, and Salt vomited.

"Give him grog."

"Give him yours."

"I have only a little."

"Same here."

Without another word, each thrust a hand thrice—rock, paper, shears. De la Luz lost. From a skin bag, he poured drink into Salt's mouth. "No lips. Keep your pox lips off." It splashed on Salt's chin, then he coughed once and swallowed greedily.

De la Luz spit a stream of coca slurry and a shudder passed through him. "We split the take." The crew was always in need of hands, and the captain paid ten quid per recruit. Whenever they could, they hotpressed, taking a man against his will—often a drunk passed out on the wharf—to serve a term on board. The British navy had started the custom, and it was especially sweet to turn the table, hotpressing Brits from captured frigates. There was always a need for experienced sailors. "Half to you, half to me."

"I saw him first." Mohammed clapped a hand to his heart.

"Then I must slit his throat." De la Luz drew his knife and touched his tongue to the point of the blade.

"Go ahead, then." Mohammed had lost his smile. "Surprise me."

"Bien." De la Luz made to stab Salt, but Mohammed grabbed his wrist in the air. "Five quid is five quid."

They sealed the deal with a handshake. In addition to earning them extra coin, the new recruit would relieve the other hands of the lowliest jobs—scraping barnacles, swabbing the sickroom. As a result, goodwill would flow back to them, the bringers of fresh meat, goodwill that would translate into favors—grog, butter, leave to plank a doxy.

De la Luz reseated his knife, and splashed more grog onto Salt's head.

Salt hacked and rubbed his eyes. Then he remembered Drinky Crow's ruined settlement, little Erie. "I...have to go home." His throat was raw, and he was angry at himself, as if base thirst dominated higher feelings and thereby reduced their value. He took up a handful of sand and pushed it into his mouth, as punishment for the mess the world—his world—had become. The sand made him retch, but nothing would come up. He was not even master of this.

De la Luz spat. "I can die happy I saw a man eat sand."

"I saw a Greek eat sand in Turkey," said Mohammed.

They hoisted Salt by the arms. "Stand up, murderer."

"Where is Drinky Crow?" Salt sputtered. Grains of sand clung to his lips.

"What we want to know. He owes money." The last part was untrue.

The pirates studied Salt. "Looks like the Captain," said Mohammed, taking in the lanky frame, boyish even at forty.

"Spitting image." De la Luz spat again. They watched Salt swallow more grog, sinews stretching in his long neck. Only the hardness to the eyes was lacking, something like pain in its place.

"Come with us, Cappy. You have a glorious future at sea."

Salt wrestled free. "I've got to go back to my wife and son." Now that he was revived, the craving for hemp returned. "The British are holding them."

"Rest easy, then. Redcoats will protect them from—"

"Redcoats? Who do you think did *this*?"

De la Luz licked his moustache.

Mohammed said, "Here is news to brighten your day. Our Captain is commissioned by the Governor of New Jersey as a privateer to seize what he may from the British waterdogs. And so, my companion, we are sworn against the same enemy, though for different reasons, perhaps."

"Let me go."

"*Tienes plata?*" asked De la Luz. "If you have ten quid you can buy your freedom."

Both were surprised when Salt reached into his pouch and extracted a few coins. The American was too green to recognize the simplest of shakedowns.

"That's all you got, Cappy?" With their cutlasses, they prodded him toward the skiff.

"Let me at least have a smoke first."

They pushed him onward.

"I had it backwards, it was a Turkey I saw eating sand in Greece."

"Stop!" bellowed Salt. Remarkably, they did. "I'll have my smoke!" He extracted a pinch from his pouch and tamped it into his pipe while the buccaneers looked on with curiosity. The moment passed, exquisitely, on Salt's exhale.

"YOU'RE A GOOD BOY." Michael Drayton spoke the words with apparent fondness. "Your mother loves you." He enunciated clearly, as befitting an officer in the British army, neither stern nor kind. There was certainty in this world, as well as doubt. Newly fitted with a commissioned officer's uniform, the boy looked sharp indeed, but for the slouch, the sullen pout, the surly eyes. "Any father would be proud. Very proud."

To James, each pronouncement scraped a little more meat off the bone. He was not a good boy. His own father said so. Did Drayton really think otherwise? Did Drayton know that James had been the one to bring down that redcoat, a bullseye through the heart at twenty paces. Is that what had impressed him, the marksmanship—or the courage to employ it? James buttoned just the middle of the three buttons on his breastcoat, as Drayton did. "I want a brace of pistols."

"When you earn them," Drayton said, as if there were no doubt that he would.

They marched through an infantry tent settlement and into headquarters—the occupied churchyard—trailed by the curly-locked corporal and his men, bearing bundles and a cart heaped with provisions. As they passed the stocks, a squadron of scruffy soldiers, including a few boys barely older than James himself, looked up from their stewpots. He caught sight of gristled tailbones—no doubt those of seized yoke oxen—and turnips with dirt still clinging to their taproots. Shot through the boys' glares, James sensed envy. A high officer leading a young American apprenticed as a British soldier was an insult.

One of the fellows spat. Another flicked a single pebble that skittered on the ground and caromed off James's fancy leather boots.

Drayton stood by protectively. "Have no fear, son."

For the first time all day, James looked Drayton in the eye, the unblinking one. Drayton was appallingly ugly, and his kindness did little to mitigate it. Was it a betrayal of his own father to seek another man's approval? "I'm not your son."

"Of course you're not. But—" said Michael Drayton. The child could not see beyond the literal. He had no notion that he might be used, in fact was being used, in the service of others. The image of Molly visited Drayton. It beckoned him and he smiled at the absurdity of it. A crush, at his age! "But I'd be grateful to have a son such as yourself."

James thought he would vomit. And yet there was something in him that craved just this sweetness.

Drayton was pleased to note that the tombstone wall had been dismantled, and that the stones had been restored to their resting places as he had commanded. The air was crisp, a note of fall in it. Crows stationed themselves on a lightning-struck chestnut, half bare of leaves. Just beneath, loosely wrapped in burlap, the corpses of the Hessians were laid out on a cart, awaiting transport. James gave them a glance, but did not break stride.

Inside the church, Cunningham sat at a table in the priest's quarters. Before him were writing paper, quills, a goblet of red wine. His face was riddled with red lines.

"Major General Michael Drayton, sir." Drayton cleared his throat. "The perpetrator has been banished, and my squad is billeted at the farm. Mr. Ebenezer Woodstock, and his, er, delightful daughter desired you to have these gifts."

The entourage bestowed freshly harvested corn, writing paper, a keg of whiskey. In the cart was half of the pig Molly had slaughtered. The side of pork looked translucent, creamy with hints of blue. Cunningham squinted, his eyes pink rimmed and lashless as a baby's. "Er, delightful daughter? Is that what you said?"

Drayton nodded. He had intended, by the word, to curry James's favor rather than to provoke Cunningham's mockery.

"Er, delightful daughter indeed." Cunningham husked an ear of corn and sniffed it. "And this, her son? Are you, er, delightful as well?"

It occurred to Drayton that his superior was sauced. One of Cunningham's eyes blinked, then the other.

"No, sir, I am not, er, delightful," said James, unable to contain his defiance. Drayton noticed that the boy was standing straight. Maybe there was something to work with, after all, in this raw recruit. If he could master his impulses. That was something every officer must learn on his own.

Cunningham nibbled at the corn, the tip of his tongue paler than his cheeks, his chin. Then, with the cob, he pointed to the side of pork. "Was that pig corn-fed?"

"Slop bucket, sir," said James. "Grease, bones, husks, peels."

"You appear to be a thoughtless lad, but at your station in life, want of intelligence is secondary to a well-tailored uniform." Cunningham leafed through his ledger, then addressed Drayton. "I have been granted a new commission, Commissary of Prisoners of New York. I will be leaving on the morrow." He smiled to himself and raised his goblet. Another sip of wine, and it seemed his face would catch fire. "You, Major General Michael Drayton, are to assume charge of this miserable outpost, and in your new duties, and with Mr. Ebenezer Woodstock's, er, delightful daughter, I wish you godspeed."

———·•·———

As NIGHT FELL, a front moved through on shifting breezes. Molly went from room to room shutting windows. Drayton had departed, taking James with him. She was alone with Ebenezer and the billeted Brits.

"They're not billeted!" Ebenezer insisted. "They're invited!"

Soldiers gambled day and night at the kitchen table, devouring ham and cabbage and scooping with their fingers last summer's tomato and strawberry preserves, tossing the empty jars into the hearth, along with chicken bones and snot rags. Every surface was piled with dishes, cups, carcasses of small game, rinds, pits, and stems. Flies and ants and beetles crept about. Cutlasses, daggers, picks and knives had been jammed into the butcher block. Ammunition boxes and powder kegs took the place of provisions in the pantry. The soldiers smoked nonstop and spat and slept in the bushes and shat wherever they liked. They shot rats and used kettles as pisspots. But until now, they had never dared climb the stairs.

"Get out!" Molly roared at the two soldiers in her bedroom. One of them was looking under the mattress for some hidden treasure. The other had Molly's underwear on his bayonet—the silky whites made in Paris that she'd only worn twice. She saw that her armoire had been rifled, every drawer rummaged through. "I'll have you court-martialed!"

They laughed. One of them grabbed her arm. She wrenched free and sprinted down the hall to Ebenezer's room, but he was not there. The soldiers stumbled after her, laughing. She swung at one of them with a candlestick. It struck his cheek with a satisfying crack and sent a loop of blood flying against the wall.

The commotion brought others running upstairs, one of them sloshing a mug of ale, another holding a pork chop. When they saw the soldier with his split cheek they laughed.

"Get out!" Molly said.

Three of them pinned her from behind, while the one removed her underwear from the blade and sniffed it. They passed the panties around, until the last put them on his head like a cap. She struggled, kicking and biting, but three men were too much, and they overpowered her.

The one with the bayonet sliced at her. She expected she would die, and waited to feel hot blood. But the soldier was so skilled that he merely rent her shirt as he intended, exposing her breasts. She made no effort to conceal herself.

"There's not a man among you," she said.

The wounded one charged first. He ripped the clip from her hair and it fell to her shoulders. Then he unbuttoned her trousers, but he was drunk and inept. Others crowded to help. In the blur she saw the green of Drayton's sash, his two pistols drawn.

"Back off, fools!" Drayton barked.

"Give us our poke!"

Drayton wheeled. "Who challenges me?"

The bayonet-wielder stepped forward. "You want her for yourself."

Drayton fired, and the man collapsed, dead. "Anybody else?" Nobody spoke. "Cart him to headquarters and clean up this mess." He took Molly by the arm and led her out of the room.

4

SALT AWOKE disjointed and headachy. His body, hammocked in hemp webbing, rocked gently on Atlantic swells. Above, against blue skies, the *Bright Star's* masts were rigged with hemp braids—from boom to spar to whelk, by loop and knot, the rope finessing into place vast sails of cannabis. Everything transporting about this sloop, the interplay of wind and water, its very movement, was made possible not by the idea of hemp, but by hemp itself. Glorious hemp! Everything was interconnected but him. And in his present circumstance, not even a hundred puffs could change that.

The *Bright Star* itself was a sleek-hulled predator, its hold filled with stolen treasure, its sharklike prow slicing the water. It ran whichever flag was convenient—Dutch, American, British, Spanish—or none at all. The crew consisted of forty-five ensigns and five hotpresses. Half the men were from New Jersey, the rest from the-devil-knows-where—Liverpool, Aruba, Araby, Cordoba, Shanghai, Suva, Bombay. And now Salt had joined them, from the-devil-cares-where. Each crew member had a stake in the future—large, middling or small, depending on his rank, shares that got traded back and forth, depending on bribes, threats and cajolery. The captain, a corncob pipe-smoking tyrant named Marbury, gripped the wheel and steered into one foamy crest after another, as if personally affronted by each wave. His arms were hugely muscled, his legs thin as sticks. He had successfully commanded three privateers, and by them had made his riches. He no longer needed money, but still he sailed for it.

When Mohammed and De la Luz had first dragged Salt before him, the captain had brought his fingers to his own face and touched it all over. "Give me a glass." He peered at his reflection in the lens of a telescope, then checked it against the man before him, then, turning the scope around, peered through it at Salt. "Damned if this hotpress doesn't look just like me, only half my size." He turned to Mohammed and De la Luz. "And for that I'm docking your commission a quid." He counted out coins from a purse strung around his neck. "Here's nine." The pirates knew better than to complain.

So Salt had taken his place at the bottom, slave even to the negro powder boy. Three years' indenture they'd given him. He was assigned the job of scraping out the victual barrels of tripe and pork brains. After that he got on hands and knees to scrub the bilge scum, mop up fish guts, and splash out the shitter, until he alone could bear the stink of himself.

All the while the crewmen puckered and blew him kisses, asking for a peek of his bloody hole, which had begun to itch fiercely. The lead ball had gone through without piercing his vitals, leaving a scab like a cork.

Sprawled in the hammock, Salt felt the sway of the sea, the spray on his face, the throb in his skull. "I'd have been lucky if you'd slit my throat, left me to the crabs."

Mohammed clapped a hand on Salt's back. "Now is when you tell me how madly you want your wife, eh, Cappy?"

"I miss her." But he didn't exactly. And saying it aloud didn't make it so. He longed for honey, and he thought often of the way they'd coupled that night in the field. These things he missed. Was there more?

"I'd kill the bastard got between me and my woman."

"That would be my father-in-law." Salt sighed. "I need rope."

Nearly every man on board, it seemed, favored a physic, especially now that the *Bright Star,* unable to unload its contraband with Drinky Crow, had lumbered into British waters in search of another avenue of trade, laden and vulnerable. The sailors were near to breaking under the stress. Marbury, pipe in teeth, was always in a cloud of tobacco. The officers were given to rum. The crew had grog, De la Luz his coca leaves. The Fijian botswain, who was said to be a cannibal with a taste for male missionaries, had kava, cold-brewed and foul-tasting. The Chinaman cooked opium. And Mohammed had his beads, which he worried endlessly, wearing them down to nubs. His singular devotion to an invisible world seemed perhaps the strongest physic of all, and Salt wished he could avail himself of it.

The negro powder boy, James Forten, was the only mate not dependent on a remedy, unless it was to busy himself nonstop making musket cartridges. Using a small blade, he rapidly cut brown paper into trapezoids about the size of a handspan. When he had scores, one exactly like the next, he wrapped each around a six-inch dowel the diameter of the bullet. He inserted the lead ball, tied off the neck with a thread, and slipped free the dowel. Into the body he tapped powder from a large horn engraved with scrimshaw of the lower Manhattan skyline—had he inherited the horn, stolen it?—and when he had filled the paper cylinder, twisted it shut. The completed cartridges, thousands of them by now, were stacked in ammunition boxes. His palms and fingertips, which were the color of rosewood, flashed against his dark, smooth skin as he worked.

"The boy can't help himself," Mohammed said.

Salt scratched his scab, then, using thumb and fore-finger, worked loose the threads of a frayed hem along the jib. When he had gathered enough, he balled them up and jammed the bolus into his pipe, then used a flintlock to light it. The smoke assaulted his throat, scorching his windpipe. He erupted in a lung-busting cough, face red, veins pound-ing. But softly, as if upon cat feet, relaxation crept through him. It was good to smoke freely. He did not miss Molly's frown, or, for that matter, her glance when he barked this order or that at James, or even her gentle encouragements or baked ham or hand-sewn hemp shirts. Or the thousand tiny obligations with which he was bound to her, for better and worse. A rover now, he had the right to take whatever he wanted. Gold. Life. Other men's wives. Not that he would.

———————

ROPE EVERYWHERE and not a whit to smoke. Salt paced. After a couple of weeks, lighting up the rigging no longer did the trick. And then he had got caught nicking the jib and Marbury had thrown him in the hole for a day and a half. Anyhow, even sail was too harsh. There was no euphoria in it. He needed bud.

"Ship sighted! Starboard." Kini the boatswain was top-mast, eye to spyglass. Mohammed stopped spindling his beads, Forten raised his eyes from his bullets. Salt, squinting, saw nothing but blue water, the horizon flat, distant, unreachable, an abstraction, the way he liked it.

"Trouble," said Mohammed. He clenched his beads and fell to his knees, bowing east and chanting in Arabic. But only for a moment, then he popped to his feet.

A whistle blew, followed by a cry. "To arms!"

The crew pulled itself into a team, heaving, knotting, loading, each man at his task with not a word uttered. An arsenal emerged: long-toms and nine-pounders, muskets, blunderbusses, pistols, cutlasses, boarding pikes, hand grenades, tomahawks, grape, canister and doubleheaded shot. Forten scrambled among the cannons with wadding, cones of black powder. It was not the first display of such speedy elegance

Salt had seen since he'd been on board, but every time was like the first. No wasted motion, the definition of economy. Salt's place was in the line that passed buckets hand over hand to fill barrels with salt water, ready to extinguish battle fires.

"Number two ship aft!" Kini barked.

Captain Marbury on the quarterdeck. "To the death, lads, to the death!"

"Number three to the lee!"

"Sponge the staves!"

"They fly colors of the King!"

"Come about!" Marbury ordered. The sailors let loose the booms and the sheets of cannabis shuddered, as if in despair. The *Bright Star* had been ambushed, fallen athwart a triangle of British warships.

"Fly the Union Jack!" Marbury's cry was echoed three times by three different voices. "Stay your arms! Peaceful stations!"

The sailors filed on deck, concealing cutlass, pike and pistol. A civilian crew on a civilian sloop, to all appearances, freighted with cargo that, war notwithstanding, sustained life. Only Forten, crabwalking so as to not be seen, continued to prime the culverins.

Suddenly De la Luz and Mohammed grabbed Salt. "Captain Marbury summons you."

The captain's quarters were upholstered in burgundy leather, the teakwood bunk burnished with lemon oil, the porthole ringed in polished brass. Tobacco smoke hung thick within, and the rasp of it stung Salt's eyes, irritated his rope-tender craw. But the captain was nowhere to be seen. Set out on the writing table were papers. Salt peered at them—a letter of Marque, Orders of Impressment—wondering which among them were forged. A post bill read:

An Invitation to all brave Seamen and Marines, who have an inclination to serve their Country and make their Fortunes.

The grand Privateer ship BRIGHT STAR, commanded by Stephen Marbury, Esq; and prov'd to be a very capitol Sailor, will Sail on a Cruise against the Enemies of the United States of America, by the ___ instant. The BRIGHT STAR mounts fourteen Carriage Guns, and is excellently well calculated for Attacks, Defense and Pursuit—This therefore is to invite all those Jolly Fellows, who love their country, and want to make their fortunes at one Stroke, to repair immediately to the Rendezvous at the ___ Wharf, where they will be received with a hearty Welcome by a Number of Brave Fellows there assembled, and treated with that excellent Liquor call'd GROG which is allow'd by all true Seamen, to be the LIQUOR OF LIFE.

If hemp moved the boat, lucre and liquor moved the men—those and sanctioned bloodshed.

"Put this on, Cappy." Mohammed gave Salt a uniform. Was this a promotion? Could the sailors already see the qualities of seamanship and courage growing in him? Salt swelled with pride; he would earn the respect his mates were showing him. He wasn't against clobbering a redcoat, if only to get even. He was ready to fight. In fact, he discovered to his surprise, he wanted to fight.

"Don't forget the pipe." De la Luz jammed a corncob pipe into Salt's mouth.

"Where's Captain Marbury?" Salt asked.

"Ha! Jolly good one, that."

De la Luz chewed furiously. With nowhere to spit he swallowed now and again, Adam's apple abob, coca ball rolling in his cheek. He presented Salt a scroll tied with a blue ribbon, a wax seal emblazoned in purple signifying the mark of the Crown. "Here are your orders, Cappy."

They guided Salt down into the hold where the booty was stowed. Casks and crates were piled high, staggered among boxes and chests and barrels and gunny sacks. Stephen Marbury emerged, guarded by Kini, who was using an Indian tomahawk as a walking stick. Marbury held a lantern and wore a black stocking cap, grimy dungarees, a woolen sweater, salt-stiffened boots. His corncob pipe emitted steady brown puffs. His eyebrows were raised in a look of gravitas, a face that could administer last rites. Now, holding the light inches from Salt's face, he studied his doppelganger. "I didn't realize I was such a handsome devil!" he cackled, baring yellow teeth in a harrowing grimace. It was the only obvious difference in their appearance—Salt's teeth were white. "Perform the task at hand, Cappy, and I'll end your indenture."

Salt wanted proof. He thought of Molly home alone, and volatile James. Salt should be there to protect them. Ebenezer, well, the old man could fend for himself.

"Here's your discharge paper."

When Salt grabbed for it, Marbury whisked it away. "Not so fast." With his dagger he cracked open a crate. Inside were Pennsylvania rifles. He pulled one out and stroked the gunmetal. "None finer. Admire her walnut butt." He plunged a hand into a burlap sack, pulled out a fistful of tobacco. "Ah, pure Virginian!" He sniffed like a dog. He added rifle and tobacoo to a crate that already held a crock of molasses, raccoon skins, and a bill of lading that itemized the cargo of the *Autonomy*, an American merchant ship sunk three months earlier.

"These are American goods!" Salt cried.

Mohammed and De la Luz continued wrapping items in burlap. Marbury smoked.

"But we prey on British ships," Salt stuttered, surprised by his patriotic indignation. "Drinky Crow would not have purveyed American pinch."

"Gob your stow!" Marbury barked. "Do you want to get out of this alive?" He inhaled a mass of smoke that seemed to puff him up like a blowfish.

"Sir, I respectfully cannot." A failure of principle had given rise to his troubles in the first place. Everything had been taken from him except his character, and he would not part with that. "I make it a point never to lie."

Marbury sent Salt a withering look. "So keep your yap

shut, problem solved! Just give the admiral this." He handed Salt a scrolled parchment, then turned to the others. "Mohammed, De la Luz, see to it!"

Mohammed and De la Luz both glanced at Kini, who raised his tomahawk. It was said that Kini's favorite bit was the cheek muscle, kebabed over an open fire. Buttocks also, preferably those of officers, being well-marbled from sitting.

"I'm to pretend I'm you?" asked Salt.

"Do I have to spell it out? Yes! Impersonate me! But not the real me. The me I would be were I a loyalist. Buy time. Give gifts. Joke about the war. Say 'Bly me'—three times should do it." Marbury puffed furiously, gasping for more tobacco. "When they let down their guard we board her as brethren and then stab them dead. I shall lead the charge. When you hear my whistle, kill the admiral with this!" He gave Salt a surgeon's scalpel to conceal in his hat band. Marbury's brow knotted beseechingly. "Everybody is to get *exactly* what he wants. You go free. De la Luz, you and Mohammed get a seven-share. Do you hear? Money! Here's a small advance!" He handed Salt a bag of coins. "There's more where this comes from! Each of you will bathe in cash. Sail for pleasure, not for toil. Enjoy your beads, your coca. Money, lads! No more wharfwench—lay a lass in lace. Freedom! Grant this god-given crate with our goddamn compliments to the god-awful British admiral and then slit his godforsaken throat!"

Minutes later, Salt, attired as Captain Marbury, accompanied by the bayonet-wielding Mohammed and De la Luz and trailed by Forten, climbed from the pinnace into the *Belisarius,* the twenty-six-gun lead ship in the British flotilla. All four were immediately shackled.

"He has a letter for the Admiral!" protested Mohammed, but a burly sailor clubbed him on the head anyway, and he crumpled to the deck, unconscious.

From the deck of the *Belisarius,* Salt watched a second ship, the *Goshawk,* sidle up to the *Bright Star.* Suddenly, the pirate sloop hoisted her sails and let loose her guns. The fusillade ripped through the *Goshawk's* spirketing, blasting its hull backwards in a froth of foam and fire. But the seven guns along the side of the *Bright Star* were no match for the return fire of seventeen along the side of the *Goshawk.* Orange bursts flowered along the gangplank, leaving behind a wreath of smoke. A tremendous explosion sent up a black billow, darkening the sky. Salt could feel spray on his face, a cold sooty drizzle. When it cleared, the *Goshawk* was listing, badly damaged, flames licking its shattered timbers.

The *Bright Star* was gone, with her American swag. At once Salt realized that Marbury had never intended anything but to cut and run, and to buy the time to attempt it, he had sacrificed the four of them.

"Captain Marbury, the Admiral warrants you'll find your quarters comfortable enough." The mariners guffawed, and led Salt and his entourage down to the hold.

In the gloom, others were already held captive, although it was hard to tell exactly how many. There seemed to be a series of stations around the perimeter, each with a ring on the wall to which a prisoner was chained, but there were more prisoners than rings, so the new arrivals were chained to each other, ankle to ankle. Water sloshed about on the floor and the air was musty, but there was no stench of excrement, which suggested civil treatment and liberal deck time to do nature's business. The timbers were slick but not carved or worm-eaten. And although the arrival of the new prisoners was greeted with groans and grumbles, as soon as the guards departed a jug of rum was passed around, followed by a barrage of questions.

"Who got blasted?"

"Where are we?"

"What's the name of your ship?"

Salt knew that in the murk no one could see his captain's uniform, yet wearing it he felt the spokesman. He told what he knew, without mentioning the *Bright Star's* stolen payload or the money Marbury had given him, which lay heavy in his pocket.

"The *Bright Star*! So you're the famous Captain Marbury?"

Salt didn't answer, but took a slug of rum.

The prisoners, dozens at least, told their stories in return. Some had been captured from other ships—the *Yearling* out of Boston, the *Swiftness* out of Connecticut, the *Darling* out of Rhode Island. Others had been taken in battle and were being relocated from the *Chesapeake*.

"Relocated?" Salt asked. "Won't we be hotpressed?"

"No, sir. Their ranks are full."

"Where are they taking us?"

"The hulks."

"SHOW US WHAT you can do, boys," Michael Drayton said. "Who wins gets pie. Who loses cleans heads."

"I left extra there for you, *America*," hissed Rupert, a rich London bully who'd read Greek at Oxford and was proud of his precocious moustache and the nickname he'd invented. James was not the lone American; a few sons of loyalists drilled alongside him. But most of the young officers in training were English scions sent by monied families.

"On your marks," Drayton said. "Go."

James sprinted into a field covered with tussocks, each hump appareled like a corpse felled in battle. Without breaking stride, he extended his arm, maintaining a bend at the elbow, pistol bobbing in time with his gallop, and got off the first shot. Rupert was three counts behind, a puff of smoke rising from the hole torn in the chest of hay beneath the woolen plaid shirt, and then another, same spot—Rupert could shoot, James gave him that. Next he slid the pistol into a hip holster and unslung the rifle from his collarbone. His precious rifle, barrel blackened by cider vinegar to cut the glint; bayonet blade too, but sharp enough to shave by. James leveled all five pounds of it, walnut stock abut his shoulder and blade dead ahead, uncoiled his thighs and lunged. He sliced open the breast of the bedraggled Continental, the gash discharging tufts of straw. Then, huffing, huffing, extending his lead over Rupert, five counts, maybe six, James somersaulted under the fence timbers and popped up on the other side in a crouch, drew a bead on a rebel sharpshooter seventy yards away, and let himself breathe. He tickled but did not pull the trigger. The enemy head exploded in a torrent of stringy white and orange pulp.

Drayton frowned at James, then uncrossed his arms and clapped. "Huzzah! Rupert! Fine shot, lad."

As James came loping back, bypassing the training course set up with obstacles, dummies, bailed hay stuffed into American uniforms, some with pumpkins for heads, others with strange gray and warty gourds, a London boy yanked taut a rope. James tripped over it and fell face first.

"America." Rupert laughed.

James ignored him.

"Young *America* is good with a pistol, better with a blade, and with a rifle, peerless," Drayton said. "It's a bloody good thing he's not gone rebel." It didn't help James's standing with the others that Drayton had made him his pet. "But you, Rupert, are the one to get pie tonight."

James did not smolder; neither did he smile.

After the field maneuvers, bathing was a naked horror of scrub brushes and tallow soap, with vinegar to rinse, and lavender oil to rub into their scalps against lice. The surgeon made his rounds, inspecting each cadet.

"Bend over and spread your legs."

"Like looking at yourself in the glass, eh, Doc?"

"A portrait of George."

"Which George, theirs or ours?"

James found the naked recruits repulsive. Their scrawny bodies, sinewy, pale and sprouting threadlike hair, looked vulnerable and larval, not worth the protection their uniforms afforded. Adding to his discomfort was his disobedient penis, which was nearly always hard, even though he beat it into submission two or three times a day, furtively wiping the issue on a bush, a tree trunk, or the earth itself, spreading his seed about meaninglessly. It had nothing to do with lust—the feeling was aggravated rather than sensuous. It was a taunt, a terror, a torment. A totem to the impotence of teenage will.

James wasn't the only one erect at bathing time, but he was the one to whom it happened most, and his persona was therefore defined by it.

"America," they teased. "You like the men, eh?"

No, in fact he hated men.

And so he concentrated intently on anything but what he felt. His rifle. His training exercises. His mother. After weeks of this practice, associations formed. His imagination was at cross purposes to his body. When he got hard he thought of guns, and the thought of guns got him hard.

Drayton approached. "Finish up and we'll go visit your mother. She'll be missing you."

"No," James said. He had his Herodotus open. "I need to study."

"Why did you hold off?"

"What?"

"You had a bead on."

James didn't answer.

"You hesitated."

"When do I get an X sash and a brace of officer's pistols?"

"Thucydides is really much better than Herodotus." Drayton paused. Then: "Letting somebody best you is not the same thing as self-control."

———•◦•———

THE *BELISARIUS* dropped anchor in the harbor of the city of New York. Under British guns, each of the dozens of captives, ankles shackled, emerged from the soggy hold. Half of them appeared to be privateers, the other half uniformed Continental soldiers. Some of them were bandaged, burned and bruised. All of them were unwashed, blinking in the autumnal glare.

"Sunshine is killing me."

"I'll kill the bastard stole my chaw."

"Holy mother of Jesus, look at the size of that flotilla."

"Too bloody light."

"What sort of name is *Belisarius*?"

The trees of Staten Island and Brooklyn were turning. The water had a tiny chop, each swell bobbing in a direction opposite the broken skylight riding on it. Foamy trails of bilge scum stretchmarked along the seams where the outgoing river met the incoming tide. Hundreds of British vessels sat at rest, both merchant and war ships, moored in the anchorage, some with masts prickly and barren as wintry limbs, others fully rigged, sails pregnant with wind. The sight gave Salt a shudder—how could the Continentals survive such overwhelming force?

Not long ago, a fourth of Manhattan had been burned to the ground by its own residents, the rest under the crush of British forces. The fire had started at the Fighting Cocks tavern and roared uptown. Rebels had set it ablaze, even George Washington admitted that. "Providence, or some good honest fellow, has done more for us than we were disposed to do for ourselves." Everything north of the Whitehall Slip was still ringed with charcoal, and nothing but sheds had been rebuilt since. Yet from here the island still looked magnificent. Plumes of smoke rose from quayside chimneys, and people scurried along the piers. The horse carts with their brightly varnished wheels looked like toys, topheavy with barrels and hams and cheeses and chickens. From here, commerce appeared neat and tidy, practical and inevitable, even deathless.

Manhattan. Salt well understood that if you couldn't have what you loved, you might kill it before you allowed a rival to possess it. But did you really love what you could help destroy?

"Some grog for an old man?"

"Get off me."

"I've got two silvers for a pint."

It had been weeks since Salt had had rope—the longest

without that he could remember, and that last only the furtive and desperate smoke of rig fuzz. His gut was queasy, stools liquid and foul-smelling. His knuckles gave him pain and his temples throbbed. Sometimes it took all his concentration to fight back the nausea. And here before him, such an abundance of hemp in the harbor—rope everywhere, some of it delicate tri-ply, some fat as wrists, the fine tawny fibers, and the lovely ephemeral sailcloths, like vowels in the alphabet. Hemp teased him inside like a melody he knew by heart but could not quite recall.

Oh, for a breath of cannabis. Oh, for Molly in a dress on his arm in New York City.

———·•·———

TWO LARGE GONDOLAS glided alongside the *Belisarius*, along with a provision-loaded barge. British military police enfiladed the gangplank. Atop the second platform stood an officer Salt recognized: Cunningham, who had sentenced him, in a blue velvet cloak. On his breast were dozens of badges and pins; never had there been a more decorated officer. He leapt onto a hill of smoked hams, each wrapped in netting. He put a horn to his mouth. "Your Continental Congress has disbanded, gents. Run amok. A few even signed with the Crown."

The prisoners stirred, some of them spitting.

"Those are the ones we made examples of. Strung them from the sycamores! The others, well, they have entered the annals of anonymity. History's garbage pail."

The prisoners grumbled in unison, as if they were a single organism.

"Warriors such as yourselves, however, the valorous but powerless, shall be given a second chance. Your so-called representatives have forsaken you in a sorry attempt to save their own necks." Though Cunningham rhymed and trilled, he was a clumsy rhetorician. "But we haven't sycamores enough for each of *your* necks." Cunningham instructed the henchmen to sluice the defectors into a ramp leading to a platform on his barge, which was loaded with the hams, rum, bread. "We welcome you!"

There were no takers, although after two hungry weeks in the dark, every last one of them was sunstruck and mad for pork, for ale. Everybody knew the British were liars, and it was unlikely that the Continental Congress had disintegrated. And yet.

"Fools, you win or you lose. Make your choice now."

Under the critical gaze of Cunningham, one captive skulked toward the British.

"Forswear your country for a corncake!" growled Salt, surprising himself. It was something James might blurt. Cunningham sneered but did not seem to recognize him in his uniform.

"You heard the news, Congress has turned redcoat," said the captive.

The rest of them, stubborn, stupid, or loyal—whether to profit or something else—refused the bribe. They were herded into the gondolas. Forten and De la Luz took places on either side of Salt. "Make way for the wounded," Salt said, again startling himself with his audacity.

"Row, you rebel bastards!" Cunningham barked.

"These must not be made to row." It was something Molly might say. Remarkably, the British guards deferred to him, parting to let pass the bandaged, the limping.

The able-bodied took up oars, and the flat-bottomed boat with its high prow and low stern plowed up the East River.

"The *Jersey* awaits!" Cunningham bellowed.

THE NORTH STAR twinkled in a sky washed with twilight, and the current of the river ran unnaturally back toward it, up with the incoming tide. The flow pulled the gondola around the bend and into Wallabout Bay, a large pocket on the Brooklyn side. The littoral reek of salt marsh mixed with the scent of cow dung from the surrounding farmlands, and the stink of rotting corpses.

The *Jersey* was anchored there, two chains fore and three aft, staying it from wind and wave. It wore its history plainly. Once a large gunboat, over a hundred feet long, it had been stripped of masts, bowsprit, and sails. The cannons were gone, their housings nailed over with knotty pine and sealed with tar. The decks were cleared of rigging but for loading derricks. The hull was eaten to the waterline by barnacles and tubeworms, and was patched here and there with iron plates. Grates barred every opening, but not the cries.

The new arrivals piled out of the gondolas onto a floating platform that served as the *Jersey*'s gangplank.

"Benjamin Frick."

"Pender Yedrab."

"André D. C. Annapolen."

"Igarz Baboo Augusión."

"John Spinks."

"Malachi Baxter."

"Peter Bentley."

"Polack Tabor."

"Thomas Wong."

"Don Miguel de la Luz."

"Mohammed Aziz Ali." He spelled it, patiently.

"That's practically a sentence," said the scribe, shaking his head and dipping his quill into the inkwell again. A straw-haired man with enormous shoulders, he sat at a tiny desk piled with ledgers, commissions, and warrants. Hessians in tattered blue uniforms, equipped with machetes, clubs, and stanchions—weapons of the lowest caste—stood watch. "How about I just put down 'Sinbad'?"

"I will rip the tongue from your head and crack each tooth one by one," Mohammed said, causing the line of captives to grin and rattle their leg irons. "Praise be to God."

"Barbary Coast goat-eater!"

"Stow your gob, writer," sniped Cunningham from his pedestal, where he was studying the face of each new arrival. Skilled or not, they were all his prisoners.

The scribe persisted. "Fool Arab, we don't want your kind, it's crowded enough without your—"

"Do as you're told!" Cunningham backhanded the scribe, trying not to show his pleasure at the scene. The *Jersey* was an odiferous wreck, already overpopulated with vile creatures and misguided heroes. These three and a half dozen new arrivals would swell the ranks past a thousand. But the greater the number, the greater Cunningham's standing. Howe would hear of it, and so, indirectly, might the King. Who would have thought that a lad so ill-omened, blowing like so much trash in the gutters of Philadelphia, could rise so high?

The scribe appealed to Cunningham. "Why can't they have regular names like you and me?"

"Because the *Jersey* is home to cast-offs and riffraff. They do not make, trade, or improve. They are pirates, runners, criminals; they thieve and murder."

Mohammed said, "I will crush your knuckles in my teeth."

A pair of henchmen went about lighting torches whose flames released gobs of oily smoke, darkening the sky. Salt was next. "Which of these names is yours?" said the scribe, rifling through documents. "Captain Scott Doyle? Sir Spenser? Stephen Marbury?"

For each officer there was accompanying paperwork, in the event that an officer was needed as a bargaining chip, to be exchanged for a British counterpart captured by the Continentals.

"Aye!" said De la Luz, gesturing toward Salt. "Captain Stephen Marbury. And a fine cappy he is."

Cunningham thrust a torch toward his face. Salt fought the urge to shrink, or to confess. What had honesty gained him? Banishment. A family broken and in peril. Oh, for an inch of rope. But no more than that.

"Give me Tong Az or give me la Luz. It's the Jeffersons and Adamses and Franklins and Marburys I can't stomach." Cunningham's face was made for the dark. In the daylight, it made you want to look away, embarrassed. And so did his ornate costume, all the badges and colored pins on his breast, his bicorn hat with three ostrich plumes. Each boot alone must have thirty brass buttons. In one gloved fist he gripped a coiled leather whip, in the other he daintily held aloft a scroll, pinky finger extended. "How could a sensible person be persuaded by this Declaration that your privileged class has endorsed?"

It was known that the signers of the document were, for the most part, rich and powerful. It was said that they were being hunted down and assassinated one by one. Salt took some small pride in the knowledge that Jefferson had written early drafts on hemp paper. He, like many people, knew a few of its phrases by heart.

Cunningham jammed a monocle into an eye socket and unfurled the parchment. "'We hold these truths to be self-evident, that *all men are created equal.*'" He extracted the loupe with a pop. "That's obviously fiction. Shouldn't it read: '*Some* men are more equal than others'?"

"Some men live to give pain," Mohammed croaked. "I am one of them, God willing."

"In that, you and I are equal." Cunningham looked pleased. "Strike him thrice," he instructed his uniformed henchmen, then winked at Salt. "What say you, Marbury? Or shall I call you the familiar, Stephen? We have made acquaintance, have we not?"

"Sir." Salt bowed as he imagined a captain would. He was watching Mohammed, whose lip was split, and thinking that Mohammed, with his faith in the unseen, did not believe that any truth was self-evident, at least to men. To him it was an affront to God to think such a thing.

The smell of shit, steaming from the hulk, rose on a breeze, along with the cry of a seagull, or perhaps an inmate. Cunningham re-inserted the monocle, peered at the scroll, and cleared his throat. "It might be argued that men are not created at all, rather that men create themselves." He peered at Salt. "Does your uniform make you more equal than your Arab?" In the torchlight, his aggrieved complexion softened. "Are you more equal than your Arab?"

"You are redundant, sir."

"On the contrary, Stephen. Repetition is a rhetorical device." Whip coiled in fist, Cunningham cracked Mohammed across the cheek. "Redundancy is repeating it again." Another crack to Mohammed's damaged mouth, and then Cunningham reached into a bag and took out a pinch of white grain. He delicately applied it to Mohammed's lips, then, using the heel of his hand, ground it in. Tears ran from

Mohammed's eyes, and his nose streamed bloody snot, but he would not weep.

"Salt is painfully dear, you know." Cunningham clapped his hands together, brushing it away. "You are common felons here. You are not prisoners of war. Even the officers among you, who may be worth something to us, criminals nonetheless." He replaced his monocle and went back to perusing the scroll. "'Endowed by their Creator with certain unalienable rights.' 'Life' I understand, 'liberty'—well, an abstraction worth fighting about if ever I heard one. But 'the pursuit of happiness'?" Cunningham fixed his lens on Salt again. Through it his eyeball was magnified, the white crawly with veins, the iris threaded with blue filaments. "'The pursuit of happiness'?"

"What is the question, sir?"

"Your declarers could have said, simply, 'happiness.' Life, liberty, and happiness. Instead they had to hussy it up with 'the pursuit of.'" Cunningham cackled. "Don't you fools understand that 'the pursuit of happiness' is the very definition of unhappiness?"

"As you wish, sir," Salt said.

"Don't patronize me, Stephen. You of all men should know what I mean. Your so-called country's so-called founders have doomed you so-called countrymen to eternal seeking and never finding. Your right is the chase, not the object, which, to my mind, is all fore, no play." Cunningham turned his back to leave, then hesitated. "Which reminds me. Your wife, how does she tolerate your absence? I would imagine she is very lonely, attending to, as it were, *country* matters without you."

Had Cunningham recognized him, or not? Salt couldn't tell. He tugged the cuffs of his topcoat, challenged Cunningham's gaze. "What makes you think I am married?"

"If you were, you are no more. Your, er, delightful wife—like those of, er, other of you sorry villains—will do well to find security in British arms." Cunningham smiled in glee, then turned back to the scribe and whispered something.

"Sign here, Captain Marbury," said the scribe, indicating the ship's ledger. "Or sign here." The scribe pushed another document forward. Salt read.

I voluntarily take this OATH to bear Faith and true Allegiance to His MAJESTY KING George the Third; and defend to the utmost of my Power, His sacred Person, Crown and Government, against all Persons whatsoever.

Salt thought about the choices that had led him to this moment: to grow hemp, to fix the fence instead of the floorboards of the porch, to say "coffee" instead of "tea," to accept blame for the shooting and plead self defense, trusting English justice. Each choice had been the wrong one. The only right choice he had ever made in his life was Molly.

He pushed aside the loyalty oath and signed the *Jersey*'s ledger, writing firmly and legibly, with robust capitals. *Stephen Marbury,* he wrote, and entered the prison ship liberated from his addiction to fact.

II

5

MOLLY STOOD on the porch, watching the sun go down. She carried a wooden serving platter that held a ceramic teapot and china cups. Her mother's things, stored in the attic for the decade since Sparrow's death. In Molly's hands they seemed like child's toys, props with which to play grown-up. "No tea, but coffee if you'd like."

"Your partisanship is showing." Sowell adjusted his wig and squeezed his large body uncomfortably into the hard pine chair. Molly had brought the dining table and chairs onto the porch, partly to get away from the soldiers who had commandeered the house, partially to keep better watch on the road.

"I prefer coffee."

"Some of us are quite satisfied with either."

"I won't serve tea until my husband is returned to me."

"A statement. Not one to stop the war, perhaps." George Sowell fidgeted in his seat, this time with a grimace. "But a statement nonetheless." Papers were stacked on his lap, waiting to be discussed. The dispensation of the farm's profits, for example—not that the point was anything but academic, there no longer being any chance of harvesting the hemp, much less turning a profit on it. And then there was the delicate matter of the succession of the estate. Most pressing, however, was the fact of Sowell's hemorrhoids, all the itchier because proper manners prevented a good scratching. He sat on one haunch until it tingled from lack of circulation, then shifted to the other.

"I'll abide by the tea boycott."

"To drive your father mad."

"If you don't want coffee, there is water."

"My dear," Sowell sighed, shifting in his chair. Bits of blistered skin flaked off the back of his neck, a spot of tar still stained his earlobe, and perhaps, Molly thought, a feather or two remained on parts unseen under his crisp gabardine coat and silk shirt. "Tea is tea, just as the law is the law, war or no."

"When force speaks, laws are silent."

"Your husband, have you heard from him?"

Stung, Molly bit her lip. "Water, counselor, will they tax that next, or will it be the air?"

The sun flattened on the horizon and on each side leaked shimmering red puddles. The yellow-leafed poplars shivered in a wind so gentle that even the skin on her arms couldn't detect it. Though autumn had arrived, the summer warmth persisted, and the earth of Salt's ripe hemp fields seemed overbaked.

"Coffee wouldn't be too awfully terrible, I suppose."

Molly smiled at him as she poured.

Rewarded, Sowell used the sugar nips to pinch sugar from a cone the size of a cat. Cones like this were not easy to come by these days, especially of such high quality, light brown and with only the barest hint of molasses. The scissor-like nips were of ornate silver, though tarnished. "You boycott tea but not sugar, then?"

"I save my honey for my husband," Molly said. "My father has lots of sugar, and I'm happy to see *that* get used up." Her forthrightness was disarming.

Sowell cleared his throat, then hesitated. "If you don't mind my saying, you look quite striking in black."

Molly was no beauty, and she knew it. But she could not forget the image of her panties on that soldier's bayonet, or of the soldier falling, and the shame of the troops the next day. What a potent and dangerous creature they had made her feel. And so today, and yesterday, and the day before that, she had brushed her hair more strenuously than usual, pulling it just a little bit harder than felt good. She had ransacked her closet, looking for what she wasn't sure, until her search took her to the attic, where among the dusty trunks containing her neglected petticoats and hose and hoop skirts, she'd found the black silk dress she'd worn to her mother's funeral. The dress was snug at the bust and hips now, but it still flattered her, perhaps more so. The tiny pearls stitched into the bodice felt like a shield, and the boots, laced and heeled, calling out some feminine authority in her. She noticed that the soldiers attended her requests with greater alacrity once she had put them on.

Sowell sipped his coffee and added more sugar, sculpting with the nips. "Your father has passed the land into a trust named for James. Since your son is native born, this eliminates potential problems in case of attempts at local retribution, or repossession, after the war. Ebenezer is playing both sides here."

"I am native born, too."

"Excellent coffee." George Sowell cleared his throat, shifted buttocks. His piles tickled intolerably, giving rise to an unbidden image of a worm sliding in and out of his anus. Or perhaps he did have worms. Pinworms. He shuddered. "Personal issues must be addressed to James's grandfather."

"Why then are you telling me this?"

"As legal guardian of James, you must sign the document."

Ebenezer appeared, boards creaking under him as he climbed the stairs. Molly turned toward her father, giving him a glimpse of her as he always wished her to be—elegant, feminine, powerful—the grieving widow. Only a glimpse, though, the rest she would withhold. Make him apologize all the days of his life.

"I want tea." Ebenezer shut his eyes hard. "Why is there no tea?"

Molly turned away abruptly, scanning the horizon. "You took from me my husband, then my son, and now you would take away my inheritance."

"Nobody took anybody."

"It has been weeks." Molly imagined James lonely, injured, or worse. The worry came upon her viscerally, pickling her insides. The chance of his misery was the law of her own. "The officer, Drayton, broke his word. Didn't he say he would bring James home every Sunday?"

Ebenezer sighed, wagged his head from side to side. "So it's he for whom you have adorned yourself? Drayton?"

"Ha!" Molly had not even thought of him. And yet, how could she have failed to see the connection others would make? That it required her own father to point out the obvious angered her more than the fact that he attributed to her such wiles.

Ebenezer turned to the solicitor. "What news, Sowell?"

"The British served a loyalty oath on Jabez Boocock—"

"The bastard who tarred and feathered you?"

"The very same, though technically he's not a bastard—he was born of a legitimate union, though of uneducated, impoverished stock—but I take your meaning. Mr. Boocock, it is said, killed an officer. Jammed a cock down the poor unfortunate's gullet." Sowell took a sip of coffee.

"A live cock?" Molly asked, incredulous.

"No, its neck was wrung."

"And where is Boocock?"

"Escaped with his life. I expect we haven't seen the last of him."

"Any other news?"

Sowell refolded his already folded napkin and let his eyes rest on the coffee pot. The moment called for delicacy, and the moment after it, too. "It is said that Drinky Crow has been killed and his"—a pause—"entire household with him."

Ebenezer blanched.

Molly, stricken, asked, "Who did it?"

Ebenezer braced himself for a surge of guilt, but it didn't come. Why not? Wasn't giving up Drinky Crow to Cunningham as bad as wielding the blade himself? He wished that his feelings would hurry and be done with him. Trembling and queasy, he shuffled indoors.

"Tell me who," Molly said.

"Smugglers. Privateers."

"Drinky Crow dealt with smugglers and privateers for decades and never came to harm by them."

"The British claim even so. Others whisper the British are to blame. Cunningham's revenge for the death of the young officer."

For a long time neither of them spoke. Finally, Molly asked, "Salt?"

"Not a word." With that, Sowell finished his coffee and summoned his carriage, a chariot of black-lacquered oak upholstered in purple velvet, wheels tall as a man, springs to absorb the shock—though, as his posterior reminded him, not well enough. It was a perc, a show. A barrister needed such transport to be taken seriously. Unfortunately, the two beautiful drawing horses had been borrowed by the British and now the thing was pulled by a single flatulent ox with bare patches on its flanks. "My dear, would you consider…"

Molly was gazing off into the hemp field, distracted. Would Salt approve of her hair, her shoes, her dress? Had she worn it for the one man who would not see her in it?

"…never mind."

"What?"

"Joining my household."

"What?"

"It's dangerous here, rife with profiteers. You could live—" *with me*, he could not bring himself to say "—in comfort and safety."

Molly stared at him, but he was unable to read her expression.

"I have means to take care of you."

Molly remained mute, and Sowell finally recognized her expression. He had seen it on the face of one straining to understand a strange tongue. "Of course you may bring your father, too, and your son." Though he wanted neither. "There is plenty of rooms. Are. I mean. Rooms."

"You think Salt's dead."

"I think he's not coming home."

She escorted him to his carriage. Flies careened around the ox, which batted them with a naked tail. Men were so easily led.

It was not an outright rejection, Sowell felt as he rolled away, wheels creaking. He turned back to look at her climbing the porch stairs. In the black dress, she put something extra into her hips. At last, he gave himself a good scratch.

———•—•———

ONE BY ONE the men were forced down the hatch, Salt the last to go. A guard shut the iron grate and locked it, muttering, "Crabs in a bucket."

The climb down the ladder brought Salt into thick, moist darkness. The absence of light felt unnatural, harmful, a curse. His being dilated, physical boundaries defined only by his consciousness of them. When he bumped something, from the opposite direction another bump would answer— or a chafe, a lick, a tickle—making expectation itself pathetic and feeble. The hold stank like a slaughterhouse. A boy screamed, terrified. A man shouted, "I *do* believe in truth!" Every timber groaned under bodies turning on their sides, shuffling about, scratching, shoving, swearing, bargaining, praying. And snoring. Salt did not know how, but some managed sleep.

"Mohammed," he called.

No answer. Hands outstretched, fingers aquiver, Salt moved forward.

"Death has no relish for such skeleton carcasses as we are, but he will have a feast upon you fresh comers."

The voice was disembodied, the syntax foreign, but without ocular proof Salt wondered if it came from inside his own head.

Air, he needed air. He began to make his way in the direction he believed the portholes to be. But the captives were packed, body to body. Every breath Salt drew had first belonged to another man, and another before him, anemic and damp and sluttish.

"Owww!"

"De la Luz?"

With fingertips Salt felt bare skin, wet like silk, sparsely haired, naked.

"Sorry, mate," he muttered.

"Stop it!"

"Do it again!"

"Newcomers making trouble."

Salt put out his elbows and shuffled toward the hope of air. His heel skidded out in front of him and he fell on a body, inert, still breathing. He pushed himself up, but his hands slipped away on reeking hot liquid and down he slammed. A pool of runny shit, and a senseless man lying in it. He imagined that excrement permeated every grain of wood of every rafter and beam, as if the boat was marinated in it. Salt wiped his hands on the man, then his forearms, the backs of his wrists, smearing rather than clearing, and leapt away.

"Mama." A whimper.

"Forten?" Salt asked.

"Mama!"

Could it be his own son? He might be here as well as anywhere. "James?" Salt grasped in the dark. "James, is that you? James?"

"He's got a bent for the boy."

"Get the nurse!"

"Get off the kid!"

"O'Nan?"

"No."

"James?"

Suddenly everything was quiet.

At last he saw the faint night sky seeping in through the barred porthole. A group of men clung in a knot before it. "My spot!" Salt, his breeches and hands slick with a stranger's fluids, a lock of his hair wet with it, patches drying to tackiness on his cheek, his elbows, muscled his way through and opened his nose to the night air.

Packed together they kept each other upright. Salt's legs gave way but he did not fall, he slid until his neck was twisted against another's back. To stand straight was more comfortable, but exhaustion prevented him from standing straight. A dog barked. Something was gnawing at his knees. Rats? Bite me and be done with it! A cock crowed. Who let loose the rooster? In this hothouse atrament of writhing limbs, birds and beasts, sacral exhortations, retinal stars, skin, wool, tongues, fevers, whatever Salt imagined was true.

Hot drips splattered his forehead, his lips, his chin. Was it blood? Spit? Tears.

The scratching sound at Salt's knees was not rats, he realized, but a fellow prisoner chewing the oak plank.

There was a scream. Then another. "Forten!" Salt

stumbled through the tentacled blackness, but could not reach him.

IN THE WEEKS since that first night aboard the ship, Salt had scarcely let Forten out of sight. On deck, the newcomers mostly kept to themselves. The old timers gambled, playing hand-drawn cards or throwing wooden dice. They were led by Ezekiel Rude, a New Jersey selectman who was said to be Cunningham's brother-in-law. He dealt tobacco and ran numbers. His yellow hair was pulled into a short tail and he directed his green eyes toward Salt.

"Join us, Captain, and bring your mates."

Salt regarded him warily, then shook his head no. When he put his arm around the boy's shoulder, Forten did not flinch. The smallest thing—a woolen hat, an apple—was worth more than this man's life, or that one's.

Mohammed said, "What I'd give for a fig."

"How's this for a jib?" Using needle and thread, Forten was crafting a miniature sail from a fold of cloth he kept tucked inside his vest. He had not spoken of the crime that had been perpetrated upon him that first night on board, and the other men honored the lad's shame with their own silence.

"Olives, honey, grapes." Mohammed cuffed Forten playfully across the head with his beads. "Pomegranates."

"Hijo de puta," De la Luz growled. *"Tengo hambre."*

"I could make them in quantity, pattern cut."

"My son thinks only of girls and guns," Salt said. "And half-penny pamphlets."

"In the first two he is like me," Mohammed said.

Forten continued his daydream. "A pattern-cut workshop would require a large hemp crop."

"I'll grow it for you." But for industry, not for escape. Salt's craving for rope had at last abated. Relief itself was euphoric.

"Pistachios. Roasted lamb."

"*Callete la boca,*" De la Luz said.

The sun was shining. A single yellow maple leaf danced across the deck. Seagulls plied the blue sky, and the water too was blue, shot through with plates of translucence. The hulk sat anchored in Wallabout, unmoved by the outgoing tide, which revealed seaweed along the shoreline and released the smell of barnacles.

On the Brooklyn shore was the Remsen farm, with a small apple orchard and brown, late-harvest fields. It was said that Remsen was a loyalist, but his daughter was a rebel. Between the farm and the hulk was a treacherous channel that ran deep under a toothy chop. Yesterday the guards had killed a desperate fellow who jumped in and paddled doggedly toward shore. They'd shot at him until long after he sank in a blot of red and the bubbles stopped rising. Nothing else to do.

The veterans, when they bothered to break from their card-playing, gazed toward Brooklyn with what might be called hope, the newcomers with resentment. The weak sat leaning against one another, or toppled over. Skin clung to bone like wet paper, ribs curved most unusually. The men shuffled and rarely spoke—to utter a syllable was tiring. They wrapped themselves in rags, two or three wore loincloths. Hollow cheeks, hollow collarbones, hollow bellies, hollow knees, hollow eyes.

Nobody had eaten anything fresh, ever.

And it was said that the foreigners and slaves in the underdeck were worse off.

"Ripe persimmon in yogurt. Sweeter than a virgin's sighs."

"Thighs, you mean," said Forten. Despite or because of his rape, he liked bawdy talk. Salt thought the child was trying to please. It was a quality you didn't want to squelch, or encourage.

"God willing."

"If not Him, me."

The air was cold, the sun warm. Everyone avoided shadows. The lee-side bunks were reserved for the moribund. This was as close to quarantine as conditions would allow. "You get a worry look on your face. I have seen it happen." De la Luz held a kerchief to his nose. "The worry face of pox."

"Maybe it's *lies,* sweeter than a virgin's *lies,*" Forten said.

"Tell me who hurt you," said Salt.

"You see how if I elongate this triangle, the jib finesses the wind?"

Somewhere, virgins sighed.

Ezekiel Rude approached. Salt took note of his new woolen britches and clean blonde hair. His eyes were bright and his cheeks were neither hollow nor withered like many of the others. Rude opened a pouch and offered Salt tobacco, and a knife made of a mussel shell that had been dropped on deck by a passing gull. "I've put out word the boy is not to be touched."

"They say your brother-in-law runs this ship."

"Cunningham," Rude spat.

"You've no pull with him?"

Rude spat again.

———•◦•———

THE BARRICADO swung open, iron hinges screeching. Cunningham loomed, resplendently costumed, face a July rose. He was flanked by a pair of British soldiers, and a pair of Hessians, as always, stood at attention two steps to his rear. "Rebels, turn out your dead!"

The Hessians clambered down the rope lattice to meet the carcass pile. Earlier, the corpses had been thrown on deck, to be sewed into bags and logged by the scribe. Later, they would be lowered into a dory along with a lucky gang of four. Grave-digging crews were envied for their hours spent on shore.

"To the rest of you passengers—for you are passengers, to my mind, and as passengers your journey's destination is ultimately the same as mine, the same as any mortal's, although we go by different ships, a consoling philosophy, yes?—I offer a delicacy. A treat from the farmer's beautiful daughter." Cunningham held aloft an apple. "Plucked it from the tree herself, she did. She told me so, with her own lips— oh, her lips! Set eyes on her lips and think, if only—" he kissed the fruit, then slowly polished it on his lapel "—what pleasure they could bestow." He bit the apple, spattering juice. "Let no pamphleteer claim that the Crown is without mercy." He tore open a gunnysack. "There are acts of kindness on the *Jersey*!"

Apples flew, skittering across the planks. The prisoners pounced. Even Ezekiel Rude and his men joined the fray. Salt watched a ragged skeleton suddenly hop up and dance about as if strings jerked his elbows, knees, and skull, a feral puppet diving after the apples with a clatter of teeth. Others fell upon him. The starving fought most viciously. The apples caromed about, skipping overboard and plopping into the river. One of them bounced off the gunwale into Salt's lap.

On the barricado landing, Cunningham posed, hands open as if holding an invisible bowl that brimmed with benevolence. There was joy in his sneer. What sport!

The wooden deck was slick with apple. Bloodied men crawled along the boards, licking. The skeleton lay inert, eyes semi-lidded, cheeks gray as clay, fingers twitching in the sunshine.

"Apple knockers, the bushel of you," Cunningham cackled.

Salt knelt, checked to see if the poor lout was breathing. Indeed he was. When he opened his eyes, the whites were yolky. His hair was gray, moustache orange from tobacco. Pox bumps had erupted on his forearms, his temples. His hands fluttered about his waist, making sure nobody had stolen the snakeskin belt still cinched tight. "What do you want from me?"

"Your name."

"O'Nan from Kentucky, you fuck-face fool." He spat blood.

Salt saw the tiny lumps growing along the man's hairline, a larger one on the earlobe. "You have the pox."

"Plenty more where that come from."

"Take this." Salt gave him the apple.

Rude and the old-timers stopped chewing to watch. Cunningham huffed, stiff with mortification.

O'Nan clasped the apple with both hands, his shoulder blades protruding like wing stumps. He devoured the apple, teeth yellow stumps, jawbones clacking. After a few swallows, he threw up.

Cunningham relaxed. No better than beasts, his prisoners, after all.

MOLLY KNEW by heart the sounds of Bury, her girlhood catalogued in every crack and stir. Clay, mud, dirt, and stone had their timbres, changing with the season. In November, warm air floating north over the Atlantic formed an inversion that bounced distant cannon fire and made battle seem internal. She knew skunks came at twilight, raccoons after dark, deer before dawn, and squirrels at sun-up. Humans came at all times, but always they came suspect.

With the demise of local government, runners had sprung up like roaches. The thieves knew to target family farms because the men were gone, fighting or killed or captured. Cash, jewelry, and luxuries like silk, spice, lace, and silver spoons were easily taken. Where the British had been lax or lenient, there were sometimes still horses, saddles, a milk cow or two, a goat or hen to be carried off. And women, some of them pretty. That they lifted their petticoats to show frilly whites as they fled, wailing, only made them more alluring.

British troops were the only deterrent, although rumor held that many of the roving gangs were moonlighting redcoats, or loyalists under their protection. But that was just talk. Most runners were apolitical opportunists, their only allegiance to themselves. Some of them, Molly speculated, might even be among the missing husbands.

Molly shuddered. Maybe nobody ever died of uncertainty.

The day they'd met, Salt was in uniform. He looked good in it, too. A courier, conveying legal writs from Virginia to New York. Thin, overlarge head, red hair, brown eyes, voice level as he thanked Sparrow for the tea.

"Tell us about Virginia."

"I saw a rainbow."

"Are the girls pretty?"

"Mother."

"May I have more honey, please?"

Her mother winked at Molly and handed her a teaspoon, which Molly clumsily dipped into the honey jar, before passing the dripping thing to Salt. She had on breeches, a blouse, and boots, same as any Long Island boy would wear. Her hair was tucked under a tricorn hat, because bonnets, well, bonnets and mobcaps were for ladies. To Molly, to be a lady was to be soft and round and in charge of folding napkins. It meant washing dishes and sewing patches and calmly accepting monthly bleeding instead of seeing it as proof that the world was unjust. Molly would not acquiesce. Ladies wore layers and powders and perfumes and brooches and cared about things like doilies. They pronounced "Virginia" with a knowing half-smile. Boys had it better. They spoke plainly and got to put on uniforms and run and shoot guns and not bleed. Boys did not fold napkins. Although this one might. This boy and his Virginia rainbow, watching her lick the honey from the back of her hand.

Sparrow broke the silence. "That's a lot of honey."

"Where do I sign?" Ebenezer took the parcel and dismissed the boy.

Months passed. But the boy came back, with his satchel of documents. And again, months after that. This time, he asked her why she wore pants.

"Show him why," said Sparrow, motioning toward the barn. It was an odd thing to suggest, but Sparrow wasn't the same woman who had offered him tea those many months ago. Lately she'd been forgetting things, like bonnets and bodices and brooches. She'd taken to wearing large hoop ear-rings and going barefoot like the slaves did, talking to her-self. When she folded napkins, she fashioned them into birds and stars.

Molly remembered. Then as now, the animals had shifted nervously in the barnyard, their odor mixing with the scent of alfalfa. Then as now, autumn leaves were piled on the ground, and though it was too dark to see them, she knew that the maple, while still yellow and pliant, were on the cusp of crispness. Already it was hard to walk through them with stealth. The giant elms still had a few green leaves cling-ing to their branches, especially their lower ones, and they thrummed in the breeze. Then as now, she asked herself what she was scared of.

"What's so special about a barn?" Salt had asked.

"What's so special about a rainbow?" She didn't feel com-petitive with him, not exactly. She showed him the butchered pig hanging from a hook. The knife she had used to do it, the water trough, the pitchfork. The milk pails, the feed, the calf, the chicks. She knew how babies got made. Her mother had taught her what the animals had shown, that love could be ruthless. And that there was romance in that.

She showed him the ladder to the loft. Not all of her poise was faked. Her curiosity did not leave her breathless. Ladies required dark of night, modesty, averted eyes. She had none of it. Off came his uniform shirt. The skin on his stomach trembled under her touch. She wanted to look. Off came her shirt. She unbuttoned her breeches' top button.

"Stop," he said.

She had not expected this. He was desperate for air. Her own breathing was fast and moist. She put it in time to his. They drew close but did not kiss. It was like riding together, neck and neck. Then he groaned and pulled away. There was a wet spot in the crotch of his trousers.

His voice cracked. "I won't do it without getting your father's permission."

"We didn't even touch."

But, oh, how she had wanted to.

Now Molly patrolled the ruined stalks in the unharvested hemp field. Why not pluck one, brown like something dead, why not roll the shriveled leaves between her fingers, crumbling them into spice? Why not wrap the whole of it into a fallen maple leaf and light it with the flintlock? It tasted sweet and bitter, not on her tongue, but somewhere inside.

They had done what Sparrow said a girl and boy should do, bundled. Salt's visits became more frequent, and sometimes now he arrived with no documents to deliver. He had come a long way and the nights were icy, so they let him stay. Sparrow did not sew him into a linen sheet, and Ebenezer did not double-check the seams, though they joked about it, and through the passing years such a story had assumed the cast of memory—James, for one, believed it true. But they had shared Molly's bed, keeping their clothes on. At least Salt had, good to his word to Ebenezer. Molly was freer. *I'll be your Virginia rainbow.* Could it have been as sweet as it seemed, looking back?

Sparrow, at breakfast, barefoot, singing:

> *Dogs and bitches wear no britches,*
> *Clothing for man was made.*
> *Yet men and women strip to their linen,*
> *And tumble into bed.*

In the end, Molly prevailed. Salt gave up Ebenezer for her, gave up himself, unbundled, in the barn loft not ten yards from the sty, streaky with daylight. Molly used woolen sponges soaked in French brandy (*I'll be your Paris, France*), Salt the Fallopius penis sheath, a sheep-gut condom tied at the base with a pink ribbon. Still, Molly's monthly bleeding stopped, and she threw up in the bushes. In secret, she stirred brewers yeast into a cup of pennyroyal tea. She would not acquiesce.

> *Quit human kind and herd with swine,*
> *Confess yourself an whore;*
> *Go fill the sty, there live and die,*
> *And never bundle more.*

Ebenezer did not make them get married. Ebenezer did not make Salt give up his uniform, his adventurous work. Molly did that. Ebenezer merely offered Salt a place on the farm, a means to provide for his child bride. The ceremony took place in Jamaica Church, and almost nobody knew that under the lacy white wedding gown, Molly was carrying.

A twig cracked behind her. Molly spun and the gun went off. She had not meant to pull the trigger. The flash illuminated a man not ten yards away brandishing a cutlass. She ran to the barn to reload. In the dark, her fingers fumbled with the powder. She shouldn't have smoked so much hemp. The punky scent of black powder got up into her nostrils. The bullet sprang from its greasy patch, falling away. She carefully placed the rifle onto the ground, unhasped the barn door, and with a swish of her skirts, slipped inside. She groped along the wallboards for the tool rack until she felt what she was after—the sickle. She tucked it into her belt and searched the wall. The pitchfork.

There was heavy breathing just outside the door. She could smell the intruder, laundry soap and lilac water, a dandy. More footsteps. Two intruders. Molly kicked open the door, slamming one of them. *"Umphhh!"*

Molly pitchforked. The victim gasped. A tine had pierced his side, the other two stuck into the ground, pinning him. She unlooped the sickle from her belt to backhand the second runner, who stood paralyzed, blade poised at his throat. One slash would sever both jugulars—how she did pigs.

"Mother." James had a pistol in her face. "How are you?"

"Fine, thanks." She caught her breath. "You?"

"Fine."

They regarded each other.

"It's so good to see you!" She let drop the blade.

He lowered the gun. "Grampa said you were fighting runners."

The impaled man groaned. Drayton, his hands gripping the pitchfork handle as if it were a beanstalk to heaven.

6

D<small>E LA</small> L<small>UZ</small> got sick.

The nurse, a slim Virginian, wore a silk shirt with a leather overcoat pulled tight against the cold, Carolina crocodile boots, three turquoise bangles, and a leather cap with a bearskin mane. His surgery practice was limited to digging out splinters, his pharmacopoeia was stocked with rum. He blocked Salt's access with a scalpel, which glinted as he gestured.

"Do not molest the infirm."

"De la Luz is my friend."

"De la Luz is my patient."

It was rare that the nurse challenged an officer. Salt considered his options.

"I want you to have this." He offered a coin from the bag Marbury had given him.

The nurse shook his head. "What would be nice—" he nodded toward Forten "—would be—"

"The boy has nothing of value to offer you."

"Would be two."

Salt extracted another coin.

Because of Forten's dexterity with needle and thread, the task of sewing the dead had fallen to him. That he was assumed to be a fugitive slave and had been buggered made him a natural for a job nobody wanted anyway. And he was dedicated to it. He fought for each corpse, trying to reclaim one of the deceased's possessions—blanket, topcoat, hammock—before it was commissioned by the nurse. Salt in turn fought for him, making sure he got paid.

It was cold and cloudy, not enough blankets to go around. In sick bay, the ill spilled from the bunks onto the floor. Plenty of work lined up for Forten, who hummed as he worked, his concentration fierce. His future was their pasts, his livelihood the end of theirs.

De la Luz was unconscious. His moustache was filigreed with white foam, and his chin was slick. Yesterday, he had ranted, "Tell me how I look! *Digame!*" Nobody would. "You get the worry face. I seen it going to happen." In the morning, he had not awoken, though his eyelids were open and his eyeballs rolled in their sockets as if he was dreaming. His skin steamed. That's when they'd wrapped him in an overcoat bought from a Hessian, who'd taken it from a dead Vermonter. Then they put him in sick bay, where he'd lain panting all day, emitting little yips.

Salt himself had the shakes again. The sprue had him shitting mucus. At least he could sit upright, and his eyeballs were not pounding in their sockets.

De la Luz had said: "Ten days burn, a thousand red spots."

O'Nan was curled up on a filthy rag next to the bunks, staring out with his yellow eyes. Most of his pox bumps had cratered, their scabs falling off. He looped his thumbs possessively under his tightly cinched snakeskin belt. "What you want now, you fuck-face fool?" he greeted Salt.

De la Luz had said, "And there is the smell. The skin gives gas."

"May I?" Salt took O'Nan's hand. Mulch. He smelled like mulch.

O'Nan's lips were an agglomeration, like pebbles in a sheath, and no matter how often he licked them they stayed dry. Another sign of the disease's passing. Most of the sick died before the lesions hardened.

"Where did you say you were from?"

"Kentucky. You?"

"Less than twenty miles away." Saying the words made Salt miss home.

"Thousands, I'd say."

Salt fingered a pustule. It felt as if it were filled with buckshot. It was always surprising who survived. O'Nan did not wince. Salt felt another, then another, searching for one not yet pelletized. "I will pay you."

O'Nan licked his dry lips and squinted at Forten, then spat. "What I want ain't yours to give."

Other prisoners had taken notice, including Ezekiel Rude and his crew, who had stopped the betting pool to watch. An audience began to collect. This wasn't unusual. An audience would collect to watch a man scratch his ass, so eager were the prisoners for entertainment.

Salt told O'Nan what De la Luz had said: "If the scabs fall off, you live."

"So I live. Take."

Salt chose a pox bump on the bicep, or what was left of the bicep. Carefully, Salt inserted the point of Forten's whalebone needle. He milked the pustule, gently rolling it between thumb and forefinger. At last it yielded a drop, shining in the sunlight like a single pearl. He squeezed sharply and O'Nan shut his eyes. Using his mess spoon, Salt collected a few more drops. You wanted pus from a survivor, because with it came both the disease and its cure. Salt had learned this from Drinky Crow, a survivor himself, who joked that though he had been saved from pox by the pus of a white man, he had been contaminated with the man's "whiteness." To Forten, Salt said, "Give me your hand."

"Will it hurt?"

Now more than two dozen men were watching, the stakes rising.

"I will be quick." Salt took Forten's hand in his own. He slid the whalebone into the pallid webbing between thumb and forefinger until up rose a bead of blood. Salt smeared O'Nan's pus with his fingertip into Forten's needle prick, and clamped his thumb hard upon it for a count of sixty. Forten blinked back tears. Next came Mohammed, who clicked his beads, grumbling, "No man pierces me."

Ezekiel Rude followed, others lining up behind him. It was too late for De la Luz. But the pus on the spoon, with its spunk of oyster, was more than enough for those not yet stricken. It was tiring work. By the time Salt looked up his ears were singing. Across the bay, he saw the figure of the girl, the apple farmer Remsen's daughter, the Wallabout Maiden, in white. He imagined for her a simple life of beauty and sweetness. What could she imagine for his?

That night the men climbed below and lay in the dark, anticipating a kind of pox minora. It was common knowledge that resistance came at a price. But the fever would be lower, the pain less acute, the abscesses smaller. If nothing else, he had given the men hope. That, and a reason to kill him should innoculation fail.

Ezekiel Rude had said, "There is no vaccine for Cunningham's wrath."

They waited in the dark. James Forten dreamed of Mohammed's worry beads. Mohammed dreamed of Forten's sails. Salt dreamed of Molly's sighs, and the stranger between them. And De la Luz dreamed until the dream was all that was left of him.

———

RAIN GAVE the river a thin, percolate skin. A degree colder would turn it to sleet. The captives squeezed under the canopy, mashed into each other, staking turf with elbow and knee. There was enough room for everybody if they stood.

But some could not stand—Salt, for instance, shivering with fever. And so he sat, at first crosslegged, and then with knees up.

Rainwater, although painfully cold, was precious. It splashed from the canvas roof into bowls, cups, jugs, duck-cloth bags, battered tin cooking pots, and canteens with paper funnels jammed in their mouths. Each cistern had an owner who kept a possessive eye on it. Salt opened his throat to the rain, letting the drops soothe.

Salt's inoculation program had not gone well. Mohammed's hand was as swollen as a basket. "Dirty dirty," he muttered, for now he was forced to eat with his toilet hand. He would not speak to Salt. And Mohammed was better off than most. Sick bay was jammed. Ezekiel Rude's fever had sent him into a delirium, green eyes rolling, yellow hair untied and wild; he still hadn't fully recovered. Dozens had died despite—or as most felt, because of—the treatment. At least, with winter coming on, there was extra clothing, contaminated though it might be.

Salt took the blame as his due. After all, failure was who he was. Hadn't Molly always thought him ineffectual? Except that he had been able to manage Sparrow when no one else could. Molly had been busy with James, an infant at the breast. Ebenezer made sure his wife was dressed and bathed, but no more than that. But where Sparrow was recalcitrant with the two of them, she gave herself over to Salt. Be still, he would say, when she sang nursery rhymes, crawled on all fours, played peek-a-boo. He got her to eat by mixing turkey with molasses. He indulged her flights of mind. Hemp helped. *The itsy bitsy spider went up the water spout.*

"Don't encourage her," Ebenezer had snapped, breaking into their hilarity. "She'll never know what's real and what's not."

But Salt had thought that Sparrow knew as well as anybody, and certainly better than her husband.

Salt shivered. Bumps had formed on his arm and shoulder, and a creeping itchiness foretold their spread to armpits and chest. A carbuncle had taken root in his cheek, he could feel the fire of it, see it in the cold eyes of Rude's old-timers. To them he was already dead.

James Forten showed no ill effects. He sat crosslegged, overcoat pulled tight, rag wool gloves cut at the knuckles, sewing a shroud. The pipe in his lips and his aquiline nose gave him a look too wizened for seventeen.

Rain fell. Prisoners smoked. Cisterns filled.

The iron barricado swung open on groaning hinges that streamed rust, and two uniformed henchmen appeared, scarves pulled over their mouths and noses. They carried a body face down between them, each holding an arm and a leg. They swung once, twice, and on three let fly, the corpse flopping on the planks.

It was De la Luz, his hand clenched as if holding a missing torch. His skin was covered with slits, a dozen plundered orifices.

"They took his pus for arrowheads."

Every rebel knew the redcoats were shooting pox-laced arrows into church congregations, although the nurse usually protected the *Jersey* dead from being used this way.

"Prisoner last year sold his pus for a bowl of gruel."

"That's a bloody lie."

Nobody made a move to attend the body until Salt crawled out from under the canopy into the rain, and Forten joined him. Together they dragged De la Luz back to sick-bay so Forten could get to work.

HOW TO MAKE love to a woman: put into words what is beautiful about her. Make her feel desired. Gentle force is not unwelcome. She will respond to what's rough in you, if the roughness is hers alone. Drayton had intended to bring Molly near to him just so, her shiny dark hair falling in long curls. That he was bedridden and pitchforked in the gut he tried to make work in his favor.

"If that night you had been dressed like a man, I would have shot you dead like one."

"Not you," Molly said. "You wouldn't have."

"Stay." He tightened his grip. "I want you."

Molly did not know whether to address the dull eye or the bright. "Am I your nurse?"

"Am I your bale of hay?"

This morning Molly had smoked hemp upon waking. Then she'd put on a dress. The soldiers had gone through her wardrobe again, although they didn't dare rifle her belongings in front of her. They were looking for loot, partly—jewels, cash, some little treasure—but she knew it was mostly something else. She could feel it when she opened the drawers. They had pawed through her undergarments, held the silk to their cheeks, sniffed her soaps.

Drayton stroked her hand. He wore Salt's pants and shirt. Ebenezer had suggested it.

"I like you better in uniform." She had undressed him with the intention of reclothing him in it, but decided instead to leave him naked, except for the bandage. He unbuttoned her blouse, at last with a soldier's boldness that boosted her confidence. She climbed on the bed to straddle him, a knee on either side, letting his hardness strain against the sheets for a while before she unbound him. Then she ran her fingertips lightly over his muscled belly, tickling his pierced side ever so slightly, a test of his military discipline, his pride. "Shall I stop?"

"No." He opened his eyes. "Shall I?"

"No." She closed her eyes. Was she unladylike? On top like this. She kept her dress on, it rode up her thighs as she spread her legs. Can a widow commit adultery? Was this the moment when she was no longer any man's wife? Or did that moment lie in the past, when Salt had disappeared into the hemp field, or in the future, when she would need to sign the death certificate? Or did it lie, like the moment of falling asleep, somewhere dreamy and indistinct?

She opened her eyes. Drayton was looking up at her with unwavering desire. Her defenses left her. She mounted him in earnest.

Before long, Drayton let out a bellow and gulped like a fish. She had not yet had her pleasure. She stayed astride his good soldier and, before he could shirk his duties, rode him to her moment.

AFTERWARD, Molly wrapped herself in a blanket and went outside to smoke more hemp. She was developing a taste for it, as well as for other things. The sky was gray and wintry, a harsh northern gust every now and again. Two soldiers on the porch watched her. Hadn't they ever seen a woman wrapped in a blanket squat in a field? Molly ducked out of the wind into the stables and was surprised to find James there, tending to the horses. She watched, unseen, as he took the hoof of a gray gelding and put it between his knees, then chipped off fragments with a pick. They crumbled away like cheese. Gauzy light filtered through the planks.

Was James a man now? What was a man? Molly could not define it, although she had a family of them. A creature who could only manage one feeling at a time—if that? So obvious in their excitement, so singular in their efforts. The way Drayton groped her, the way Salt tried to know her thoughts. How could he not know after eighteen years? There was no man capable of loving Molly the way she was capable of being loved.

She had loved Salt's courier's uniform, the duty and adventure it bespoke. She had loved the rail-hard boy who went places, unstayed by rain, snow, dark of night. Molly herself had never left her father's farm, had never been anywhere. Salt had had his travels, and other women before her, Molly was sure of it. Everybody bundled, not just courting couples. Who hadn't he slept with in Trenton, in Baltimore, in Williamsburg?

But over the years Salt had yielded his backbone to Ebenezer. He did his father-in-law's bidding. Whatever sense of purpose remained had frayed like rope. Salt had forsaken *uniform* for *rainbow*. And she was circumscribed by who he had become. He seemed not to consider that she, too, had given up other possible lives when she had married him. Maybe she would have married a diplomat, gone to live in France or London. Maybe she would have been nobody's wife at all.

When Salt complained about her father, she'd urged him to strike out on his own. He'd worked for himself once, he could do it again.

"There's a war going on, Molly. And I have my hemp."

"Work for the Continentals."

Salt was stunned. "You'd go against your own father?"

She'd offered to go with him, to Virginia, to Philadelphia. And he had refused. He had rejected her gift, this stranger, her husband. She cursed him and his stupid hemp. And every damned rainbow, too.

James finished the task and gently put down the horse's leg and straightened up. She had to give the British that, they had corrected his posture. And the uniform, red though it was, bestowed manliness. His face was clearing, the pimples giving way to a beard. He made her proud. And yet...what she had wanted for Salt she did not want for her son. In James, she wanted more *rainbow.*

"Now they have you attending their beasts?"

James looked up. "Why are you wearing a blanket?"

She opened it to show that underneath she was properly dressed. But when James saw her black silk dress, still wrinkled from Drayton, he said, "It's not the horses' fault."

Molly was chastened. So much blame, nowhere to put it.

When she returned to the house, Ebenezer shuffled about, beseeching her. "Have you seen my riding boots?" "What happened to the butter?" "Is it cold out, do I need a cloak?"

JAMES SAT on his haunches in his father's hemp field among the fallen plants. A trio of pigeons investigated. Outsider birds; the locals knew there were no seeds to eat here.

James wanted to be a good son but he didn't know how. Other children said what they meant. Often, James did not recognize meaning at all. He made up for this lack by listening hard. What did he hear now, other than wind, whistling through cannabis?

Father always said, "Love is mankind's highest law." And, "Work is back-making, not backbreaking." And, "Help your mother." And, "That's the last rope I'll ever smoke."

Mother always said, "Love you." And, "I love you." And, "But I love you."

Grampa said, "God rest her tolerant soul." And, "Have this." And, "All I ever wanted was for you to have this."

James sat himself on the broken-down fence—the very one that had started all this trouble. Pillaged to keep some tea-sipping redcoat's toes warm. Why couldn't his father have left well enough alone?

The pistol gave him comfort. In this it hadn't failed him yet.

Around the bend came a Quaker on a big-boned horse, hooves a-clack, hauling a wagon. James knew all his neighbors, and this man was not one of them. He sat Quaker-straight and had Quaker mutton-chop sideburns, Quaker white, and a tailed topcoat. When he drew near, James saw that his freight was chicken cages, each of them occupied, tiny feathers floating on the gently expanding, gaseous stink they brought with them.

The Quaker lumbered off his horse and stood before James. He licked his lips, the lower one hanging like a plum in an oddly familiar way. "Is this how you greet a Friend?"

"Boocock." James took a step back and made a show of not raising his pistol. "You actually fool people in that get-up?"

"Don't be shy!" Boocock exclaimed. In his surprise, James allowed himself to be squeezed tight. He could feel Boocok inventorying him for weapons, and took advantage of the moment to return the favor, noting what felt like a dagger and a pistol tucked into the belt, beside a cudgel. At last they broke apart, gazing at each other with what a stranger might take for affection.

"If they see you here they will ask for your papers."

"Don't think this Quaker doesn't have papers. I've got passels of papers. Ha-*ha*!"

"I should arrest you."

"Nice uniform. Heard from your daddy?"

"Heard what?"

"A man's man, your pa." A look, perhaps of sympathy, perhaps of bemusement, crossed Boocock's face. "Wouldn't lie to save his family."

"Unlike you?"

Boocock pulled a parcel from his bag and unwrapped it, revealing two roast drumsticks. One he thrust toward James. "Take!"

James took.

They ate in silence, staring at each other.

"I never met a man didn't like chicken," said Boocock, tucking a shred of meat back into his mouth. "I've got a business proposal for you."

"What business would I have with a chicken farmer?"

"They say your father raised a cock in the churchyard. That make him a chicken farmer?"

"I'm not listening." James flung the leg bone into the deserted hemp field.

"Got a hold on you, this place, eh?" Boocock said.

James eyed him warily.

"That redcoat." Boocock took three steps into the field, then turned and pointed his drumstick at James. "Pop!" He clutched his breast. "Was standing here when he was gunned down. About right?"

"About."

"By that very pistol, would be my guess."

"You have chickens to sell? We'll buy six."

"I saw the hole. A fair piece of shooting. Plug through the heart."

"They say you killed an officer yourself. With a rooster."

"As I said, I never met a man who didn't like chicken. Except maybe that one."

"What's your proposal?"

Boocock took a sharp breath. "I'm sorry, boy. It's none of it your fault. This war is about realm. As in *coin of the.*" Boocock raised his eyes in sympathy. "Have you any corn whiskey?"

"There's a cask in the barn."

"Let's have at it!"

"Quakers don't drink."

"This one does."

James hesitated.

"Come. I don't expect your trust. But my proposal will benefit us mutually."

James had an idea what he wanted for himself. So he led Boocock into the barn.

———————

THERE WERE no longer guns in the gun room. But its location at the aft of the ship between decks kept it out of the throng, and there was a porthole for air, and a little room to lie about. Although Cunningham's guards paid no mind to rank, the prisoners did, loosely basing it on their status when captured. Salt was on high. But title alone did not get a prisoner into the gun room; you had to be invited. Ezekiel Rude, with seniority, was in charge of it, and that made him the biggest gun on board.

"You cost me dearly, Marbury," said Rude. Health restored, his green eyes again shown bright, his yellow hair again neatly tied into a tail. "Those lives you saved."

In the end, more of Salt's patients had lived than died. The success of the inoculations had strengthened his standing with the other prisoners. "You bet against me?"

"I bet with the odds."

"But you yourself were inoculated."

"A hedge."

The furuncles cratering Salt's own arms and shoulders had deflated, and those on his face had begun to itch. He was able to piss, and hungry again. Not just for food but for escape, escape for himself and scores of others. But how?

Salt handed three gold pieces to Rude. Invitations to lodge in the gun room, though an honor, did not come free.

Rude accepted the coins and pulled out tobacco. "Share a smoke with me?" He dealt only in high-quality Virginia leaves, not the twigs the prisoners and guards usually contented themselves with. You didn't get tobacco like that without connections. Redolent and tangy, it brought to mind Salt's hemp fields. Curiously, the memory came without longing.

"You'll take no offense if I don't," Salt answered. "How is it your brother-in-law hasn't killed you yet?"

"Can't get away with it." Rude said. "My wife has powerful connections of her own."

"Then why doesn't she get you off?"

"I won't sign the loyalty oath."

"Do you speak with her?"

"Bastard censors our letters," Rude said.

Salt extracted another coin and traded it for another pinch of tobacco, which he tucked into his waistband.

Later that night, he would pass it to a guard, a large-skulled Scottish brute named Carple, who would nose the pouch, sniff, grunt, spit, and finally accept it. A favor in the bank, to be drawn against later.

———•·•———

THE EAST RIVER was the mightiest of rivers; the East River was no river at all. It depended upon the sun, moon, stars, who sailed. When the Atlantic flowed up, bringing salt air and memories of the horizon, the warmer seawater rose in the icy river and mixed with the streamlets of Hudson freshwater rounding Manhattan's southernmost point, bringing hints of conifers and tilled fields, of cattle and baled hay, of quayside horseshit and fish guts and the garbage of Wall Street. When the waters were rising, the *Jersey* strained at her chains.

As payback for the tobacco, Carple granted Salt access to the quarterdeck, along with Mohammed and Forten. Shackled, the three of them maneuvered to a small, fenced pen. A pig rooted about in manure and three chickens pecked at water droplets. The Farm, the guards called it, where they kept animals before slaughtering them for their own consumption. While Mohammed and Forten attended to the fishing tackle, Salt surveyed New York harbor.

A man-of-war blasted its cannons toward Staten Island in a drill too commonplace for the prisoners to care about. Hundreds of British ships, with their crews of thousands, their goats and sheep and pigs, their hogsheads of rum and bags of nutmeg and casks of gunpowder, lay at anchor in the harbor, and the upflow brought a bouillabaisse of surprises. Broken weapons and shredded uniforms floated by, and this morning, a wharf doxy, blonde hair billowing with the currents, covering her face, pulsing like seagrass, a white petticoat sealing her hips and legs, fishtailing lacily at her ankles.

"*Jersey* Mermaid."

The men gazed, hoping for a look at her face, relieved that her hair covered it. She floated slowly away.

The incoming tide also brought fishing luck, Mohammed had discovered. Forten stood at the ready with Mohammed's pork ration, saved from the day before. It had been spoiled even then, but the others had eaten theirs, ravenous for meat.

"Bait!" Mohammed snapped now.

Forten cut it into chunks and skewered them onto tiny hooks made of chiseled whalebone. Salt had braided hemp thread into fishing line. He attached a baited hook and looked at Mohammed.

"Here?"

Mohammed shook his head no.

"Here?"

Mohammed pointed, and Salt angled the line there. "We could catch lobsters," Salt said. "The Dutch eat them."

Mohammed spat. "Cockroaches of the shore."

Before long, Mohammed had caught several fingerlings, which they used to bait larger hooks.

"If you eat fish that eats pork, then aren't you indirectly sinning?" asked Salt.

Mohammed didn't answer. They fished in silence, watching the belows. Dozens of them emerged blinking in the cold brightness, clenching their mess tins. Mulattoes, Indians, French, Spaniards, Chinamen. Not the good people of Jamaica, or Brooklyn, or Hempstead Plain. Swarthy, shaggy, gaunt, haunted. Very few were dressed warmly enough. They huddled close to each other, blowing into cupped hands. The wintry air gave them croup. Shackled and ankle-deep in pigshit, Salt shivered. Pulling his overcoat tightly around him, he wore his privilege uncomfortably.

"I look at them and don't feel anything." Mohammed kept his eyes wide open.

The belows passed around a punk to fire each other's smokes, and before long a haze settled over the *Jersey*. It smelled like burning hay. Salt scanned their faces. A lipless old man of perhaps sixty, eyes swallowed by wrinkles. A black man with white hair like an exploded thistle. An albino, wagging his head back and forth, gazing skyward, babbling in French. An Indian scratching, scratching, scratching. Out of habit, Salt looked to see if it was Drinky Crow, but it was not. Still, he knew that these were fathers, sons, brothers.

Mohammed said, "If you want to get out alive you must look the other way."

The urge to smoke crept back. It felt as if the craving was rooted in Salt's chest. He began to roll shreds of Rude gold into half a brown leaf.

"She's back," Forten said, peering down into the water where the *Jersey* Mermaid floated, her feet bare, the undersides of her toes like blue marbles. The body bobbed against the boat, turning supine, and the luxurious blonde tresses flowed to the side, revealing a lump of flesh gnawed to the teeth. Seagulls dove after the crabs, which scurried back to the safety of the underside.

"Crabs," Mohammed said, "make excellent bait."

Salt finished rolling the cheroot and placed it in his lips, unlit. It was a half mile or so to shore. There the Remsen wheel turned slowly in the creek that provided fresh drinking water for the *Jersey*. Salt hoped for a vision of the Wallabout Maiden to offset the image of the *Jersey* Mermaid, but only the waterwheel moved, promising nothing but the passage of time.

Save yourself: Mohammed's counsel.

The drop down to the water was farther than it had looked from the deck. Salt spent a long time in the sky, falling, watching as if outside himself, until he crashed head-first into the icy tidewaters. Surfacing, he splashed wildly toward the waterwheel. He could see it over the swells, the white-caps. Shots pinged nearby. The guards had poor aim, but he could not outswim the snipers. A lead ball hit him in the shoulder, searing. Blood unraveled like a silk thread in the river. Another bullet like a mulekick to the chest. Salt sank into the darkness. It was cold down here, frigid. Something bumped against him. The *Jersey* Mermaid! Beautiful brown eyes gone, black sockets in the skull, teeth wide with maxil-lary glee. So happy to see him!

Something yanked his line hard, and Salt snapped to.

Mohammed rushed to assist. The hemp thread held. They heaved together, rocking back and forth. Their catch was a large brown sturgeon, its snout long and spoonlike, with three whiskers of flesh sprouting from each side. It would feed many. It flopped on deck, frenzying the pig and chicken in The Farm. The belows stared up. The snipers were watching, too, along with Carple.

Salt gave the cigarette to Mohammed, who placed it carefully in his lips. A guard tossed him fire. He torched his smoke and inhaled deeply.

That night in the gun room, Salt could not sleep. The daydream nagged at him, as if he were still under water. He must do something to free himself, to free his fellows—*his men*, he was surprised to find himself thinking of them. A board beside his bunk was loose. He pried it loose with the mussel-shell knife. Below it was another layer of wood. How many more lay between him and the outside of the hull, freedom? Mindlessly he began to chisel. The crude instrument made for slow progress, but the work itself made him feel hopeful, and it killed time.

If any of his bunkmates were awake, they knew enough to keep still. Salt collected the sawdust in a pouch and brought it aloft the next morning, where he sprinkled it overboard. Guards hardly ever made their way below, but he would give them no reason for suspicion.

———·•·———

"SALT AND the powderboy, going at each other like a couple of apes," said the nurse.

There were three kinds of lice. Crabs were large, even the old grayhairs with fuzzy eyes could spot their eggs. Each man pinched his own. Headlice required a partner, which, like covert love, required trust, or pay. For those who could pay, the nurse offered the services of a stable of lice-pickers. Gamblers honored debts by picking. The cook got the hungriest boys to do him in exchange for extra butter. In this way, lice furthered the cause of civilization on the *Jersey*. Having lice was not a stigma, nor was having yourself picked clean of them, but ridding another man of them could mark you as his girl.

With his filed nails and sharp eyes, Forten was expert not only at sewing but at nitpicking—which he practiced now, in the brittle winter sunshine, snagging the little eggs and sliding them off the fine hairs at the back of Salt's neck.

O'Nan said, "The Captain don't care who thinks what."

Ezekiel Rude said, "That can be a good thing."

"Vermin."

Body lice lived in clothing, blankets, hammocks, rope. They were too small to crush between fingertips. You had to get them between fingernail and spar, squish until the skin under your nail went white. Even then the little bugger would sometimes spring up and scuttle away. You could burn them with a hot iron. You could drown them in rum, and leave yourself wanting. But their eggs, laid in seam stitching, were nearly impossible to kill. You couldn't get to them except by unraveling your clothing.

Salt had seen them under a lens. On six hooks—where any reasonable creature would have hooves, or paws—they scuttled along human skin, honing in on the tenderest spots, into which they sunk pincers and a tube to suck blood. The bite didn't hurt. Their spit lubricated and thinned a man's blood, which in its natural state wanted to scab. In this way, they were like an occupying army.

Forten hummed while his fingertips worked gently on the back of Salt's neck. It tickled and felt nice, as if all the time in the world were not a torment. Salt had heard Sparrow say that for a man, love began with touch; with a woman the opposite.

"Look how they enjoy it."

"Anybody else do a negro like that he'd get a knife in the ribs."

"He might yet."

"Vermin."

Lots of men had "girls" on ship. The rule was that a man's girl satisfied him, but his girl satisfied herself. A man took, not gave. In this way, equations of respect were balanced. Until now.

For the past month, every louse Salt and Forten had collected from each other got tossed alive into a matchbox. Lice lived only three days without feeding on blood, so there were dead ones mixed in with the crawlies. They were tobacco-colored, with pointy rears, greasy eyes, stubby antennae. Lice fever, pediculus delirium, struck at least one prisoner daily. Salt considered body lice Cunningham's little warriors. When the dead were brought up each morning, he had seen them abandoning a cooling corpse like sailors a sinking ship. Salt collected these also, constantly renewing his supply the way a boy collects arrowheads, for no purpose. Or some possible purpose.

———

TWO PREACHERS paid their monthly visit, an elder and a younger.

"God vendors," spat Ezekiel Rude, but the prisoners generally welcomed them. They arrived with clothing and food; they left with letters home.

Escorting the party was Cunningham in a plumed hat, breast laden with pins, badges, and clips. He flicked a luxurious tress over his shoulder with the backs of his fingertips and nickered like a horse.

Mohammed said, "I can die now I saw a man henna."

Six guards stood ready, armed with bayonets.

"Today we offer you freedom!" Cunningham announced.

Rude spat.

"First offer, freedom from the cold of winter!"

Gifts were unveiled—boots, blankets, mittens. The elder, wrapped tightly in his stole, blessed every taker, admonishing a debt to the Lord, an obligation the men were quick to accept with genuflections and knuckle kisses, while the younger stood aloof, as if counting the hairs on each man's bowed head. When the neat piles of clothing had been depleted, religious interest waned.

"And now for another freedom!" Cunningham peered over manicured nails. "You, slave boy. Get over here. Yes, you!"

Forten got to his feet, looked over his shoulder at Salt, then approached with an economy of movement that wasted no grace. "I am not a slave."

"In America every black boy is a slave."

"My father was born a free man."

"Yours and your mates'—" a sweep of the arm, a flip of the hair "—but not mine. My father before me was born to a father indentured. There is no shame in humble origins." Cunningham bowed slightly, the decorations on his chest jingling. "What were you before capture?"

"Powder boy."

"Do what the boss tells you?"

"What he asks of me, sir."

"For pay?" Cunningham unrolled a paper.

"Yes sir, and—"

"Sign here to free yourself of the prison ship and get back to work for twice the pay in the Crown's currency."

"—and for experience."

"Experience."

"Yes, sir."

"Experience?"

"Experience."

"Very well. Sign here and *experience* freedom. It is in writing. The Crown rejects slavery."

Forten gazed at the offerings before him. A brand new uniform. A shiny pistol. A musket fitted with a bayonet. A self realized. A dream—someone's, if not his. Salt willed Forten to take them, to prove to him that any son could be bought. Wouldn't James have jumped at the chance for a gun, a uniform?

"I volunteered to be a powder boy," said Forten.

Cunningham smiled. "Not to sign an oath of allegiance is to volunteer to die."

Forten stood silent. The others looked upon him curiously until Cunningham, exasperated, stepped back. The god vendors stepped forward to dispense more apples. At gunpoint, the men didn't riot this time. Apples in hand, they filed past the cook, who took a slice from each apple and tossed it into a cask. He would make moonshine with it, fermenting the mix with the yeast from the spit in his mouth.

7

MOLLY STOOD on the porch, the rifle barrel in one gloved hand, the butt in the crook of her elbow. She was wearing a heavy black coat over a black dress, plundered from Sparrow's wardrobe stored in the trunks in the attic. The gown was tight, but not terribly, and she was in the mood for mourning.

This morning when she woke, Drayton was already in uniform. "It's getting harder to put off your son," he had said to her. "The lad has a thirst for battle."

"I know you'll not let him," she had said, wrapping herself in the quilt and sitting up.

"He has made himself into a skilled warrior. He's a credit to you."

"Let him come home," Molly implored, allowing the covers drop ever so slightly.

"Come home?" said Drayton. "I have made him battalion leader." He patted her shoulder, then put on his pistols and left.

Now Molly stared out at the frigid landscape, morose. She had squandered her sexual capital and gained herself nothing. The estate was more decrepit than ever—crops moldering, fences plundered for firewood, heaps of garbage outside every window, bedpans emptied there by the occupying soldiers. Soon James would be in charge of louts like these.

A figure emerged from the hemp field, a strapping fellow in a coonskin cap. There was nothing stealthy or furtive in his movements—war had made her fluent in such body language—and so she decided not to shoot him.

As he approached, Molly could see that he wore a pistol in a holster, and a blunderbuss hung by a strap from his shoulder. He was rugged-looking, with amused eyes and a square jaw. In his hands was a plump parcel, wrapped in paper and stained with grease. "I come bearing gifts."

"Mr. Boocock?"

"This pullet was fed on cornpone and molasses, and by God you can taste it." He did not lick his lips, but something in his eyes suggested the gesture. "Not some tom brought up on crickets and deer pellets. Especially if you like dark meat. Do you . . . like dark meat?"

Molly switched the rifle from one arm to the other and sat the butt on her hip, letting the barrel swing out.

He spoke again. "Nobody carves a pork chop like you."

"What?"

"Word is."

"Whose word?"

Another offering, this one wrapped neatly with a red ribbon. Still she held her pose, until with his workingman's fingers Boocock plucked the ribbon, put it atop his cap, and and aubergine, glazed with butter and sprinkled with salt and rosemary. "May I join you?"

"What do you want?"

Boocock smiled, and the expression appeared to cost him some effort. "How often was I asked that question in the last six months and never answered the same way twice?"

"Why did you say that about pork chops?"

"Your husband boasted about them. May I?"

"Yes, it's cold out. Let's go in the barn."

It wasn't much warmer in the barn, but it was sheltered from the wind. In a far corner was an old blacksmith forge that could be used as an iron stove. Molly built a fire inside it, using dried cornstalks for kindling. Boocock set the chicken on a small table and unwrapped it, golden brown and flecked with seasoning. "Smell that dill? Too much can cut the nuts off an old rooster, pardon my French, but just a little puts your nose on."

She ate. Since Salt had left—had been taken from her—nobody prepared her meals. It was comforting, it was welcome, it was delicious. She could taste the corn and the molasses in the meat.

"Some favor breast. I like thigh."

Boocock's vulgarity amused her. As did the red ribbon atop the coonskin. And the man himself, blunt and generous. He had some powers of attraction—dexterity, for one, and enjoyment in sharing. "And how would you answer this time?"

"What?"

"The question you never answered the same way twice."

"I'd say nothing but more of now."

Molly leaned toward the fire, now going strong. "They say you killed a redcoat with a cock."

"Heavens." He licked a greasy thumb. "Have you any ale?"

"Corn whiskey."

"That will do."

She disappeared, returning with a jug and two glasses. She poured Boocock a tumbler full, then one half full for herself.

"I admire a gal likes her mash."

"Where is my husband?"

Boocock drank. The ribbon fell from his crown. "I don't know."

He picked up the ribbon and placed it gently on the lapel of her coat. Her hair fell to her shoulders, smooth and shiny. Her eyes were a bit bloodshot, and she did not grimace when she swallowed whiskey. Nor did she sit with her knees together, but spread her legs like a man. She was as likely to meet his jokes with a hard stare as laughter. And the way she had slung that rifle from her hip, half threat, half invitation. There were rumors about those soldiers, especially that scarface Romeo, Drayton. Even talk of Sowell. The widow slut.

The war had created scores of them.

What currency did they have but sex? Boocock was not above trading chicken for it. But he knew Molly would require more than candlelight and a roast chicken.

"Let me help your son."

"James doesn't need help anymore."

"The boy has practically memorized *Common Sense.*"

"Him and a hundred thousand others."

"But they are not British officers," Boocock said.

"Bring him back to me."

"He's a murderer, you know."

"Even if he were, the British are not punishing him for it." She sipped her whiskey.

He would have to do something for her. In fact, he was surprised to discover, he *wanted* to do something for her, for no thought of anything in return.

———•·•———

ALTHOUGH STARBOARD was more productive, Mohammed fished off the lee, the better to hear the Wallabout Maiden. Now and then, her melody got lost in the wind, each man's ear straining to fill in the haunting gaps. The gondola was running from shore to ship with its usual freight of sweet water. In the other direction, tiny plumes of smoke rose from a hundred Manhattan chimneys, each plume shuddering before taking flight in the gusts blowing from the northwest. The wharves were bustling, horses and carriages and wagons piled high with cargo wrapped in burlap. Ferries plied the river, scooting aside the ice floes.

The chow bell rang.

"Potatoes!" called a guard.

"Potatoes!" echoed another.

Cunningham appeared at the landing, his arms around a gunny sack. "Po-*tay*-toes!" he enunciated.

How long had it been since Salt had seen a potato, much less held one, the chapped brown skin on his fingertips, the fine layer of earth made edible by what underground magic, the eyespots, beginnings of tender shoots, and when you cracked it open the translucent crunch was enough to make you believe in something bigger than yourself, if only until the next bite, and the next.

"Nightshades from your friendly neighbors, the Remsens!" Cunningham unknotted the burlap neck, slowly, teasingly, failing once, failing twice, finally clasping the bag between his knees and using his eyeteeth to loosen the knot and rip it open.

The potatoes rumbled onto the lower deck, thudding, skidding, one of them spinning upright. But the prisoners did not pounce. They watched in silence, squatting on their haunches, unmoved and unmoving. Whatever dynamic property the potatoes had, it vanished as the last rolled slowly to a standstill on the deck. Finally, two men rose, O'Nan and Rude. Between them they held a piece of sackcloth, each gripping a side, and swept the deck, collecting each spud.

They brought the lumpy bundle to the center and set it down in front of Salt. He saluted a thank-you in the direction of the farm, and every prisoner aped him. There were not enough potatoes for each man to have one, but there were two for each mess. Salt cut each in half with his mussel-shell knife. The prisoners lined up and each took his half-potato without complaint. The remainder were halved once again, until all the men had exactly the same portion.

Most men did not wait to cook theirs; they simply munched. And, judging by their faces, by the way they wiped their mouths with the backs of their hands, the potatoes were good. But not worth going to war over.

It was Forten's job to retrieve the rest of the rations. Off he scrambled to get them. By an agreement General Washington had negotiated with Lord Howe, each prisoner of war—or detainee, as Cunningham would say, a bit of fine print that allowed him to ignore jurisprudence—got a ration two-thirds the quantity allotted a British seaman:

SUNDAY AND THURSDAY: 1 lb biscuit, 1 lb pork,
   half pint peas
MONDAY AND FRIDAY: 1 lb biscuit, 1 pint oatmeal,
   2 ounces butter
TUESDAY AND SATURDAY: 1 lb biscuit, 2 lbs mutton
WEDNESDAY: 1½ lbs flour, 2 ounces suet

A menu that would starve even the scrawniest British conscript. And "two-thirds" was an accounting gimmick anyway. Who was checking if the pound of meat was mostly bone, or the suet green? Unlike a prisoner, a sailor with money or an occupying soldier could get his hands on rum, oranges, sugar, beets, carrots, apples, fowl, squash, ale, pie and sometimes olives, figs, pigeon, haricot verts, cheese, cake, pheasant, and bread. Potatoes.

The cooking for prisoners was done in the forecastle, a rickety shack that housed the galley. At its center was the Great Copper, which was enclosed in brickwork about eight feet square. Large enough to contain three hogsheads of water, it was partitioned. In one side, the peas and oatmeal were boiled in fresh water. In the other, which had begun to corrode, meat was stewed in saltwater drawn from alongside the lee of the ship. To whom did it matter that the saltwater used to boil the meat was fouled with the incoming tide, funked with the waste of hundreds of tall ships and the mighty city of Manhattan itself?

To Salt, for one. He retrieved a two-gallon jug from a locked chest bequeathed to him by a man for whom variolation had come too late, and handed it to Mohammed. While many dangled their meat to cook in the Great Copper, Salt and Mohammed set about preparing a fire from scavenged kindling and set a bent tin pot to boil upon it. Each mess—five or six men—who had the means cooked their meals in freshwater like this, building little fires directly upon bricks laid atop the floorplanks around the forecastle's perimeter. Salt's little cooking fire whipped in the bitter wind that pierced the charcoaled plank wall, but the water was boiling by the time Forten returned with the day's rations, pork on a string, peas in a paper cone.

"What about the biscuits?" Salt asked.

"What biscuits?"

"Today's supposed to be biscuits."

"T'ain't no biscuits."

Just as well, thought Salt. The last had been inedible. Forten had pinched his nose and gnawed as if he'd been chewing bugs. Which, in fact he had been—tiny brown weevils, with long snouts and waving antennae.

After mealtime, the prisoners were allowed their deck break. Great gobs of ice clung to the stump of the amputated bowsprit. Glaciated gargoyles perched along the railings. To the derrick clung a wintry scrim. The hawsers were enameled, glistening in the bright sun, which hung powerless and low over the Staten Island narrows.

Cunningham produced a deck of playing cards. They were new and glossy, and the face cards depicted King George and his court. Another guard passed out lacquered chips, blue, red and white.

"What about Rude?"

They looked at Rude. This was an incursion on his turf, a direct attack. Cunningham said, "To the house goes fifty percent of the weekly take, not to be less than forty quid a week. Any man object?"

Again they looked to Rude. Rude turned his head and spat, then lit a cigarette.

Someone said, "Rude folds." And, recognizing the cards

and chips as the shiny bait they were, the gamblers took them anyway.

That night, as every night, Salt returned to his chiseling.

Outside the gun room there was scuffling and a cry. But Salt's bunkmates snored on. The creaking of the timbers and the slight rocking of the boat comforted him, reminding him that the hulk would not last forever, and put him in a meditative state. Night in the hold was the definition of black. A boy's game: Salt would hold his hands in front of his face, bringing them slowly closer, as close as he could without touching. He could stick a finger in his eye and never see it coming. It was surprising that you could be so close to something, even to a part of yourself, and not be able to perceive it.

By the time James had turned five, Sparrow no longer spoke. She couldn't walk, didn't sleep, ate only strawberry jam. She recognized nobody. Ebenezer imported a wheelchair for her, all the way from London, made of cane and wicker, with large spoked wheels. But Ebenezer was too impatient to attend to her, and left her strapped in it for hours at a time. One day Salt found her abandoned in the garden, her cheeks badly sunburned. Ebenezer bought silver paste balm from Argentina and hired a nurse, an ex-slave from the island of Jamaica. Salt had asked her about the hemp they grew there, which he'd heard was powerful, but she knew nothing about it.

Finally, Sparrow lost the ability to swallow. Even water would not go down, but spilled off her chin.

They buried her in the Jamaica churchyard. It was the first time James had seen his mother cry, and he was frightened. Salt explained to James that death was like sleep, you dreamed on, whether or not you remembered, but James was not consoled. He'd taken to crying out in the middle of the night after that, scared of the dark. When he cried out, he called for Salt, not for his mother. And Salt had gone to him, every time.

Salt chiseled on, as his mates snored, sighed, and scratched in their sleep. He began to see himself as a vessel of dreams, his own and others'.

WHAT COULD Sowell offer a woman, especially one whose bare arms showed so enticingly through a crocheted shawl? The last feather had ages ago worn off and the tar was long gone, but an air of humiliation clung to him. His wig and collar made him seem a doughy eunuch. He did not see that a man who has been stripped, shamed, and shunned by his kind, yet picks himself up and powders his cheeks and links his cuffs and gets back to business, is a man a woman could respect. Especially a woman who has bartered sex for security and come up short in the bargain.

At first Molly and Drayton had settled into the rhythm of Drayton's visits, and the thrill of wanting and being wanted carried her into the heart of winter, the pleasure at first outweighing the guilt of betraying Salt, and her son and self. By some strange logic, she even felt that by sinning against Salt, she somehow kept him alive. But as the icy months passed, the heat between her and Drayton had begun to dissipate. By spring, as the weather warmed, bringing longer daylight and daffodils but no James, a chill set in between them. Drayton claimed a throat ailment and dosed it liberally with rum, which did little to repair the rift between them, or to rekindle desire. And yet he came each week to her bed, if only to fall asleep there, with his boots on. And here was Molly, disgusted with herself, saddled with yet another helpless man.

"Do you think my husband is dead?" she asked, cutting short Sowell's reverie.

Sowell hemmed. "We must obtain his certificate of death."

"But what if he's not dead, Mr. Sowell?" Molly pronounced it like "soul," and he never corrected her. Her curls now fell past her shoulders, and her black dress swished as she climbed down the porch stairs.

"It is imperative. His death certificate unencumbers you. It frees you to claim what's rightfully yours. James. Property, I mean. Bury. Succession."

"There's no body."

"It's just a piece of parchment."

"So is a marriage certificate."

"If something, heaven forbid, were to happen to your father—if he were to drop dead of apoplexy, or trip and fall on a bayonet, or get tomahawked by a runner, or burn up in a fire, or jump from—well, you get the gist, Molly, my dear—you would be stuck. You'd have to rely on the courts, or what's left of them, for disposition of the estate, and the transfer of assets. Do you see?"

"I don't know for certain that he's dead."

"It's my job to imagine the worst."

"That's a mother's job."

"I will get you Bury, and secure James's future."

"How?"

"Appoint you James's exclusive guardian. That will give you say-so over his trust—the Bury trust. Any decision regarding disposition will necessitate your stamp of notary, at least until the age of majority, which is a matter of stipulation. Shall we say twenty-one? At the same time I write James a will naming you as sole beneficiary."

Molly looked at him. "So go ahead and write."

"My dear, let me tell you how I can protect you." Sowell tugged one cuff, then another. Carefully, he peeled off his wig. It was startling to see the thin black and white locks plastered to the side of his skull, the skin there pale and clammy in the spring light. But the shape of his head was surprisingly fine. He held the wig in both hands and peered into it as if it were a crystal. "I have no arms but language. The power of the word. A poet I'm not. I cannot describe the sun going down, nor a virgin's kiss. Me in a pulpit is a catfish in a poplar. What I can do, however, is to fashion a suit of armor from sentences. With twenty-six letters and a sleight of syntax, I can guard you and those you love, so that the slings and arrows of outrageous fortune fall away harmlessly. With my help, what is mortal in you, that messy glory on which so many depend, can beat freely."

Molly was astonished to see that his eyes were wet. She took his arm and he drew nearer, a pale, moist creature un-used to the sunshine. He unscrolled a paper and smoothed it flat, set a quill and bottle of ink alongside it. "In myself I have had to sacrifice the very feelings I am paid by others to safeguard." He inked a quill and handed it to her. "Until now."

"To sign is to murder."

Sowell whispered in her ear, "No, my dear. To sign is to deliver."

Molly took the quill in hand, and the hand was steady.

8

"SNAKE FOR MARBURY!" A shout was passed, like a bucket of water, from man to man. "Snake for Marbury!" The gun room door banged open, and in came a tether. "Snake for Marbury!"

Caught. Salt fumbled with the mussel shell before hiding it in his blanket. He puffed his cheeks and blew away the sawdust.

"Nothing good ever brought the snake," Rude muttered.

"Wait for me," cried Forten.

"Stay!"

The snake was a rope with a headknot. He whom it called had to hold onto the headknot and be yanked by the guards from the hold. The last prisoner who had been singled out by its midnight strike was hanged, and then his rectum was sliced open to reveal a greased tube made of tin containing a diamond brooch and ruby earrings stolen from a British magistrate's widow. Or so the story went.

"I've got ahold!" The snake pulled him through the mass of men, many of them growling words of encouragement as he caromed off them—"Steady, Cap," "Courage, sir"—although some merely echoed the order, "Gang way, Marbury up top!" And one man whispered, "Hope they slit *your* arse open with a dull blade." Salt coursed through the maze by feel, letting the pull of the rope guide him, giving wide berth to chamber pots and threading his way past supine bodies—Marylanders, Rhode Islanders, South Carolinans, all clinging to the dreams of riches, patriotism, love, or who-knows-what that bad luck had killed by bringing them here.

A torch flickered at the entrance grate. Carple, the Scottish guard, used a skeleton key to unlock the grate, its iron hinges squeaking painfully.

The early summer night was mild. Salt longed to linger under the sky, an extravagant celestial spill. It would take a lifetime of nights to count each star—a man would most certainly fail trying—but just now it seemed a worthwhile endeavor, and not because the stars held a man's destiny, but because counting would focus his consciousness on each, if just for a moment. Wasn't each, even that faint one that skittered away as he watched—especially that one—worthy of absolute attention?

They took him past another iron barricado and down a narrow passageway into a large room. In the center was a writing desk piled with several large bound volumes. There was also a crucifix, a pedestal, and thumbscrews. "Parole office," Carple explained. Salt had heard the rumors. So this was where the furloughed prisoners reported for duty, the lucky men with cattle, munitions, and other coveted provisions to supply the British—men with monied wives, who in return escaped serving aboard the prison ships and were quartered at home.

They stripped him. Salt regretted losing his coin pouch and his matchbox, with its carefully hoarded livestock, but there was nothing he could do. Carple led him to the room's edge, where a sawed oak barrel had been half filled with water. It was barely tepid, not nearly warm enough to quell the goosepimples on Salt's arms and legs, the skin stretched tight over his ribs, but it felt unimaginably luxurious nevertheless. Salt went to work with a bar of rough soap, scrubbing hard, drawing deep draughts of cleanliness, his pleasure almost obscene.

"What did I do to deserve this?"

Carple said, "You did good."

After he had dried himself, Carple issued him a new set of clothes—simple Quaker britches and muslin blouse, plain Friend. The square-toed shoes were a size too large, but they had shiny buckles and new soles. The sight of the new clothing flooded him with hope, which felt disturbingly like fear. Was he to be set free? Had somebody come to his rescue? Molly? Or—and here his heart sped—Ebenezer, with his open purse? Instinctively he reached into his pocket for his own purse, before he remembered it was gone, and encountered there instead, to his surprise, the matchbox. He looked at Carple, but the guard only returned his gaze with a steady stare.

Carple led him to the rear of the ship. It had bay windows and leaded panes silled with copper, turned verdigris in the salt air. Curtains of purple velvet were gathered at either side. There were wing chairs and a settee, upholstered in the same purple velvet, and on the plank floor purple rugs. The door handles, cabinet knobs, and curtain railings were brass, lit up and dancing with the reflection of a coal fire burning in the hearth, under a teak mantel that featured a carved sea serpent baring fangs.

In the center of the room was a round teak table with the remains of a ravaged feast. Squab carcasses were ripped apart, grimy goblets held the dregs of claret, boiled cabbage gave up its too-intimate odor, seedcake crumbs adorned all. Beyond the table Cunningham was joined by a preacher in a white-ringleted wig, along with two women, a fat one in a mobcap and a lanky one with a mesh veil over her face. Two attendants busied themselves, one with a quill and record book, the other with a decanter. No sign of Molly, nor Ebenezer.

Three men in civilian clothes entered from the side, each bowing in turn as Cunningham called his name and rank for the record keeper. Despite their dress and the grim imprint of incarceration on their faces, they seemed to be British officers.

Cunningham addressed them. "You have served your country with distinction, and for that we are grateful," he said. "In accordance with Washington and Howe's agreement, we have bought your freedom in exchange for that of three prisoners of high rank on this ship." Salt wondered where the others were, and why the exchange was taking place on board the *Jersey*, rather than on land. Then he noticed one of the attendants sketching the scene, and marveled anew at Cunningham's genius for self-promotion.

"How did the Americans treat you?" Salt whispered to the last of the officers as he passed.

"Just better than dirt," he hissed. "*Dirt* I can understand. *Just better* you will pay for."

After they had gone, the elder stepped forward. Silky white hair fell in bangs, framing a round pink face. He wore a tight black waistcoat with three fabric-covered buttons, and a thickly hemmed white collar that fell from his throat halfway down his chest in two rectangular tails. With the back of one hand he slapped the Bible he clutched tight in the other. "God holds you over the pit of hell, much as you hold a spider over the fire."

Cunningham raised his eyebrows gleefully.

The elder again slapped the book. "He abhors you, and is dreadfully provoked: He aches to throw you down."

The thin woman lifted her veil, revealing the face of a mere child. She smiled conspiratorially at Salt.

"Abhors *us all*."

"Amen," whispered the mobcap.

Cunningham winked at her. "If any are exempt, I daresay you are, Sister." He addressed the threesome. "Lord Howe will be pleased to have his officers returned to him.

The Crown thanks you for your assistance with this exchange of prisoners."

"So then you'll let Ezekiel go?"

"It's his rank that dictates Rude's value," Cunningham explained to the elder, "not his marriage to my sister."

"It hurts me, William, this war between us," said the mobcap. "Who was it walked me down the aisle? Whose arm gave me away? William, you're my blood."

It was hard to believe she and Cunningham were related, she in her plain petticoat and square-toed shoes, he with his auburn tresses and uniform bristling with medals.

The elder spoke. "Where is this Rude you speak of?"

"He will be delivered at sun-up, you have my word, along with the third," Cunningham said. "Night time, as you can imagine, presents a logistical problem. It is difficult to extract a handful of rebels without disturbing the nest. God may see them as spiders, but I see them rather as hornets."

"After what Ezekiel's family did for us," hissed his sister. "The house. The farm."

"Are there women on board?" The lanky girl, undaunted, directed her question to Salt, but Cunningham answered.

"Not yet, no. Will there soon be? Perhaps."

"Who is this one?"

"A captain," said Cunningham. "Captain Marbury of the pirate ship *Bright Star*."

"Has the…Captain…eaten?" asked the girl. Something about her was altogether too familiar. Her eyes searched the room and came to rest on Salt's face. "He's had the pox."

Reflexively, Salt ran his fingertips along his cratered cheek. He had forgotten.

"Have the men medical care? A surgeon? Are they fed?" The elder peppered Cunningham with questions. Salt felt like a specimen, to be peered at, poked—and then? He stood there, blinking and drooling.

The girl persisted. "Look at his bones. You can see the skeleton showing through."

The fire popped.

"Bring my ward a plate of supper!" Cunningham roared. Then, more softly, "Neither I nor the Crown compel a soul to do what is beyond its capacity. It gets what it has earned, no more and no less, and is responsible for what it deserves."

Salt was seated at the table, and the visitors studied him as he ate. He had forgotten what crystal felt like against his lips, how claret tasted, three rubies of firelight in its heart. The perfume entered his nose and got caught up behind his eyes, but he could not slow himself. He swallowed it all in one gulp. The plate was bone china, and it greeted his fork with a friendly clink as he cut into the roast pumpkin, drenched in butter and drizzled with molasses. It fell apart delightfully in his mouth, and he jammed in another huge slice. Next came roast squab, its skin crisp as toast and flecked with salt and pepper—oh salt and pepper!—the meat succulent and steaming, breaking apart along the juicy seam where opposing muscle grains met.

"Is everything to your liking?" Cunningham asked.

Salt grunted and licked his fingers as tears ran. The onlookers were embarrassed. The black-cloaked elder averted his eyes. Fat Lady Rude, ample bosom thrust forth, murmured, "Look, he weeps."

The girl said, "I never saw my father weep. Not once."

Salt was these benefactors' good deed, the food, by Cunningham's agency, the benefaction. This Salt understood— the scene distilled to a sketch and paragraph to be run in a London newspaper and reprinted in New York, assuaging consciences and worries on both sides of the Atlantic. But the girl, what about her? Where had he seen her? She was pretty in the way a pretty young girl might sketch a pretty young girl, wide-eyed, features untroubled by any complicated past, every emotion met with curiosity.

"Captain Marbury, these fine citizens have secured your freedom." Cunningham waved some papers. "These letters, addressed from General Washington to our Lord Howe, detail a list of grievances concerning the treatment of prisoners of war and—"

The elder said, "I'm sure you do not abide the abuses listed therein."

"My hand is severe but my intentions benevolent."

"Seneca said that."

"He got it from me." Cunningham sniggered, then sniggered again when no one else laughed. He nodded to an attendant, who poured brandy all around, placing a snifter before Salt as well. Cunningham held his own glass high. "May hostilities end, and brother embrace brother." A nod towards the women—"and sister."

Salt stared at the amber liquid, its resplendent color already intoxicating.

"Come, Marbury. As of this moment you're a free man."

Salt picked up the snifter and swirled, watching the liquor map the inside of the glass. The fire crackled. The purple velvet curtains glowed, the burnished teak gleamed. Color. How many nights had he lived without it?

He addressed Cunningham. "Sir, if I may, I wish to exchange my grant of liberty for another on board, a youngster whose mother—"

"Amen," whispered Lady Rude.

"Hold your tongue—"

"—and I'd like it notarized in the witness of present company—"

"—I don't negotiate with—"

"—let him speak—"

"—by leave of the Crown—"

"—that the prisoner's name is James Forten!"

Cunningham showed his teeth. "The little negro who sews?"

"Yes, sir."

Sconces threw steady gold light, casting three shadows of Cunningham. Each slid in opposing choreography across the floor and up the walls as he paced. "One doesn't trade bullion for lead. General Washington will certainly desire an officer for an officer."

Salt had expected this tactic, and was prepared for it. Cunningham did not want to lose this chance to pawn off

Salt, the troublemaker, and call it a good deed. "It will improve upon the story."

"As I recall, Marbury, you believe all men are created equal," Cunningham said.

"In a political sense."

"A politic answer."

"Politics is war."

"Your countrymen politic for slavery and call that freedom. I should hazard a guess that you personally own a negro or two, and drive them to realize your dreams. Or would if you could."

For the first time in a long while, Salt wondered if Cunningham recognized him for who he truly was. He had been no slaveowner, but only for lack of means, and Ebenezer's approval. Somebody had to beat the hemp. But now he said, "I have renounced slavery."

"And what does the little negro do with his earnings?"

"Gives them to me."

"I see."

The elder and Lady Rude exchanged glances. The writer scribbled notes. Even the child frowned.

Salt added, "It can be rough below. Desperate men get violent."

"The very definition of a rebel." Cunningham's shadows played on the walls, one growing, another shrinking, each a different shade of dark.

"The youngster needs protection."

"And, Captain Marbury, how will your own family accept

your largesse? Will they forgive your rejecting them for the little negro?"

Salt winced at the suggestion—James abandoned, Molly spurned again. But his conscience had gone beyond tyranny; it called itself justice and required sacrifice. "Never."

Cunningham shuddered and scowled. "Smells like boiled cabbage in here. Clear the table!"

"The cords of love are stronger than iron fetters," said the elder, but it was unclear whether he was extolling a virtue or lecturing the girl.

"Amen," said Lady Rude.

The servants cleared the table, and Salt took advantage of the distraction to extract the matchbox from his pocket, open it wide, and flick the contents between the velvet drapes drawn open at Cunningham's bunk.

The girl saw him do it. She crossed her eyes and stuck out her tongue. Salt felt the corners of his mouth pull up, conspiring in her silly mirth. The adults in the room continued their peculiar study of him.

"This will not be well received by my superiors," Cunningham said at last. "Exchange an officer for a powderboy? A negro no less."

So the decision had been made. Salt would stay on board, and Forten would be set free.

"Let me remind you that these men are criminals in the eyes of the Crown, Mr. Remsen," said Cunningham.

So the elder was Remsen, of the Remsen farm! At last, Salt identified what was so familiar about the girl. Her voice.

Remsen's daughter, the Wallabout Maiden! Not at all the siren he expected.

"We hear you singing," Salt said to her. "We wait on it."

She jammed a finger in each ear. "Boring," she growled.

———•·•———

EACH DOOR in the house was hand-hewn. Heaven's doors, Ebenezer called them, because those who were given to such things saw in their panels a cross on top, a book below. Not that Ebenezer was given to such things. Like most people, he prayed when threats, bribery, and cajolery had not worked. What mattered to Ebenezer mattered to God; he never imagined otherwise. But not even for the Almighty would he get on his knees. That he would only do for James.

"Don't go!"

"I'm already gone." James slammed the door behind him.

Ebenezer, kneeling, sputtered and gazed at the book, the cross. Punish me! he thought. Get it over and done with! Still he waited for the onslaught he knew was on its way. How had he, who opposed the enslavement of the darker races, given up Drinky Crow to worse? And for what?

Somewhere inside the house another door slammed shut. And another.

———•·•———

UNDER BLUE SKIES and puffy clouds, the trees fresh with new green, honeybees and butterflies danced over the river to grace the hulk with a whisper of gardenia. The first to say good-bye was Ezekiel Rude. He had given his clothes, his gaming ledgers, his bricks of Virginia tobacco to Salt for distribution among the ranks. Salt in turn issued them to Mohammed for safekeeping. Mohammed had traded half a sturgeon for a storage chest with a working lock. Because the barbary religion prohibited usury, he operated as the most favored bank.

"Better me than him," said Mohammed.

Salt stared at him. "Was that humor?"

"He could at least have given me his spot in the gun room," Mohammed sulked.

But a Bostoner had paid off Rude to take his place, and invited his friends. They were said to have performed heroically at Lexington. Most important, they brought with them two jugs of rum.

O'Nan was already in the gondola, thumbs hooked under his snakeskin belt. The sickest and the sorriest, Salt had convinced Cunningham, would reap him the best publicity.

"Why O'Nan?" said Mohammed. "*Everybody* hates O'Nan."

"He gave pus," Salt said. "What did you ever do?"

Last to board was James Forten. He said to Salt, "I will rescue you."

"Ha! *That* was humor." Mohammed pushed Forten gently down the gangplank.

Later, as they were about to descend for the night, the guards, as usual, barked, "Stand and be counted!" Salt took his place at the end of the line, prolonging the simple pleasure of fresh air. A honeybee bobbed around his head, allured by what? There was nothing attractive in him. "Go ashore," he bade it.

"Short count!" The guards scrambled. "Man gone!" Carple slammed the barricado and sent snipers to their marks.

"Where's the Arab?"

"Can he swim?"

"Mohammed?" Salt asked, but it sounded like calling his name.

The prisoners were stripped and queued, counted and re-counted. Hours passed. Long past midnight, they were allowed to dress and go below, Mohammed still missing.

In the gun room, they were passing around the rum. "Somebody will be made to pay," said the Bostoner, his accent brassy.

"I'll not argue with you," Salt said.

"We agree on that, then."

FIVE DAYS LATER, the exchanged prisoners returned. It was the fourth of July. Humidity smudged the line between bay and sky, everywhere a fishy gray steam into which the bow of the ship disappeared. The world was hot, interior, not subject to laws of perspective. Twelve flags hung from the boom. One was light blue, with a picture of a thorn-bush and a hand, the motto *Sustain or Abstain*. Another was yellow with a boar and spear, *Aut. Mors. Aut. Vita Decora*. Another yellow one had an arm extending from a cloud, the hand clenching a sharpened dagger: *Resistance to Tyrants is Obediance to God.* Most had the standard thirteen stripes, red and white, and in the upper left a blue patch with thirteen six-pointed stars arranged in a square, one in the center, although even these were crudely stitched, no two alike, as if executed by children. Then someone raised a thirteenth flag, this one yellow with a rattlesnake coiled thrice, its red forked tongue sticking out, riding above the cry DON'T TREAD ON ME.

Salt knew prisoners from nine of the thirteen colonies, and knew how badly one missed a place when you were forced from it. But he was surprised by the passion the men put into making the flags. The urge to celebrate independence. All day prisoners had been raising cheers, singing. *"Yankee doodle went to town, a riding on a pony—"* a new Kentuckian, Bobbs, fingerpicked a banjo *"—poked a redcoat up the arse and called it alimony."*

Carple grinned, made a show of stomping his foot in time. Even in jest he was unable to hide how music moved him.

"Take down the pennants!" Cunningham growled. Today he wore wings on the shoulders of his uniform, the French pistols braced in Spanish leather, the long tresses girlishly pretty. His grin, lipless as ever over the perfect teeth, suggested that joy was a practical joke played on the human race. It was rare that he deigned to walk the deck, but here he was, surrounded by armed guards.

"They're only flags, sir," said Carple.

"No reason then not to take them down."

"Of all days, let it pass, sir. A little merriment never hurt anyone."

Cunningham's was the smile of a mandarin. "Of all days, this is the one day on which I can't let it pass."

"Ship to starboard!" cried a guard. Cunningham disappeared inside to Captain's quarters. Forten stood at the bow, nose aloft, others behind him plying the long oars as the gondola slid alongside the *Jersey.*

Salt stared from the deck. "Is this Cunningham's joke?"

Forten wouldn't look at him. O'Nan went off by himself for a smoke. Ezekiel Rude's hand was wrapped in a wet rag, a frown stamped on his face.

"What happened?" asked Salt.

"My wife signed the damn loyalty oath."

"So what?"

"*So this!*" He smacked a fist into his bandage, pantomiming a blow. "I beat her and left her on the wharf."

Slowly, Salt learned what had happened. When General Washington, somewhere in Maryland, had learned by messenger the identities of the freed prisoners, he became enraged. Continentals had given up British lieutenants, whose capture had cost buckets of American blood, and for what? Diseased knaves of dubious patriotism—a yellow-eyed militia man, a nepotistic profiteer, and a seventeen-year-old black powderboy with a nose like a French king's? A trick! Washington complained to Howe, and Howe came down hard on Cunningham.

Cunningham was forced to release three officers. Then he doubled prisoners' rations—with maggoty tripe.

———•–•———

THE GUN ROOM was overrun with Bostoners. One of them said, "Say what you want, the Arab found a way off this floating esophagus."

"Sarcophagus, the newspaper said."

Rude sat in the corner, seething. Mohammed's trove had been trashed, and Cunningham had usurped him. He had been ousted from the center, marginalized. All that saved him from poverty was the Virginia tobacco, which he had been able to exchange for mutton, peas, and butter, but most of which he gave to the Bostoners in order to rent his little corner of the gun room. He would likely be ousted altogether unless he could persuade his wife to get him more tobacco. And that was unlikely in light of the bandaged hand, and his refusal to sign the oath.

"Bastard Arab stole the smoke!"

This time when the Bostoners said, "Have yourself some goddamn rum," Salt took the jug. The fire in it burned going down, and hit his gut with a sizzle. The next swig killed the pain, and the killing felt so fine a third pull was in order. Next came a smoke, which Salt sucked into his lungs to the point of bursting. When he exhaled, he asked, "What newspaper?" He hadn't known the question was in him. "That said sarcophagus?"

"The *Boston Herald.* Said nobody escaped ever, or would.

Said the Brits were no better than savages. Said somebody would be made to pay."

When the rum came his way again, Salt drank. How could he have forgotten what feeling good felt like? Oh, for some rope. The simple fact of wanting it was proof of, well, what? He would have to find rope. Drinky Crow might know where to look. But Drinky Crow was dead.

That night Salt didn't bother to chisel. When he closed his eyes, he felt the boat move, and for a moment he thought the ship had sails again, and the men on board were not prisoners but passengers, on a wind-borne journey to...

He awoke in the dark. Or maybe he was already awake, sleep had come in shards. He needed to urinate. He shut his eyes again, battling needs. You could ignore stiff dick; it got easier as you got older.

How to picture Molly. Unclothed. Sitting on the bed, upright, knees together, breasts compressed by her bracing arms. Twice or three times a week, say one hundred thirty times a year, that would be twenty-three hundred or so. How like a man to count. When they were newlyweds, Sparrow had teased them mercilessly, mimicking, "O, don't stop!" Molly had wanted it more often, but Salt wanted it deeper. For her it could be as matter-of-fact as a string of sneezes. For him the pleasure was in the prolonging, especially as he aged. To fantasize was to torture himself. When you are married to a woman for eighteen years you know how far she will go, what she won't do, what you can't do. And it's those things that become your fantasies.

In the dark came the leathery stealth of a footstep, a familiar tiptoe. Drinky Crow crawled into the hammock with Salt.

"But you're dead." Yet there was nothing ghostly in the presence lying next to him, already naked, or half so.

"Hold me."

"Forten? What—"

"Please?"

"Get out."

"But I thought we—"

"Get the hell out!"

Salt fell back to sleep. Sometime before dawn, he had a nightmare in which Forten was shrieking over and over, "Daddy! Daddy!"

———·•·———

"REBELS, TURN OUT your dead!" Cunningham's reveille.

The dead had already been turned out, so the phrase served as a requiem. But today the seven corpses lined up neatly by sick bay were not yet shrouded.

"Why hasn't Forten sewn their burial gowns?"

"Got himself raped again."

Salt looked again, more carefully. Forten's was among the corpses.

———·•·———

COURT WAS convened Sunday morning.

Twelve men were selected for jury duty, each of them

getting a pinch of tobacco for pay. They were empanelled in two runs before the gunwale, crowding together, as dozens of their fellow prisoners looked on, impatient to get back to their cards. Salt sat bench, half an empty powderkeg turned upside down. Sick at heart, and sick of himself, he had tried to decline, but the others had insisted.

Across the river, the Wallabout Maiden sang. The melody carried on the breeze, notes dropping suddenly, then a measure suddenly near and clear. The Maiden herself was hidden somewhere, maybe in the orchard, or behind the outbuildings.

"Bring forward the suspect," ordered the bailiff.

Yellow-eyed O'Nan was dragged forward.

"Three to two O'Nan." Rude kept track of the bets, restored to a fraction of his former glory. At least this wagering was free of Cunningham's deal tax.

"Guilty!"

"A hundred dollars says not." In other circumstances allowing jurors to bet might be considered a conflict of interest, but about the prison ship, no one would serve otherwise.

A Bostoner gave O'Nan a cigarette, and O'Nan sucked it as if it were his mother's tit. A juror addressed him. "Want ye a lawyer to plead your case?"

"*Ye?*" O'Nan spat. "Why ye say *ye* on Sunday and only on Sunday?"

"*Ye* is history!" shouted a gallery drone.

"Come to order!" Salt called, and the gallery quieted.

Salt held up the snakeskin belt. "Is this yours?"

"You know it is," O'Nan said. "That very copperhead bit me."

"It was found around the boy's throat."

"He wouldn't stop crying. *Daddy, Daddy, Daddy!*"

"Why was he crying Daddy?"

"I didn't do nothing."

Salt said, "And that made him cry Daddy."

"Daddy Daddy Daddy."

"Then what?"

"I made him stop."

"With the cottonmouth belt."

"*Copperhead,* damn it!" O'Nan had smoked the cigarette down to the nub. "It was play." He slapped his lapels and ran a purple tongue over his oily moustache, ruffling himself like a filthy pigeon.

Salt said, "Since you have confessed, this court pronounces you guilty of rape and murder."

From the gallery, a cry went up. "Death!"

"Death," Salt said. He hated O'Nan as much as he'd hated anybody, ever. But any pleasure he thought revenge might bring was not forthcoming. With what he hoped was gravity, he muttered, "The law requires it."

Now to carry out the sentence. Rude produced a pouch containing Cunningham's lacquered chips and laid down the rules. Nobody was excused from the draw, not even the judge. The man who drew the black dot would be executioner. If the lot was drawn by the man you'd bet on, you won. If you bet on yourself and won, you were exempt from carrying out the sentence but won nothing, and lots would be drawn again.

"Who's in?" A Bostoner threw a chip into the pot, and a cascade of cigarettes and chips clattered after, with Rude once again keeping the ledger. The good-hearted, the prudent, and the cowardly bet on themselves.

"Draw your lots!" Salt ordered.

It was his chip that had the black dot.

A cheer rose up, mixed with whistles of relief. Nobody had bet on Salt, including himself. When the pot was distributed, a silence fell over the deck. Even the seagulls seemed to hover in mid air, their wings outstretched.

"Do you want to appeal the sentence?" Salt asked O'Nan.

"Hell no," said the prisoner, returning Salt's gaze. His face was the texture of cheese, his clothes stiff with smut. There wasn't anywhere on him that wasn't scurfed, stained, or otherwise marked by appetite and its gratification. "You of all men understand what I gave the boy."

Salt fingered his chip. To the east, he heard the Maiden's song again. "Prepare yourself." A Bostoner handed O'Nan another cigarette while a scribe arranged to record a last will and testament. The heavy-lidded guards looked on, hands tucked in pockets.

"The boy's pleasure was my pleasure." O'Nan puffed and nodded. "Them is my last words."

Again the melody pulled and pushed, syncopated by the tidal breezes, the stress on the weak beat, like a tune you know but can't give voice to. Salt grew angry. What right did the girl have to sing, when just half a league away men were struggling to sort themselves from beasts? Salt regarded O'Nan with loathing. Just because a boy wants to die doesn't mean a man should grant him his wish. He asked himself what Drinky Crow would do. "Rum!"

A jug was sent hand over hand. With it, Salt lured O'Nan to the gunwale. O'Nan took the jug and gulped until his eyes watered and a flush spidered across his cheeks.

"Easy or hard?" Salt asked, when he had finished.

O'Nan looked down. "I cain't swim."

"They say drowning doesn't hurt."

O'Nan took another swallow of rum, another lungful of the cigarette. He cowered against the gunwale, and staring wobbily at Salt: "I ain't jumping."

Salt shoved.

O'Nan toppled head-first, arms flapping like misshapen wings until he splashed into the water. Salt's palms tingled where they had touched him. The guards never took their hands out of their pockets. Across the channel, the girl sang on.

ALTHOUGH SHE MIGHT have wanted to, Molly could not wear breeches to her own wedding. Instead she wore a gown that fell, scandalously, just below her knees. None of the hundred guests had ever seen a dress so short, though there were pamphlet accounts of them. And her calves, though hosed in French net, looked, said other girls, manly. The men said otherwise. Was she or wasn't she? Except for the chaste Quakers, perhaps one in four American brides wasn't.

Salt was handsome in his suit. It was black and crisply tailored, a white cotton shirt and black tie. It looked a bit like a uniform. He had refused Ebenezer's request that he wear a wig, so his red hair, backlit, glowed. Good looks weren't the only reason to choose a husband, but it was an important one. You had to like the face in front of you. You did not have to honor and obey. But Molly decided she would.

Even the ladies got drunk. There was rum, Barbados pineapple, hairy coconuts split and filled with blueberries, a thousand raw oysters on great slabs of Hudson River ice that had been stored in hay in the cellar since winter. And boiled lobsters, spit-fired capons, roast pig and beef, Jerusalem artichokes and cress salad, pie and cake and tea. Fiddlers played. Sowell had been there, Boocock too. Sparrow, her illness not yet distinguishable from ebullience, had danced with almost every male guest.

But Molly had nibbled only bread, tried to keep from vomiting. She was carrying. And not even Salt knew, as she remembered it.

Of course there was no way he could know now, either. Her sickness was not so bad as it was when she had been pregnant with James. Her sense of smell, though, was heightened. Pisspots, cheese rinds, unbathed soldiers—even gunpowder got to her. Maybe this time she was carrying a girl.

"Rebels, turn out your dead!"

Now that Forten was gone nobody took the time to dress the corpses. They were sewn roughly into their hammocks or simply cast naked into the billows. Bones were left on the beach, bleaching in the tides.

Salt stumbled on deck to fair skies and a humid wind from the south. On the planks was a human gut, unstrung. It gleamed opalescent green and pink, as if glazed by the hand of a master potter. Seagulls fought over it, though there seemed to be plenty. It looped around sick bay and festooned the derrick, then stretched thin where it disappeared under a pile of corpses. On the other side, it connected to Mohammed, who sat upright, legs splayed out. His eyelids had been sliced off, and his beads dangled from his nostrils. Whoever had replaced his skullcap took no pains—his ears stuck out. Bits of seagrass and grains of sand clung to his beard.

When Salt lifted him, the corpse broke in two. Out of its abdominal cavity spilled the bricks of Rude's tobacco. The gore did not stop the other prisoners from helping themselves. They crowded Salt away and picked the body clean, scavenging even the beads.

Salt wrapped what remained in the shredded caftan.

———·——

Everybody wanted shore duty. Bare feet on sand, the ferment of marshgrass—sweet!—the spitting clam burrows—salty!—the rushing phalaropes with their reverse knees—run! Land ho! You had to laugh, and not because anything was funny. You were coupled with a partner, yoked to each other by ankle irons. The *Jersey* system required that a weak man go with a strong. Two strapping inmates were not likely to escape, but they were likely to try, which caused extra work for the guards. Salt was now among the weak. The shackle clanged his leg bone, no flesh to cushion it. The wet sand between his toes was too wonderful, and sent them into spasms. He had to pry them back with his fingers and remember to breathe. Slowly, they settled. Even if he had wanted to run, he couldn't.

Salt and the Bostoner he was shackled to finished burying Mohammed.

"Say a few words?" asked the Bostoner.

"Seventy virgins," Salt said. Mohammed's vision of heaven. "And good fishing."

The other prisoners were a hundred yards off, filling the hogsheads with fresh water from the pool near the wheelhouse, according to the standing arrangement that let Remsen play both sides: Americans were kept alive, and the Crown paid for the water.

The Bostoner let Salt wander up a knoll. He plucked a dandelion, scattering the seeds, wishing. To see Molly before he ended up in the sand next to Mohammed. Had she forgotten about him? Given him up for dead? He tossed aside the dandelion and pulled up the root, the loamy scent of earth reminding him of home.

"Don't wander away now," said a guard. "It's my back will take your flogging."

"Where's he going to wander? He's halfway to dead."

The Bostoner and Salt hobbled up the small creek toward the farmhouses.

A butterfly lighted on Salt's shoulder, then flew away. Under a stand of pin oaks, a black squirrel gathered an acorn in its forepaws and threw a nervous backward glance as it scrambled up a trunk. Salt picked up another acorn and gnawed it, savoring the bitter pastiness. The sunshine was a balm, the shade, the bright treble of the creek, the birds. The Bostoner sucked one dandelion stalk after another. Too astringent for Salt—they seared his gumline. But honeysuckle he could stand, the sweet nectar on the tip of his tongue. Maybe if he could string one instant of happiness to another, he could go on.

Then he saw her.

She was bathing in the stream, her dress hitched, crystal droplets splashing her calves. The bodice fell off one shoulder, exposing a chest nearly flat, a crescent of nipple as brown as an egg.

The Wallabout Maiden. Her hair bounced in the sunlight, butterflies everywhere. Too much of a good thing, Salt thought warily. A squeal from her meant death, or worse.

The girl looked up suddenly, right, then left, but she seemed not to have noticed them. Through her skirt, she adjusted an undergarment. Yellowjackets scrambled the damp bank, agitated and agitating. What did they thirst after?

James never should have stirred them up.

The Maiden paid them no mind. It was the butterfly

that interested her, its yellow wings as large as her hands, blue tails lit up. Salt had seen one on the boat, maybe this very one. It was not a graceful flyer. The overlarge wings clapped again and again, the wormlike body dropping fast between each beat as it made its way to him. The Maiden's eyes followed it there.

When she saw the two of them she paused, but made no show of modesty, no effort to cover her shoulder, her stick-like calves below the bunched dress.

She said, "I watch you sometimes."

This sent the Bostoner into a fit of nervous liplicking. She tiptoed forward. Her toenails were lacquered an exquisite pink, in the way of the English gentry. At the sight of them Salt giggled. She turned out her bottom lip ever so slightly and curled her toes away from his eyes.

"There is ham in the smokehouse. Biscuits. Cornmeal you can boil, blackstrap to add. Smugglers ply the Sound. Hempstead Bay, too, Father says. Plenty of them are patriots, though you wouldn't know it. They put in after dark. Three nights' walk will get you near enough."

The Bostoner panted, but Salt declined. The young guards would be made to pay. His fellow prisoners.

"What kind of man refuses freedom?"

"A captain." The Bostoner meant it kindly, but the whiff of vanity hung in the air. He rattled the chain, the iron banging painfully against Salt's shin. "Old man, if you won't save yourself, won't you save me?"

The Maiden's fingernails were painted differently from

her toenails. They were pearly in the French way. There was a wildness about her, in her lionlike hair. Or maybe it wasn't her hair at all. Maybe it was her eyes, fixed hard on his own. Did she know what aiding and abetting meant? How Cunningham would make Remsen pay for his upstart daughter?

The Bostoner, frantic now, reached into the stream and hoisted a rock, its underside slick with moss. He was about to strike the chain when a shot rang out. A puff of smoke rose from the hillock where two guards broke toward them at a run, one leveling a rifle.

THE GUARDS were arguing even before they reached the body.

"Straight through the heart at fifty yards," said the sniper. His uniform was tattered, but his weapon was immaculate.

"More like forty." His companion poked the Bostoner's ribcage with his bayonet.

"Fifty. I paced it myself." The sniper wormed the spent powder from his rifle barrel. "First taste your blade's channels ever had is the blood of a dead man." He turned to Salt for confirmation. "A crack shot, eh, Captain? Not a half inch off the mark."

"Now the Captain, there's a target. He's nothing but skin and bones."

"I could thread his needle at sixty."

"Load of shit."

"Bet your rifle on it."

"Against your musket?"

"And a beaver pelt."

"You're on. Unchain him. I'll pace out sixty." The rifleman extracted the ramrod, examined it, rescabbarded it. He was just puffing his cheeks to blow the mechanicals when the Maiden reappeared.

"Release him!"

The soldiers consulted each other's faces, but there was no assurance in either. A female pretending to power was more a curiosity than a threat. Still, they were conditioned to authority, and she was Remsen's daughter. The water they drank was his, as was the earth under their boots.

"I command you!" she said. "Unlock his leg iron!"

"We don't have the key," mumbled the guard, wiping his knife on the grass.

Salt half expected the Maiden to stamp her foot. Instead she said, "The Americans have defeated the British at Virginia, Exeter, and Roundable. The war has been decided. Everybody knows this."

A squadron of redcoats came galloping. When they saw the Maiden, each in turn doffed his hat, their leader bowing deeply. Quickly, they set to work on the ankle iron with a maul. They strapped the Bostoner's corpse on a horse and hauled him away. They made Salt walk.

9

ALWAYS THE BLACK of night in here. Salt chiseled, his breath, anemic, depleted. The smell of decay surrounded him, but his nose was numb to the stink, so familiar by now that he couldn't smell it, any more than he could hear the yawns and groans, the scratching and swallowing, the heaving of timbers against each other and the tides. The taste of his spit had the tang of iron. The tip of his tongue explored the holes in his gums where his teeth had fallen out. His knuckles were swollen and tender, his knees stiff and unbending, his neck barely able to hold up his head. Still, he chiseled.

The mussel-shell knife struck something hard, impenetrable. He jabbed again, and felt the unmistakeable resistance of metal. He pounded in frustration. "No!"

"Stow it!" muttered a Bostoner.

By dumb bad luck he had struck one of the iron plates riveted to the exterior of the *Jersey,* part of the quilt of wood, metal patchwork, and iron bars that barely held the hulk together. He banged the shell against the iron.

"Quiet!"

Exhausted, Salt lay back. De la Luz, Forten, Mohammed, the Bostoner, all of them, gone. The image of O'Nan floated by, followed by that of Molly, but in his mind her hair was blonde, like the Wallabout Maiden's. Molly's hair had not been blonde at all. Had it?

———•◦•———

"Rebels, turn out your dead!" Bodies thumped onto the deck. There were three, one seamed into a woolen blanket, another in linen rags, the last in a hemp hammock. Prisoners swabbed the deck with vinegar, guards tended to the vegetable plot on the quarterdeck. Late-season carrots grew there, and radishes, stunted basil and marigolds. The pig snorted, perked its pink ears, translucent in the slanting sun. The chicken scratched its scaly feet, hunched its wings and uncoiled its neck, striking at the sky.

A visiting Quaker tossed a handful of sparkly dust. "You want a bird to thrive, you've got to feed it vitalments." The chicken pecked it. "Mica. Pica. Granite. A twig or two. A gizzard ain't got teeth but them you give it."

A guard watched apprehensively.

"Boocock. Jabez Boocock, chicken farmer." The civilian extended his hand and the guard shook it. "Where's Lord Cunningham? He's got business with me."

"The Lord is in his lair."

Boocock watched the chicken go after a butterfly. "It sees the caterpillar in him still."

In the captain's quarters, the velvet drapes were drawn against the stern windows. Candles flickered, expensive beeswax with its honeyed scent. Even in the dark, Boocock could see that the man's face plagued him—purple as a cabbage, threaded with crimson veins, the nose misshapen and bubbly, as if it were boiling under the crust. His body seemed to plague him too. He scratched furtively at his underarms, his chest. Maybe the skin under there was the same.

"Hurt?"

"The surgeon told me to avoid sunlight."

"That an order, or an abdication of duty?"

"Shoo. How'd that moth get in here?" He clapped once. "Where are your chickens?"

"I got crates of them. Where's the payment?"

"You said you'd take it partially in Continental Army issue bonds."

"Any patriot would."

"You are a patriot, then?"

"I come as a Friend."

Cunningham slid a document across the desk, then dipped a quill into a pot of ink and handed it plume-first to Boocock. "An order for two hundred and fifty chickens. George Washington told Lord Howe that he would match his treatment of the British prisoners of war to what he hears about the treatment of the Americans. Suddenly there's boodle for cock."

"Fat ones, and tasty, too."

"Where from? Every chick within a hundred rods is spoken for."

"Not every." Boocock thought of Molly and sighed. Then he scanned the paper, and finding its terms satisfactory, graced it with his signature and pushed it back. From a large pile, Cunningham counted out thirty coins, which he stacked into a column for Boocock. Then he slid across the table dozens of papers stamped with the seal of the Continental Congress. "And here are fifty worth of Continental Army bonds."

"Taken from prisoners?" Boocock asked.

"They trade them for cigarettes and pork."

"I'll take them at one third of face."

Cunningham placed his fingertips on his cheeks and grimaced. "Ouch."

"Those bonds are worthless to you. I'm doing the Crown a favor accepting them."

The bonds were hard to read because the quilling was formal, and the language thick with nonsense. They would be worthless should the Americans lose. But Boocock hoarded them, speculating the opposite. Here was one with the name Ezekiel Rude, guaranteeing payment for two stints in the Continental Army. Another for O'Nan. A third for James Forten. Boocock frowned. "This one's a forgery."

Cunningham grabbed the paper. "How can you tell?"

"The border of the stamp's a fake."

"The little negro was a forger?" Cunningham scratched his crotch.

"You been took, eh?"

"A slave on the run, after all. That lying seamstress had everybody thinking he was born free."

Boocock said, "No sunshine by surgeon's orders, eh?" He glanced at the pile of coins Cunningham kept for himself, the bonds of the dead prisoners used in their place to pay for the chickens to feed the prisoners, but possibly to be resold for profit. "Maybe he just wanted to save you from shame."

"Save me from shame?" Cunningham murmured. His lips, what there were of them, were paler than his cheeks. "I know by heart what the righteous can't imagine!" Cunningham slammed down a fist. "But one thing I am not *ashamed* of is my god- damned face!"

"Then why are we conducting business in the dark?"

For several moments, there was silence. At last, Boocock spoke. "I go by a regular mirror."

"And if you'd pay it a glance, you'd note that the self you see belongs not to you but to the times. Unless you are, as you appear, a simple Friend. Isn't there another document you want to show me?"

"It's a separate piece of negotiation."

"Bloody lice!" Cunningham attacked his crotch, his underarms, his collar, scratching first with fingernails, then lighting upon a quill and using that. "Bloody moth!" He opened the door, letting in a stream of light that made him cringe, and batted at the butterfly, which escaped, flying up into the blue sky and over the deck of the *Jersey,* alighting on the garden rail.

Two prisoners were busy lowering the water cask to the gondola. After that, they heaved ho the bodies. The younger of them said, "A shame to waste that hommack."

The older, gray in the stubble, replied, "It's not a hommack, it's a hammock."

"Where I come from it's a hommack." The boy twitched, like getting his mouth around something, then he did it again. His skin was green, his eyes blue, his fingernails black.

"Where's that?"

"Carolina." The boy twitched, and halfway through it twitched again. It was not part of his character, the old man saw, but something visited upon him.

"Not what it's called from where I'm from."

"Where's that?"

"Carolina."

The boy spat. He ran his hand across his mouth and then along the seam where the hammock had been stitched closed. "Well then, we come differently from the same place."

The older man said, "Crudely stitched. Like he sewed his own self inside."

"Did you see that?" Now the boy was twitching uncontrollably.

"I didn't see nothing." The older man stepped between the boy and corpse. He bent at the hips and, keeping his back straight, hugged the big cocoon upright.

"It's breathing."

"Where I'm from the dead don't breathe." The old man dumped the corpse over the gunwale and it fell horizontal and unnatural until it went thud on the gangplank where the others were already scattered about. The boy stared. The old man stared, too. But to all appearances the body inside the hammock was behaving like a dead man, and they were satisfied.

ONSHORE, the Carolinans went about their work. The old man took the legs, the ankles giving easier purchase. The body landed with a soft thud in the sand.

The single butterfly was joined by another, then four, then eight again, and twofold more. Tiger swallowtails alighted on the beach and uncoiled their black tongues, flickering about, searching out the grains.

"Are they thirsty?"

"Maybe they like salt."

"Where I come from they like sweet."

The boy and the man, not allowed shovels, gravedug bare-handed, shackled together. The old man scooped deep while the boy wasted time trying out and discarding pieces of drift-wood until he came upon what looked like a human bone.

"That a shoulderblade?"

It made a serviceable spade, though, and finally they dug down to where the groundwater seeped in and the walls began to crumble.

The first corpse was stiff, no longer vulnerable to the insults flesh is heir to, and the boy in particular treated it roughly, tossing his end into the grave, startling the butterflies and causing the other prisoner to stumble.

"You want to show a modicum of respect." He set down the feet gently.

The boy gnawed at the air, spat, and gnawed again. "Can't feel a thing."

"Says you and what pope?"

"Stop rattling my chain, grandpa."

The old man growled, "Young people."

They grabbed the next body. It was clad in muslin rags like a carnival mummy. A whiff of decomposition hung in the air. The butterflies opened and closed their wings slowly in the sunshine, like dozens of winged heartbeats.

"Always do a thing like you're being watched, I tell you. Not a thought in your head ain't but heard aloud."

"Tell it to them crabs." Hundreds, perhaps thousands, of tiny crabs held motionless, legs retracted, waiting, waiting, guts like metal filings showing through translucent shells. When the man and the boy turned to the next grave, the crabs picked themselves up, clicking and foaming at the mouth parts, and advanced slowly en masse.

More bones littered the glades just above the high-water mark, scattered about like bleached driftsticks. No body stayed in the shallow graves for long. A humerus and a femur jutted together in a V, a dozen ribs logjammed behind them. Hundreds of the white pebbles were not pebbles but teeth. Their feathers soiled with blood, beaks sharpened by bone, gulls waited, the pecked-upon sorriest of them, who couldn't fend for the harbor's sweeter offerings—oysters, menhaden, bread crusts tossed by the British fleet.

The boy twitched. "The dead grow hair."

"You don't want to look at that."

"See?"

"Last one. Hurry up now."

They slopped sand on top.

"Don't cover the hammocked one."

"Hommacked."

"Hammocked."

The Carolinans hurried away, chains clanking, without turning to look back.

———·◆·———

A HAND EXTENDED through the hammock, thumb and forefinger grasping about like a beaked thing in no hurry. They found what they were seeking, a thread that had three tiny knots at its end, and pinched it tightly, then pulled. The hammock yawned and gave up its guts. Salt rose, coughing.

The crabs scurried. The gulls cried in protest and hopped away. Only the butterflies were unperturbed, continuing to sample the sand and gently fan their wings in the late orange sun.

Salt coughed again and again. His windpipe felt like tacks, his head filled with cowbells. He stood up, clutched his chest, and fell down.

III

10

I N NEW YORK harbor dozens of ships were anchored, all nosing north into the outgoing tide, which brought with it the fresh scent of northern woodlands. Only the boats in Wallabout Bay had hawsers at each end, in permanent defiance of the currents. In the dusky light, Salt could make out the outline of the *Scorpion*, a small hulk that the newspapers called a hospital ship. Nearer to shore, the silhouette of the *Jersey* suggested a pretty picture of a boat, even stripped of its sails. Two lanterns glowed astern, one abow, but the iron-barred windows of the hold emitted no light. Manhattan twinkled in the background.

He rose but the gulls stood their ground, feathers more stalk than fluff, greasy beaks snapping at him as he passed. Salt tried to step over them, unsteady, flapping his arms clumsily. He fell into a fit of coughing. The effort wearied him and he trembled, running a dry tongue over chapped lips. Oh for a drink, but the tide mill looked a quarter of a mile away.

He stopped to kneel. How many thousands had been buried on this beach? What were their names? Nobody was keeping any list, no one visited their graves but more dead, and those who brought them here. To die unacknowledged, Salt had felt it impossible. What he said and what he did only happened now, and now, and now. For so long there had been no reality outside prison ship, and prison ship wasn't reality at all. On the greater world Salt left no mark. An autumn breeze was more substantial; a falling leaf, these shifting sands carried greater consequence.

He found a rib. It was good and solid, not yet bleached to a crisp. If sharpened, it could hold an edge.

Wallabout Bay was a half-moon, a natural enclave protected from the harsh pull of the estuary, and its open shape gave up every secret at a glance. There was nowhere to hide, every point being visible from every other point. How many times had he scanned this shore from the *Jersey*'s deck? He knew there would be dozens of pairs of eyes searching at any given time. Ten yards inland, however, there were bogs and thick stands of cripplebush. Salt slunk into the vegetation and discovered that what appeared from offshore to be a solid mass of flora was in fact clumps of briars connected by a maze of interlocking sand trails. He found a spot that afforded a view and sat. He began to rasp the rib against an outcropping of schist. Ship bells rang out, calls to mess. He rested, waiting for nightfall.

Somebody approached along the water's edge, caped and wearing a tricorn hat, leather boots turned down at the calves, a broken-handled shovel in hand. The hat was cocked forward and he could not make out the face, but when the figure squared off toward him, he knew at once who it was.

"Do you aim to stab me with that?" With the shovel, she gestured at the rib clutched in his fist. The shovel handle had been sharpened too.

"If you aim to turn me in."

"I haven't already, have I?"

A cough and a wince, then a crowing intake of breath. Salt began to slide the rib into his waistband, then thought better of it and kept it in hand. He felt weak and parched and wobbly. "You have been digging."

"I have been digging." Sand clung to the toes of her boots, and water marks stained each knee. Her arms were bare under her cape. She shielded her eyes from him under the rolled brim of her hat. A braid had been pinned up in back but it was coming loose in an untidy loop.

"There are no rings, no bracelets, no charms, no pearly buttons. In daylight you could see for yourself that none of our teeth are gold." He swept the blade across the sand. "The gold ones get pulled right away."

"You think I'm scavenging like a common gull."

"I go by instinct." Polaris shone, bright among the other stars, all of them terrible in their changelessness.

"The tide unburies you." She looked up at him at last, and at last Salt had the relief of being seen. Then she lowered her hat, concealing. "I dig you back."

At that he put the rib away, believing.

"Come with me." She led him through the brambles on a trail that gave way to a marshy lagoon matted with choke-weed. From there she climbed a steep, grassy hill eroding in bald patches and drainage fissures. Salt followed on all fours. At the top there was an apple orchard, branches still holding leaves but harvested of fruit.

The Remsen house had two stories, with a steeply pitched roof that flattened like a brim over a wide veranda. Pillars made it grand. Wood smoke curled from one of the three chimneys; sour oak, sweet maple. The first floor windows glowed orange, flickering with hearth light, and a man's shadow passed over the drape.

"Officers are quartered inside. Follow me."

Out back was a large barn. It had three doors and hayloft and a large yard, clean and tidy, fences and fixtures intact and well-tended. She lifted the latch and pulled the door open on oiled hinges. Inside the air was warmer and smelled of straw and manure. As she lit a lantern the horses glanced backward and flicked their tails, stirring flies that buzzed lethargically in the dark. She grabbed a pitchfork from the wall and slung a bale into a corner, spreading the hay about with her hands. "Lie down." She fetched a tattered old quilt that smelled of mildew. Salt pulled it up to his neck, shivered once, and lay back, exhausted. He heard the squirt of liquid against tin, and before long she returned with a pail. She placed a hand on his back to help him up, then steadied him as he lifted the pail to his mouth. He drank, but not greedily enough, and milk spilled down his front, foamy with cream, and warm as the inside of his mouth. Some of it got on her fingers and she licked them.

She left, taking the lantern and closing the barn door behind her.

After a while, he stopped coughing. The animals breathed in the dark, calm, every now and then a chewing sound. He wrapped the blanket tightly around him. It was wonderful to be dead.

Hours passed, or maybe it was minutes. It wasn't days, of that he was fairly certain.

"Take off your clothes." The girl had returned with a wheelbarrow containing two oaken buckets, steam rising out of them, a porcelain basin. Daylight flooded the hayloft and filtered through the planks.

He hesitated. The pox marks. The filth. The bones poking through the skin. She began to unbutton his shirt.

"How old are you?"

"Old enough." The briefness with which her brown eyes held his gaze before they flicked away might be innocence, or it might be invitation. She folded a muslin cloth and submerged it in the bucket. She rubbed a piece of perfumed soap on it and dipped it again, then started at his shoulders and worked her way down his body, washing, then dipping, then washing again.

He wasn't worth this expensive soap. "If they catch me they'll kill you."

"You're safe here as anywhere."

"I'll go."

"You won't get far. There are checkpoints round every bend. Drop your britches."

She scrubbed his legs, the skin on them stiff and black as cowhide. He took the cloth from her, dipped it in the hot water, turned away to clean his privates. When he turned back, she had filled the porcelain basin with water and set a razor and a small earthenware pot next to it. She wetted his face, then opened the jar. He inhaled the scent of lanolin, twined with lavender, as she smoothed it over his cheeks. Then she placed her fingertips on his chin and began to shave him.

"You are skilled with a razor."

"I have slit throats."

"Sure you have."

She pressed the flat of the blade against his neck. "Don't laugh."

How unlike Molly she was. Molly, who had severed the jugulars of a hundred pigs, and was graced with the good sense not to boast.

She had brought him a linen shirt, breeches of thin wool, boots, and an overcoat. He frowned at the breeches, which would mark him as a loyalist; patriots wore leather to boycott the British wool trade. But the choice was probably prudent, and he was touched at her anticipation of his needs. The overcoat was green, with gold piping. The boots had square toes, and held the narrow shape of the prior owner's feet—a slave?

"Have you no moccasins?"

She left, shutting the door behind her. He went back to sleep.

Next he woke to her humming, and the sunshine pouring like syrup through the open barn door. He blinked against it and the door swung shut, muting the humming. She had left him a basket—bread, ham, celery, cabbage, gingerbread, a pint of rum, a bottle of water. There was a candle and flintlock too, and a brass candlestick.

When he had eaten, he lay back and closed his eyes again, trying to follow the humming among the other sounds outside. There was the restless stamping of cattle, the clatter of hooves, the hiss of breeze in trees.

And then he opened his eyes into darkness again, amid the heavy breathing of stabled mammals that was becoming as familiar as the scratching and groaning of his *Jersey* bunkmates. He lit the candle she had left for him, and made his way to the door. It was locked from the outside. Both of the other doors were locked also. The milk cow mooed and rolled her eyes, agitated by him, and he shushed her.

Imprisoned again.

He went back to where the tools were kept and found the pitchfork. He jammed the handle through a knothole and pried, until the plank creaked painfully and the nail that held it in place yielded with a rusty gasp. The space was just big enough to slip his wasted body through.

The air was chill and smelled of crushed apples. Somewhere nearby there was a cider press. Two sentries stood in front of the house so he dared not go closer, but even at a distance he could hear someone playing scales on the pianoforte, breaking into fragments of waltz now and then. There was a clatter of china, and a shriek of female laughter. Then the sound of the Maiden's voice, singing a cantata. Outside the accompaniment was muffled, and the lyrics, in German, were opaque to his ears, but the phrasing ranged high and low, invoking love and loss.

Salt found a rock to urinate on, the splash of it satisfying after months of the *Jersey*'s communal slop pot.

He circled around to the front of the barn and unbolted the door, then slipped back inside. He drank the rest of the water, then started on the rum. It pickled his tongue and filled the cavities of his head with vapors. He found a dry heel of bread, washing it down with more rum. Then he went back to sleep.

———•·•———

SALT PLACED the tin pail beneath the cow and grabbed a teat. She flicked her hoof twice and contented herself with the inevitability of a stranger's hands. The teat was fleshy and firm, and the milk pinged against the tin as he pulled. When he had enough, he stepped back and poured the remained half-pint of rum into the frothy liquid. Wallabout syllabub, better than any lord's.

And a lord he felt himself to be, especially after last night, when the Maiden had visited him. She came after digging, shovel over her shoulder.

He lit the spermaceti candle, scented like bleach, like butter. "Take your hat off."

She leaned the shovel against the wall and set the tricorn hat onto its broken and sharpened handle, then untied her braid, hair tumbling loose. She removed her boots, slowly unpeeled the socks, no longer hiding her polished toes. Her cheeks were red, her lashes darkened. A hint of rose oil emanated from her skin. Naked but for the cape, she said, with a knowing, half smile, "Virginia."

"Rainbows," Salt said.

"Where the fighting is. Somewhere down there. They say it's over but for the gunfire. England's pulling out." She spun around, cape flying. "Why'd they name it that?"

"You tell me."

She braided herself a crown of hay, and gripped her cape as if at royal lapels. "Bow down before me."

So long deprived, Salt obeyed.

"I command you." Off came her cape. Off his suit of armor.

Every morning there was a basket of fresh gingerbread, along with apples, buns and jam and butter and sometimes ham or boiled eggs or cheese. There was fresh cider now too, along with the rum and water. And every night, after her digging, the candlelight tryst. The barn a castle, stabled with angels. She danced and spun and issued decrees. Sometimes she hummed, but never would she sing.

One morning she brought English tea, strong and black.

"I want coffee," he said.

"Jamaican or Brazilian? Or from the darkest jungles of Africa?"

"I want honey." Salt was tiring of play-acting. He longed for Molly, straightforward Molly. What might she be doing now? Stocking the root cellar with carrots, apples, preserves. Salting cod. Smoking hams.

"If you leave I'll hunt you down," she said, as if reading his thoughts.

"Sing for me," he said.

"I sing when I'm called upon," she said.

"I'm calling upon you," he said.

"When I'm happy, when I'm sad. These are call-upons."

"You sing when your father calls upon you."

"That's not me singing, that's his child singing."

"Grow up."

"Tickle me."

"I must go home."

"Tickle me first."

What he needed she had given: safety, a nest, food and drink, cheer. What he had given her was herself as she wished to be seen—sparkling, brave, in charge, independent. He saw that she liked to think she was a girl who did as she pleased, hands calloused from her digging, but at bottom she was a child with the means and freedom to pretend with abandon.

When she was gone, he pushed aside the loosened plank

and let himself out of the barn. The sky was gray and the wind blustered, but no rain fell.

———•——

WHEN HE COULD, Salt traveled under cover of night, but it was too easy to get turned around, especially after the moon set, or when clouds obscured the North Star. More than once he unknowingly circled back on his trail, and frequently he stumbled. After the first few nights his shins were bruised and his face thrashed.

But daylight brought danger. Even in his woolen trousers and scarlet ascot he knew that his pox scars might betray him, or his stiff-jointed gait. When he opened his mouth he no longer knew what words would come out, or who might be speaking them.

The clouds broke to blue skies, and the temperatures stayed mild for autumn. There were still a few leaves on the trees, many of them retaining their green color, dull and depleted but extracting the last of the waning sunlight. A wild rose bush clung to a pasture fence and it, however, was blooming. The flowers were pink, their scent mild but unmistakable, and they put Salt in mind of the girl, perfumed with rosewater.

On a grassy knoll he came across a beehive constructed like a chest of drawers. He reached for the handle of the top drawer, and the bees crawled through the webbing of his fingers and onto his wrists but did not sting him. He pulled open the drawer and broke off a piece of honeycomb. The wax capsules broke apart in his mouth, releasing the sweet, golden liquid.

"I'm like to stick your sorry thieving ass." The beekeeper emerged behind him, brandishing a hoe.

"God save the King," said Salt.

"Nobody else likely will." The beekeeper spat, eyes following the stream of brown juice, then tongued the plug to the opposite cheek. The skin bordering his lips was stained orange. "What are you doing on my land, loyalist cullion?"

"I'm an American, escaped from the *Jersey.*"

"Honey filcher. Load of steaming worsted crock."

"I figured all that's left in these parts is Tory. Why I took this honey. I'm in enemy territory and take whatever I lay hand upon." Salt reached inside his sleeve for the sharpened rib. "This I do not call stealing."

"Either side says that, but it don't amount. Poaching is poaching." The beekeeper spat. "War's all but over. The last of the fighting is down yonder in Virginia. The goddamn redcoats are getting out of Long Island, and none too soon if you got to ask." He extended his tobacco pouch to Salt. "Chew?"

"No thank you, sir. I no longer have the teeth for it."

"A man don't need teeth for quid." He jammed a four-finger pinch into the vacant cheek. "They told me about you. Remsen elder sent word. He's stalking you. Vows a *'merican captain* took something from him."

"The clothes I'm wearing."

"Got his daughter with him."

————

SETTLEMENTS THINNED out the farther east Salt traveled. Now and again, he encountered British troops marching west. When he saw them coming, he ducked off to the side of the road and crouched among the sedge. The soldiers were unseeing, and he had little to fear from them. They advanced scowling, exhaustion tugging at their limbs. Their uniforms were frayed at the cuffs, patched in the elbows and knees, threadbare in the back, plain worn out.

He made his way through miles of scrub pine, the ground beyond the road duff-covered, pine cones everywhere. The pine nuts were bitter, but made his spit run thin and his blood too, easing the pain in his joints. After several days he emerged to cleared fields overgrown with grass. At sundown, he slept curled up in a culvert, covering himself with his fancy overcoat.

A rowdy gang of boys woke him, playing or fighting, he wasn't sure at first. They pounced on the smallest among them, stripping off his clothes and slathering him with molasses. Next they grabbed up handfuls of foxtails and tossed them at him, fists full of the spikey seedheads. Some stuck, some floated to the ground.

"Tory, the war is over, time to pay. Your side lost."

"Ungrateful Yankees! You'd scrag the one sired you!" the little one bellowed ferociously.

When they saw Salt they froze. The runt scratched at

the foxtails clinging to his ribs and summoned his courage. "We know you."

"Who am I?"

"A runner."

"Not a runner, but on the run."

"A Tory."

"No Tory us."

"There's no us, there's just you."

"A score of dead men ride with me."

"Where? I don't see 'em."

"Can't see the heart that beats inside me either."

"Ghosts?"

"No. Real dead men."

"Did they die fighting redcoats?"

"Every day for a year and a half."

The boys looked at each other, then the little one stepped forward. "We heard the story of you."

"How does it end?"

"You escaped hell afloat. The only one. The Brits are hunting you. The girl and her daddy, too."

"What girl?"

"Everybody knows."

"Who?"

"The girl who got something stole."

———•·•———

DRAYTON BANGED open the root cellar door. It was cool, dank, crepuscular, a streak of light falling upon a cask of molasses, an exudate of crystals at its joinery. Molly sat on a high stool, her dress bunched above her knees, her bare feet dangling above the hardpan floor. Over her head a ham swung gently, suspended from the ceiling.

He took a step toward her, but she stopped him with a look.

"Where is James?"

"Organizing the march south. I made him Lieutenant."

A step nearer, and he got a whiff of ferment—apples, butter, molasses, pumpkin, salt cod, pork. And something else.

And then he saw what he'd been searching for—Sowell, lost amid the baskets of withered apples, potatoes sprouting eyes, pumpkins quietly deliquescing. His hands tucked and buttoned, his wig was missing.

Molly stood and pushed past Drayton, to the open door. "The war is over."

In the empty air, the ham still swung.

———•—•———

ON THE SEVENTH DAY Salt at last found himself in familiar territory. In his prior life, these rolling pastures had defined the outer limits of his world, as far from home as he ever got, but for the rare trip to Manhattan. He didn't know then to whom the farm belonged, nor did he now. The fences were long gone, burned for firewood most likely, but they were no longer needed. There were no straggling cows left to eat the hay someone had carefully scythed and stacked and bonneted in what they called Dutch caps. He climbed under one to get out of the wet.

A sound like a crash of cymbals woke him. More redcoats, accompanied by horses pulling wagons loaded with pots and pans and rakes and pitchforks and stoves and ovens and casks and urns. On top of a flatbed was a harpsichord crafted of varnished wood. Sheep and pigs were tethered to cows and oxen, all of them on the march. Soldiers sagged on their soaked mounts. Wheel after wheel stuck in the mud, and officers with matted plumage cracked whips, as if that were all it took to free them. Salt watched from his shelter as they approached.

"Get that feed!" commanded an officer, his grand moustache unable to disguise the youth in his voice and cheeks.

"We already have enough feed for these beasts, sir, and fifty head more," said a soldier.

"Get the feed!" screamed the lieutenant.

"We have nowhere to put it."

"Burn it! Scatter it! Ruin it!"

This was the British army, now, ragged, bitten, a wounded animal.

"I can't free this wheel," complained a soldier, shoulder to a stuck wagon.

"Toady me!" bellowed the lieutenant.

Rain fell.

The lieutenant grimaced. Water dripped from the tips of his moustache. The war was nothing like he'd expected. The buttons on his green overcoat had been replaced with disks of tin. The fresh blacking on his boots could not hide their deep creases and the crude cowhide patch on the sole was more bothersome than the hole it replaced. More galling was that the Major General had awarded top commission to his little pet. *America.*

"Soldier on, Rupert," Drayton had said, arm around his shoulder. "I need a good make-do man in the field." But fresh supplies went to James.

"Push, you lickspittles!"

More soldiers waded into the mud, heaving unsuccessfully.

"We're going to have to leave the cart behind."

The lieutenant pinched one side of his moustache, then the other, wringing out the rainwater. "I'll be damned if we leave the rebels so much as a thimble." He slapped the horse's hindquarters. It would not budge. Disgusted, he spat. Then he drew his bayonet and lanced the creature's flanks, and quickly did the same to its mate. They started and reared, then lurched forward wildly, toppling the cart and scattering the goods. The lieutenant thrust his bayonet toward it, in a rage.

"Wreck it," he said. "All but the harpsichord."

The soldiers went about the task methodically, without chatter, as if they had done this before, stomping, hacking, smashing, and rending.

When they finished, the lieutenant shouted, "Blow me! Scatter the hay!"

A group of soldiers veered off into the pasture, making for the first haystack. A man with a sabre sliced the cap free, and the team went at it, windmilling with hands and legs until the hay was sopping and strewn about. Through the slanting rain, Salt watched the faces—stern, unshaved, soaking—approach his hiding place. Had he come so far only to die in a haystack?

When they were nearly upon him, Salt emerged slowly, hands raised above his head. The soldiers merely stared. They had seen too much new in this war to be surprised.

"Deserter?" asked the sabre-bearer. "Shall we save time by killing you now?"

They searched him and quickly found the sharpened rib bone. Then they marched him back to the lieutenant, who tested his thumb on the point of the weapon and said, without looking up, "Kill him. But don't waste a bullet. Use a knife or pike or some such." He held up the rib blade. "Better yet, use this."

"I can help you," said Salt.

"Every deserter says as much."

"I'm not a deserter, sir."

"You are wearing three layers of clothing like a deserter. You are skinny like a deserter. You are in Long Island, where the only Americans are deserters or spies or both, sniffing for widow."

"You accurately if incompletely describe me." Salt noted that the men were eyeing his boots, the gold piping on his green overcoat.

"Shame to kill an honest man. Kill him nonetheless." The lieutenant stroked his moustache, then turned his horse aside as if to go. But from the opposite direction came a squadron of redcoats, trotting fast. They were cleanly attired, their horses fresh and newly shod.

The lieutenant pulled up short to await them. There were ten of them on horses. As they drew nearer, the lieutenant spat again. *"America."*

He seemed to mean their leader. Salt looked, and saw a strong young officer——why did the British insist on making officers of boys? This one was impeccably uniformed, tall in the saddle. Across his chest, a brace of pistols were cross-holstered in a gleaming green sash. James!

"Rupert."

The lieutenant returned a half-hearted salute.

James took no notice of Salt. His attention was on the ruined cart and its damaged horses, who stood trembling by the side of the road. At the sight of them, James's own horse reared and tried to back away, but James would have none of it. He guided the mount forward.

"These beasts suffer," said James disapprovingly. He drew his pistols from their holsters, held them steady at arm's length, and pulled their triggers. The horses slumped into the mud, and the acrid smell of powder filled the air.

"A shame to waste good bullets," smirked the lieutenant.

James surveyed the roadside debris. "I thought you'd decamped."

"What we can't take with us we destroy."

James dismounted. "This is not enemy country. This is our own country. Our orders are to treat it as such."

"No offense, *America,* but some of us weren't born here. And some of us don't feel the love." The lieutenant spat. "Sir."

Salt could not get enough of looking. Quietly, he began to weep.

"Who's the captive?"

"A deserter, so he says," said the lieutenant.

"Why do you weep, sir?"

"I am sorry, son."

"Do I know you?" James asked, not unkindly.

Salt saw himself as James must see him, his face cratered and sunken, his back bent, the light leaking out of his eyes. But how could a son not know his own father? "I gather not."

"Familiarity from a stranger smacks of deception." James forced a laugh. "I have not seen the practice before, I'll give you that."

"Take him into the field and shoot him," said the lieutenant.

"Leave him where he is," ordered James.

"What's he to you?" said the lieutenant. "No wonder people doubt your loyalty."

"Who doubts my loyalty?"

"You give cause."

"Nobody is more loyal than I."

The lieutenant enunciated as if addressing a child. "Then prove it now by killing this old man." He offered the sharpened rib, handle first, as if respectfully.

James took the rib and approached Salt, his gaze penetrating. "Interrogate the deserter."

THE INTERROGATION took place in the command center tent near the center of the encampment, which held the overflow from the Jamaica Church. Thousands of British were staging for the long journey south, to Virginia, or Carolina, the likely setting for what many felt would be the war's final battles. Most would go by boat, the remaining would make the long march. Drayton had charged James to lead the exodus, which was to get underway the day after tomorrow.

He entered the tent, tying shut the doorflap behind him. It was made of hemp cloth and supported by five poles, ten feet high at the center. Even somebody as tall as himself could stand straight. A scribe sat at a desk furnished with quills, papers, stamps, and sealing wax. Everything James did he did scrupulously, because somebody was always watching. It was the lot of an American-born British officer, and he had come to terms with it. The deserter sat, hands bound to the ladder-back chair behind him

"Why are you wearing three layers of clothing?"

"To protect myself from what comes."

"And does it?"

"So far."

"Why did you leave your family?"

"I didn't want to."

"It's a rare man who does what he doesn't want."

"First I was hotpressed. Then taken prisoner."

"Could you leave no word?"

"I left to save my son."

"How is it that leaving saved him?"

"He killed in self defense. I took the blame."

"Are you sure it wasn't murder?"

"No."

"And this…son. Do you love him?"

"More than anything."

"Anything?"

"Anything."

"Your own breath?"

"What I feel for him will survive me."

"Some put the love of strangers above family."

"A man deprived of his own may seek familiarity among strangers."

The adjutant paused and looked up, puzzled, until James continued his questioning.

"Who do you love more, your wife or your son?"

"Both."

"And they love you?"

"I want to believe."

"Wouldn't a son despise a father who denied him his dream?"

"What dream?"

"Say the son dreamed of serving his country. Say the son dreamed of making his father proud."

"The son would make the father proud whatever he chose to do."

"Even if he betrayed the father?"

"How?"

"By serving his country."

"Even if."

"Put the spy to death. Execute him on the morrow. Broadcast it, make a spectacle of it. Perform it in the churchyard."

James seemed almost giddy. After all, wasn't this the very substance of revolution, to destroy the body that sired you? What came before kin? Never country, in the history of the world, till now.

———— ·•· ————

"I did as you asked." The girl was no older than fourteen. She wore a bonnet of yellow silk, a dress of blue linen. A string of pearls hung in twin cascades from her neck, the skin there creamy. James had adorned her, selected her, paid for her, an indentured servant from Dublin, buying out the remaining four years on her contract. She was a caged bird, pretty, ornamental, curious, a responsibility, his. She spoke trippingly.

"I unlocked the grate and told him, 'Flee, flee, flee for the chance of your life' but he would not go."

"Would not go?"

"He says, plainly, that he will not go until you yourself command him to."

"Kiss me."

The Irish lass kissed him softly, and he ran his hands down her roughly. It was lovely to be surrounded by people who awaited his orders. It made them feel safe; it made him feel safe and powerful. What was power if not wanting and getting?

He broke away from her and picked up a bell, ringing it angrily to summon his footman. The adjutant appeared instantly, wringing his hands in the vestibule. "Your orders, sir?"

He must engineer his father's escape. There was no other way to pull off the scheme he and Boocock had planned.

"Assemble the troops, and the two neighboring armies. Who says the war is over? God save us all."

11

JAMES PACED his tent. It was white and new, the hemp-cloth virgin. It had not seen anything but clear skies in its short and happy life, and its bleachy freshness suggested a world where filth did not exist. The fixtures were all first rate. The mattress of down—nobody else had one, not even the General—was cloud-light and cloud-soft. The folding chair and desk were crafted from birch, the wood caressed by hand—if under threat of whip and chain—to coax out the subtlety of the grain. James had never allowed himself to fantasize about reaching a position such as this. Lieutenant. With dozens—no, hundreds of foot soldiers—at his disposal. The power. The Irish girl naked under the blankets.

"Get out!" he rebuked her now. When in his wildest imaginings would he have kicked a girl out of his bed? Why did so good feel so bad? "Wait!"

She cowered, like a dog expecting discipline. He sniffed her hair, laved in rosemary oil to repel the lice and fleas that infested a standing army, her neck perfumed with lavender tincture. There was nothing musky about her. She was too young to stink. Once he had told her she was beautiful, and she had flushed in humiliation. "Bathe and return to me."

From the hickory chest he extracted a file of correspondence. Among the commissions, plans, tributes, receipts, and bills of lading were letters from home. He treasured those from his mother, even the ones to which he had never replied. He liked to reread them, trying out different interpretations, reading for tone. When she wrote, "We had a wonderful ham for Sunday dinner" she may have meant just that, or she may have been signaling trouble between herself and Drayton, because eating ham necessitated butchering a pig, and she knew he knew that she butchered when she felt trapped. James paid particular attention to the closings. For instance, what was the meaning in *Love always*? A hedge against the death of love, or deathless love itself? *Love always* was aloofly at odds with the sentiment itself, more formal than a simple declaratory *Love*. But was *Love* really *Love,* or just convention?

James drew the duplicator toward him. It was a simple but ingenious device—a mechanical arm that held a quill, its elbow accordioning through balsam supports to a second quill that by this device mimicked the movements of the first quill as James directed it. He spread his mother's letters alongside the device and scanned them. When he found a phrase that fit his plan, he traced it with the first quill, and it appeared on the second parchment as surely as if the ghost of his mother were writing. And in a way, she was. James was merely taking the essence of her expression and recomposing it, in her hand, for another audience.

Sadness and anger washed over him as he read and reread, searching for the patches from which to make his quilt. Any words could betray new readings. *Never forget this: Your father left because he had to leave to save us* could be made to say, *Your father left because he never loved you.* The statement *I know you are angry but you will come to understand* might just as easily read, *Your father left because you are angry.* And perhaps *Oh, James, I loved you not enough* really meant, *I love you too much.*

If the familiar language of mother to son was so slippery, how then to write to one's beloved? *The suitors are testing my stamina.* He crossed that out and wrote, *The suitors come.* That didn't sit right either. *Drayton and Boocock and Sowell want my hand.* He continued: *James says you have escaped from Hell Afloat and, though he is too young*—No. Callow? Shy? Mad?—*headstrong to admit it, he is very proud of you.* And finally, *Hurry home!*

James melted the red sealing wax with the candle. He dipped his fingers into it and let it congeal, then ran his fingertips over the desktop, the leather chair, the upholstery tacks, enjoying the numbness the barrier imparted. Finally, using a plain, circular stamp, he sealed the back of the envelope. Then he climbed into bed, joining the girl. He wanted to hear her Celtic lilt. But she slept the slumber of a child. He deserved her; she deserved better.

"It was born thus," she mumbled, her hair rumpled, dewy heat emanating from under her gown.

He shook her.

"Green, I suppose," she murmured.

"Deliver this letter to the prisoner."

She opened her eyes, her breath still deep and steady. When she saw him she smiled. She liked being shaken awake. It showed how much he thought of her.

He gave her a cloak and a bundle of fatwood, to give her the appearance of one of the females—wife, or washer-wench—who lived in bush huts at the camp's outskirts. He had left a jug of rum with the sentinel who could least resist it—there were plenty of candidates—for insurance.

"Take a candle that the prisoner may read by. Leave the cage door ajar, but bring me the key. And do not speak to a soul. If anybody says anything to you, simply nod. Am I understood?"

A while later she returned, flush with pride at a mission accomplished. Her display annoyed him, he preferred the languor, of which there was so little in his life. He knew that a word of gratitude would fall on her like a blow, so he told her she looked like a common jade in that cloak and to re-move it at once, which she did brightly, and he realized it was not her hips and lips he liked best, though he did indeed like them very, very much.

A woodpecker was hammering, the individual blows too rapid to distinguish, the trill of its industry tiring. The sun was yet to come up, but the eastern sky was gray as boiled wool, and it lit the tent unpleasantly. The encampment began to stir—the crack of wood, a sniff of smoke, a banging kettle, a curse, and then, what James had been expecting, a panicky cry:

"The old man has escaped!"

———•·•———

ALTHOUGH he hadn't lived there in more than a year, James still called Bury home. His roan knew the way, and rode there hard, aware that sugar cone awaited her, as well as the water trough. Salt, hands tied behind his back, tailed along on a splay-gaited gelding. James had easily overtaken him, and Salt had not resisted capture, but now his wrists burned.

"How about we remove the binding?"

"Can't."

And so the charade continued as the miles passed, no longer for the safety it offered from outside suspicion, but for the protection it offered from their mutual estrangement.

Smoke curled from the chimney. Molly must be home. Salt's heart beat, *Not yet, not yet, not yet.*

In the letter, hand-delivered by a mysterious servant girl who wouldn't explain, Salt had read, in Molly's hand, *Many townsfolk think you ran to save your own skin. I tell them it's not so.* But he knew that a thing repeated often enough insists on its own truth.

The fields were weedy and the fences around them gone but for one, and that rebuilt crudely, with unstripped branches that still held shriveled brown leaves. The iron balls on chains that once kept the gates shut had been taken for shot, the gates themselves burned for cooking fires. The few remaining animals had free run, and it showed.

She had written, *Your son thinks you have turned your back to him.* Salt looked in vain for a stray hemp patch, but so thoroughly had his dream been stamped out that it was as if it had never existed at all.

She had written, *I confess that I too have felt betrayed by you. I forgive you but not myself.*

James's roan picked up the trot and Salt's gelding stumbled behind.

She had written, *Come lie with me.* It was in her hand, that he would swear to.

Salt's heart beat, *Yet, yet, yet.*

Bent and withered, Ebenezer stood next to the porch, tending the ivy, which looked exaggerated and lush, as if it were not an unremarkable plant but a coddled hothouse exotic. It annoyed Salt now in exactly the same way it had annoyed him then.

When the old man noticed the visitors, he stooped and squinted. His eyebrows had grown shaggy and tangled. When he saw James, he beamed almost violently. Not waiting for James to dismount, Ebenezer hugged the young man's leg, holding on as if to keep himself from going under.

James bore his grandfather's dotage patiently. Then Ebenezer shuffled toward Salt, cataract-ridden eyes darting about. "Water your horses and go."

Salt said, "You know me."

"What I know," Ebenezer pointed to his nose, "is that you stink." The old man peered over his shoulder. Salt followed his gaze to the front door. At the double-hung window next to it he thought he saw the curtain quickly fall back in place, as if somebody inside had been spying out. He had always been fond of that curtain lace, handmade in Ireland and patterned with feverfew. Not once in all that time onboard the *Jersey* had he given it a thought. Yet here it was, that lace, that ivy, their continued existence proof of the finitude of his own.

"Stink!" The old man waved his hand about, then ran the palm of his hand over his bald pate. "You stink like burnt hair!"

James stepped forward. "Lodge your complaints with me, Grandpa."

"That the pistol I gave you for your birthday?" asked Ebenezer.

"And plenty of excellent use it's gotten, too," answered James, as he had said before and before and before, more than a hundred times. "Thank you." *Thank you* worked better than chamomile, better than laudanum even. They were the words his grandfather sought out in every encounter, his pride leaving no room for anyone else's.

"I know damn well every gift I ever gave." Ebenezer snuffed. "Put it away."

"Yes sir." *Yes sir,* another thing his grandfather had taught him. *Yes sir* kept him from having to put the pistol away.

"Your ivy thrives," said Salt, unable to help himself. He hadn't meant to spleen. Homecoming called for grander emotions.

"Get off my property!" Ebenezer's agitation had turned palsied. "Get out of Bury!"

"Bury is mine now, Grandpa," James reminded him.

The old man quaked. "I gave you Bury because I love you." He stomped and punched the sky, a slow charge to attack. He reached to pull Salt from the saddle.

Without looking up, James raised the pistol and fired a shot skyward. The blast rang in Salt's ears like a baby's cry.

"I gave you everything," Ebenezer sputtered.

James reloaded, tapping gunpowder from his horn into the barrel and jamming home ball and wadding. "You gave me everything in case the British lost." James licked his fingers. The gunpowder was bitter like hyssop, and this was a good, strong, clean batch. He took another lick. "You made, it would appear, the right bet."

"But you're a British lieutenant."

"Among other things."

"I worked hard for this land," Ebenezer cried. "Ungrateful bark louse!" Not getting any reaction, he added, "You take after your father." Still no reaction. "He gave you up."

Finally, James winced.

Ebenezer pushed his advantage. "Put that pistol to good use and shoot him!"

"You gave him up."

It was Molly, standing on the porch. How long had she been there?

She was dressed in a fine silk petticoat, pearls around her neck, her uncovered hair falling shockingly down her bodice. Her breasts rose with each breath. Salt took in the cleavage, the swell of the belly.

———————

DRAYTON NEEDED coffee, but there was none to be had. His head ached and the jitters visited him this morning, as they had yesterday, and the day before that. Tea didn't help. All he wanted was to feel normal. Which required rum. Which he splashed into his syllabub, and then poured another proper jigger. Nothing else would quiet the twitch of his eyelid. He gulped his frothy breakfast, determined to kill that little spasm. But what if, instead, he listened to its message? He had lost weight, so much so that he'd had to punch a new hole in his belt, which he cinched tight. He had frequent bowel movements, hydrous and easily expelled. Out, *out!* He wasn't made for the domestic life. Jug in hand, he headed for the door, ill-prepared for the scene he found outside in the yard.

Ebenezer stood with his arm around Molly, who in the struggle to push him away was spilling out of her bodice, one variegated nipple visible. Her ripeness was magnificent to Drayton, and repellent. That the baby was his elated and terrified him.

And there was his old nemesis, astride the gelding. Salt seemed to be made of dowels and rope. His skull seemed over-large, the brow and hollows of the cheeks overpronounced. The red hair had darkened, and he was scarred with pox. But his eyes burned with a new light, a light Drayton had seen in soldiers on the battlefield.

"Listen to me!" Ebenezer thundered.

"I'm done listening to you!" Molly wrung her shoulders free of his grip.

"This wasn't what I imagined," Salt said, looking at Drayton, then Ebenezer, then James, and finally Molly, who blinked away something. What had he expected? Warm gin-gerbread and hot embraces?

Molly cupped her belly as she descended the steps. She had long ago stopped imagining Salt's homecoming, and the sight of him angered her now. Where had he been when she had needed him? She had accomplished with one stroke of the quill what the entire British army, with its pistols, pow-der, Parliament, and prison ships, had not: she had killed her husband. The war would be over soon, and she, a woman of property, would taste real independence—to dress as she pleased, to do as she liked. Why then was she crying as she drew near Salt?

"I warned you no good would come of your carrying on!" cried the old man, his voice reedy and wheedling. He struggled to pull Molly away.

But Molly crumbled into her husband's arms. It was her father, not her husband, who had been the ruination of them, she knew. His derelict lordliness, his land, his lucre, each of these he spread like a disease. He had driven out Salt, had put the pistol in her son's hand, had brought Drayton upon them. Even the way he clung to her now, peppering her cheek with kisses, patting her back, revolted Molly and left her revolted with herself.

The skewbald lifted a rear leg to stomp a fly away and caught its hoof in the rope tethering Salt, pulling him off balance and setting aflight a passel of flies. Instinctively James sprang to him, and Salt let himself be grabbed about the waist, the chest. At last he was in his son's arms.

To James it was like holding a bundle of kindling. His father consisted of knots and points. The only thing remotely soft about him were the hands, which fluttered about before landing on James's back, his sides, his nape. He did not stink as Ebenezer claimed, but smelled like saddle leather, like a father. James heard a sob, and recognized it for his own. He squeezed tighter, his arms both capable and undefended, as if in forgiving he was himself forgiven.

"It's not too late," Molly told Salt. Theirs was an anxious, ill-fated, and dangerous love, but still she chose it. If still she could.

Drayton steeled himself. Veteran of countless battles, he found the violence of the emotions unfolding around him terrifying, the shifting allegiances appalling. How could Molly choose over him the husband she cuckolded and had written off as dead? Why was James embracing the father who had abandoned him, when it was Drayton who had made him a man? Drayton hadn't the stomach for this mess, the heart, the head. He must get back to his regiments. To guns, powder, rank, uniformity, formations. To strategic goals and their accomplishment. This was his calling.

He slid his saber from its bootblacked sheath, a clean-edged thing, the slash of it pleasing to the ear. He held it in the sunshine. Peacekeeper me. But nobody was paying any attention.

Ebenezer eyed the pistol in James's hand, its walnut handle and silver buttcap, the expertly forged brass flintlock. Its worksmanship displayed hours of labor, years of practice, a decade of apprenticeship, a lifetime of devotion to craft. He said, "I gave him all!" Or maybe, "I gave him up!" Or "Give it back!" It was hard to tell as he lunged for the gun.

A stallion would have stood firm, but not Salt's gelding. The leather straps that bound the animal to him groaned, then went slack as the beast let the momentum carry it forward, allowing Salt to slip his wrists from the rigging and snatch at the pistol, which Ebenezer already had a hand on.

In reflex, James grabbed for the pistol too, and flung it away, butt meeting skull en route with a crack that in battle would have been pleasing. Salt went down, cheek to ground, nostrils filled with timothy, sweet timothy that should have been scythed long ago. Blood spattered everywhere, red as the cochineal juice Ebenezer dyed his woolens in, from caterpillars from Mexico—because there was money enough and because blood was only really crimson when wet.

Salt couldn't breathe, couldn't get up. But the pistol lay in the grass, and he could reach it from where he lay. He needn't stand to shoot. But first, a breath, and a second, like the millions before, somewhere the count was kept. The third breath came with a gurgle, like a baby's. Salt's hand was unsteady, and he shut one eye. No, his son would disapprove. One must learn to aim with both eyes open, maintain the binocular advantage.

The eye looking down the barrel saw Drayton climbing his mount. The other encompassed Molly, cupping her hands just under her breast, signaling, *Here, here.*

A boot kicked the gun away, and it discharged by itself.

EBENEZER WAS falling, falling, but strong arms caught him. He looked up, into the black and grizzled face of Drinky Crow. *There you are,* he breathed. *I had given up on you.*

There is no such thing as a secret, Sparrow said. Sparrow, too! She wore a yellow dress and a brimmed straw hat with matching yellow flowers in its band. She smiled indulgently. *You silly soul, let this be a lesson.* She helped him to his feet. *Let's go,* she said. And they went.

JAMES LOOKED down at his father's head. The strange red hair was thinning at the crown and the scalp showed through, pale as eggshell. The ears were beginning to look like old man's ears, cartilaginous and rimmed with wiry hairs. But he was stronger than he appeared, this father who called work backmaking, who wouldn't lie to anyone but himself, not even to save his own son. James himself knew a thousand ways to lie without even speaking. But not to himself. Not when concealing pistols or reciting pamphlets. Not when popping off at any target, or no target at all. Which was the lesser hypocrisy?

Stay, James thought. He had grown into a man to make his father proud, and what happened next, however it came off, would change history.

Lips and chin quivered, doing strange things to Salt's smile. His lips worked as if mouthing a prayer in church, not believing. But the blazing eyes fixed upon James believed.

HALF A MILE down the road, Major General Michael Drayton felt free. Happy to be rid of them, even James. A good boy, a responsibility nonetheless. As for Molly, well, the memory of her was a trophy, to pull off the shelf and remember fondly in his dwindling years, not now.

Suddenly, he was set upon by a swift-hoofed posse. The leader wore a raccoon cap and rode a big-boned dray with blinkered eyes and shit-stained flanks. The others' horses were a battered and mixed lot rigged with cast-offs from the British Dragoons and the American cavalry.

"Jabez Boocock, chicken farmer," said the man in the coonskin cap as he pulled even.

Drayton reached for his pistol. He could get off a

shot without letting go the reins. It was a move he had practiced hundreds, no, thousands of times. American militias were composed of candlemakers, squirrel hunters, cabbage mulchers, and goddamn chicken farmers. What they lacked in skill they made up for in ignorance.

The posse made to draw their guns, but they were too late. Drayton drew quicker, firing before any of them so much as had a weapon clear of its sheath. Boocock got hit between the eyes.

Or would have, had the pistol been loaded. But it merely clicked and fizzled.

Boocock examined a fingernail.

Stupidly, Drayton looked down the barrel. Even in his sorriest, mash-addled state, he had always kept his gun cleaned and loaded. It was black down there, nothing to see. But the balance of the piece was wrong, how had he failed to notice? A gram of stability was missing from the fulcrum, the lead ball, and he knew at once that the pistol had been unloaded. Somebody had gone to the trouble.

James! James had betrayed him. Drayton had underestimated the boy. He threw down his pistol and drew his saber.

"Too late for heroics," Boocock said, taking a coil of rope from a peg on his saddle. Dozens more Americans rounded the bend, perhaps fifty in all. Many were armed with British muskets, others with Pennsylvania rifles, still more with swords, a militia in mismatched, ill-fitting uniforms, including a score brandishing rakes and pitchforks and riding upon mangy asses. Their disorder galled Drayton, the primitive clubs and hoes, not so much as a nod to defilade or military execution. A mob, no more, led by a sarcastic cockswain.

Boocock was fashioning a noose. "You understand, of course, that I'm *bound* to make an example of you. We'll string you up from this here sycamore. Like a weathervane."

More troops were coming, on foot, marching in chaotic cadence. Among them were oxen drawing victuals, tents, cookpots, lanterns, cannons, and carriages bearing women and children, and loaded with corn, cabbage, tobacco, butter churns, barrels, pigs, goats, chickens in crates. The return of refugees.

"There are thousands of us." Boocock said. "Strung from a branch you'll be good for morale. Mine at least."

Too late, Drayton realized the extent of James's betrayal. Why hadn't he seen it coming?

"You're worried about your men, aren't you?" Boocock asked. "Boats are arriving for them, to be sure. But not to convey them south, no sir. The boats will take them home, if in hell they'll dwell. They'll see the Union Jack, they'll set up a cheer, and—" Boocock clapped "—they'll all fall down. Those who fight get grapeshot. Those who run, well, those come right into our arms, so to speak."

The men raised their weapons and let out a roar.

"I give you my sword." Drayton proferred the handle to Boocock.

Boocock sat upright on his horse and let the beggary pass over him. This was power, and he had better get comfortable with it. "That quaint redcoat surrender ritual doesn't play with me."

————— · —————

JAMES RODE toward the big red sun, so exhausted he had difficulty holding himself upright in the saddle. Pregnant Molly and frail Salt hadn't been much help with the digging, but they'd helped him settle on the grave site, in the side yard, next to the fence. War kept Ebenezer apart from his wife; Jamaica Church and its yard were off limits, a rebel staging area now.

They planted a slip of ivy in the freshly dug earth, then the three of them went into the house. From Salt's closet James chose buckskin leggings, a hemp shirt Molly had sewn, moccasins. The father's clothes now fit the son, and it was time for the son to go. One side or the other would kill him as a traitor if he stayed. Only Boocock understood his allegiances, and Boocock would execute him too, if he could wring public approval from the act.

Was it exhaustion, or was that British officer dangling from a sycamore yonder Drayton? James drew closer. Dead, Drayton had a peaceful look on his melted face, his head crooked as if he had nodded off. Someone had gone to the effort of straightening his lapels and tucking in his shirt tails. He examined the rope. Hemp, and nice handiwork, too. Boocock's, likely. That man had civilization sickness, what a politician called right.

An old preacher rode up, followed by a girl on a chestnut mare. He said, "Now there's a proper noose."

"What happened to his face?" asked the girl. She had a lovely voice and steely eyes.

The preacher was sucking a strand of hay. "We're searching for a Captain Stephen Marbury. Do you know the man?"

Before James could answer, the girl broke in. "Father, look at his moccasins," she said. "May I have some like those?"

Afterword

MY OFFICE is in the Brooklyn Navy Yard, on Wallabout Bay in the East River, just across from Manhattan. A few years ago a security guard pointed to the water
and said, "That's where the British tossed ten thousand dead
Americans." Did I know that during the Revolutionary War
more people died on Brooklyn prison ships than in all the
battles combined?

No, I did not.

About a dozen floating prisons were anchored in Wallabout Bay between 1776 and 1783, the most notorious of
which was the *Jersey*, moored about a hundred yards off the
Brooklyn shore. No one knows for sure how many were held
there, or how many died. Historians put the death toll somewhere between 8,500 and 11,500 men. (I found no credible
accounts of women held prisoner.) By my rough calculations,
as a percentage of the total population, today's equivalent
would be about 1,000,000 to 1,300,000 dead.

The salient feature of the Prisonship Martyrs' Memorial in Brooklyn's Fort Greene Park is a tall, fluted column. It was designed by the most famous architect of his time, Stanford White, built at huge expense, and unveiled to great fanfare a hundred years after the war ended and the *Jersey* gave up its last prisoner, was abandoned, and sank. And it's a failure. Its "eternal flame" in a bronze urn at the top was either extinguished in the 1970s, or during World War II as a wartime security measure, or never lit at all; accounts differ. The bronze eagles that guarded it are in storage in Manhattan, but two may be returned shortly, or may not; accounts differ. Civic groups and city agencies are committed to restoring the monument. While it may not succeed as a public memorial, its peculiar beauty can inspire intense private moments. Underneath the expansive granite stairs is a crypt. Not long ago, I paid a visit.

Two New York City Parks Department employees sawed through a steel plate that had been welded over a copper door to protect the crypt from vandals, and allowed me inside. The tomb was clean-swept and made of bisque bricks. There rested thirteen caskets, each representing a colony. On top of one was a real human jawbone, with teeth, and a red plastic hibiscus, evidently left as a remembrance. It took an effort, but the three of us managed to lift the lid. Inside were bone chips and dust. Whose?

To get a clear picture of the era I turned to, among others, *Founding Brothers: The Revolutionary Generation* by Joseph J. Ellis, *American Scripture: Making the Declaration of*

Independence by Pauline Maier, *1776* by David McCullough, *Common Sense* by Thomas Paine, the letters of John and Abigail Adams, Jefferson, Washington, Franklin. Further research led me to first-hand accounts by two former prisoners, Thomas Dring and Thomas Andros. They were written decades after the fact and subject to jingoism and the vagaries of memory. But in them and in other sources tantalizing fragments and mentions abounded: Plagues of lice and smallpox, and the deployment of both in biological warfare on board. Bread that even weevils couldn't eat. Piles of cash, of cadavers. Boys crying for their mothers. Rum, privateers, mercenaries. Small acts of kindness. Bond market speculation. War widows. Premarital sex. Song, fever, and gunpowder. Rope—how it bound, how it freed. Hemp, and the fortunes it created. The contemporary equivalent might be oil. Transport and communication depended upon it—rigging and sailcloth for seagoing vessels, naval, pirate, and mercantile, including those bearing sugar, spices, and slaves. Hemp oil lighted lanterns, hemp seed fed chickens. The fabric woven from it clothed people, the paper made from it was used for bills, legislation, currency, pamphlets. *Cannabis sativa* was the raw material of a free press. If the plant's intoxicating strains and properties had not yet been exploited, its role in colonial life was nevertheless mind-altering.

Reading history, one thread kept pulling at me: how many ordinary people were simply caught in the wrong place at the wrong time, and how they were radicalized by the experience. I was reminded how incredible it is that my country was founded not on race, religion, or borders, but an idea.

What, then, about the dead? They continued to haunt me.

The Society of Old Brooklynites compiled in 1888 a list of eight thousand prisoners said to have perished on the hulks. From it I took the name Ezekiel Rude. Other characters—William Cunningham, Aaron Lopez, George Sowell, and James Forten, for example—I loosely based on the historical record. In the novel they meet different fates than did their real-life counterparts. But what about someone whose name was not written anywhere, someone completely forgotten? What happened to him, and to those whom he loved and who loved him? He is Salt.

Acknowledgments

THANKS TO my agent, Cynthia Cannell, who has stood by me for eighteen years and three novels. Thanks to my editor, the extraordinary Becky Saletan, whose presence is in every sentence of this book. Thanks to assistant editor Stacia Decker, publicist Tricia van Dockum, managing editor David Hough, jacket designer Kelly Eismann, interior designer Cathy Riggs, copy editor Ken Fox, and everyone at Harcourt. Thanks to friends and early readers, Neil Gordon and Monica Jenicek Lyall; to my co-workers and colleagues at Cumberland Packing Corp.; to the Brooklyn Public Library and its Brooklyn Collection. Thanks to my parents, Joan and Jim, and to all the Drinkards. Thanks to my parents-in-law, Barbara and Marvin, and to all the Eisenstadts. Thanks to my wife, Jill, and our daughters, Jane, Lena, and Coco. And thank you.